BRIDGE OF SIGHS

BRIDGE OF SIGHS

Priscilla Masters

severn House

This first world edition published 2018
in Great Britain and 2019 in the USA by
SEVERN HOUSE PUBLISHERS LTD of
Eardley House, 4 Uxbridge Street, London W8 7SY.
Trade paperback edition first published
in Great Britain and the USA 2019 by
SEVERN HOUSE PUBLISHERS LTD.

British Library Cataloguing in Publication Data
A CIP catalogue record for this title is available from the British Library.

ISBN-13: 978-0-7278-8838-9 (cased)
ISBN-13: 978-1-84751-963-4 (trade paper)
ISBN-13: 978-1-4483-0173-7 (e-book)

All Severn House titles are printed on acid-free paper.

Severn House Publishers support the Forest Stewardship Council™ [FSC™],
the leading international forest certification organisation.
All our titles that are printed on FSC certified paper carry the FSC logo.

MIX
Paper from
responsible sources
FSC® C013056

Typeset by Palimpsest Book Production Ltd.,
Falkirk, Stirlingshire, Scotland.
Printed and bound in Great Britain by
TJ International, Padstow, Cornwall.

One more unfortunate
Weary of breath
Rashly importunate
Gone to her death

Take her up tenderly
Lift her with care
Fashioned so slenderly
Young and so fair

'The Bridge of Sighs'. Thomas Hood, 1799–1845

This poem was a favourite of my grandfather's, William Watkins – or Tad'cu. I can still hear him reading it in his sonorous Welsh voice. Thank you to him for sharing with me a love of literature, language, poetry and the natural world, and to Mr Hood for such a heartfelt and inspirational poem. One is always touched by the tragedy of suicide. A feeling that friends, family, the entire world has somehow failed them.

The poem continues with questions:

Who was her father?
Who was her mother?
Had she a sister?
Had she a brother?
Or was there a dearer one
Still, and a nearer one
Yet than all other?

Questions which form part of any coroner's investigation into a suicide.

An attempt to answer the question . . .

Why?

ONE

Now!
It was the middle of the night when Gina finally realized that this was the time. She sat bolt upright in bed, for now giving up even the idea of sleep.

Terence would be deeply asleep; he would not wake. She threw back the duvet, her thoughts racing towards their conclusion. She had been moving towards this point ever since . . . In the darkened room she blinked back a tear for what might have been. *Ever since.* The bolt of realization had found its target. She had known there was no escape and now she had reached the end of the line. With her analytical brain she had explored every single possible escape route and found none. She had explored every possible route, thinking up explanations, justifications . . . but in the end she had known there was no way through. It was a blind ending. Softly she stepped out of bed. She didn't want to take the chance that he would wake. That would have twisted the knife too far. She slipped her track suit on. Every night it had been laid out, ready for the moment. After a swift glance at the screen she flipped her phone back on to the bedside table and padded out through the bedroom door, pausing for just a minute outside her son's bedroom. There was not a sound. She couldn't even hear him breathing. She pressed the palm of her hand to the door, as though it had palm recognition and would swing open. She was tempted, even now, to open it, to check he was still alive. But she knew *he* would be. She knew *he* would be OK. Better without the shadow she would have cast over his life. She now pressed her face to the panel painted *Terence's Room* and kissed it. 'Be happy,' she whispered. 'Have a good life, better than mine. Goodbye, my darling. I love you more than you can ever know. Believe me. And this is why I go.'

She hadn't left a note for her mother. For her to understand the full story would be to drag her into the slurry pit that her life would become if she stayed. It was not a choice. Not her choice anyway. She must go, vanish. She had no option.

She told herself this on every step as she descended the stairs, each step taking her farther away from her life until at the bottom she felt she was already in freefall. She let herself out through the front door, closing it behind her with the softest of clicks. And now she was outside in the cold clear night of early March. She could see stars above, identified the Plough, maybe Cassiopeia. No time to search for the rest. No time left at all. Her car was already facing down the drive in readiness. She had known as she had driven home from work and manoeuvred the three-point turn that this would be her last night on earth.

She eased herself into the driver's seat, buckled up and started the engine. If she could have done that quietly she would have, but engines make their own noise. They do not alter through grief or exuberance. There is no volume control on the internal combustion engine.

She had reconnoitred her spot too, driving along the A528 north out of Shrewsbury, knowing the road to be winding and in some parts treacherous. In fact, ideal. She had found her blind bend with a wall ahead. Perfect.

Driving through the still night she encountered few cars. One or two making their way home after a night shift, another heading into work for a very early shift. She passed them, envying them their ordinary, un-dramatic lives, their futures, their having some-where to go whereas she had nowhere. Except the wall.

She sensed when she was nearing the spot. And then she saw it, the road sign heralding a sharp and dangerous bend. TAKE CARE, it advised in bold letters. She smiled. She would.

She had worked it all out step by step. Almost a week before she had explored all the possibilities to see if there was a way out, looking at each alternative from every angle, using her lawyer's brain to search for that chink of light. But her conclusion had been inescapable.

She must not survive.

For a moment her thoughts veered towards self-pity. Why me? In the end she had answered this one too. Because you earned it. You popped your head above the parapet, became successful, wealthy, famous, one blessed by the gods. And you wonder why you got targeted? Don't forget, little Gina, those whom the gods wish to destroy they first make mad. She smiled. The real answer was not madness but visibility. She had become visible and attracted attention. A high-vis person. A target. And now the only way to stop herself from being the bull's-eye was to exist no more, to remove herself body and soul.

But the word 'soul' had uncomfortable connotations. It had conjured up her mother – mouth open, her tongue ready to receive the sacrament, head scarfed as she prayed. She seemed to look straight into those warm green eyes, kind eyes, the salt and pepper hair and the stoop which was a recent acquisition and gave the only clue to her age. Her mother was an Irish Catholic who believed as firmly in the soul as she did in hell and purgatory. Gina shivered. What if her mother was right?

Suicide was a sin. Destroying what God had created.

She was there. A jumble of thoughts pushed her foot further down on the accelerator, underlining her determination. There was no alternative. The Information Super Highway – she was zooming along it and the road pretty fast. As she released her seat belt only one thought snagged her brain: Terence. And yet even now, at the back of her mind, was the sweetness of stolen honey. Then resolutely she gripped the steering wheel so tight her knuckles shone like moonbeams. She squeezed her eyes tight shut, pressed her right foot down to the floor and waited for the impact, hearing a howl of protest from the engine which she overrode. Faster. Faster. Harder. Harder.

The car smashed into the wall, glass, plastic, metal splintering as it screamed. She heard the noise, felt the crushing pain and then nothing.

TWO

Friday, 10 March, 3.18 a.m.

Graham Skander was dreaming.

He was diving the coral reef in Tobago where he had been only one short month ago. A fish was ahead of him, jewelled scales bright blue. He felt the sun on his back, heard his breathing rasping loudly in the snorkel mask, as he sucked on the pipe. He pursued the fish, camera in hand. He wanted to—

Bang!

Startled, it took him a while to surface, to leave the coral reef, open his eyes and process the sound, wondering whether it had been part of the dream. He lay for a minute, still confused, and then he heard a hissing sound. He knew what that was. Not part of a dream.

He threw back the covers, planted his feet on the floor and crossed to the window.

The Grange was an eighteenth-century house, symmetrical, red brick. It had been there long before the A49 had become such a rat run. It was his wall that cars had to manoeuvre and one or two had hit it before. He knew the sound and it made him angry. The insurance companies might rebuild but they never did it quite like it was before. Graham lived there alone since his wife, Rita, had left, citing his irascible nature which apparently was peppered with 'boringness'. Her word, not his.

Peering through the window, he recognized the signs instantly. A blaze of lights obscured by a cloud of steam. He could hear the hiss from the radiator, smell the stench of burning tyres as he breathed in petrol. Another bloody car taking the corner too fast now embedded in his bloody wall, he thought crossly. He slipped his bony feet into his slippers, tied his dressing gown around his waist and stomped down the stairs.

Fumbling for the key, he spared a fleeting thought for the driver. But when he reached the car and shouted, 'Hello, are you all right?' he saw that the damage to the car was much worse than usual. The bonnet was completely crumpled but, worst of all, he saw something he had not seen since seat belts were made compulsory. Someone . . . A woman? Slumped half through the windscreen, her face embedded in the wall. Blood everywhere. And her face. Oh, God, her face.

His 'Hello' died in his throat. He didn't need to have a medical degree to see that she was dead. And, he harrumphed bravely as he turned back towards his house to ring the emergency services, looking at the state of her face, thank God she was.

But he couldn't say that to the operator when she asked which service he required and what had happened.

For a moment, he couldn't speak. 'Umm.' It was as far as he got at the first attempt. He cleared his throat. 'Graham Skander here.' He could hear the shock making his voice waver. 'From The Grange. Preston Gubbals. A car has . . .' Again, he cleared his throat. 'Embedded itself in my wall.' He recovered himself a little. 'Not for the first time. A woman driver. I think . . . I'm afraid I think . . . I think she's dead.'

The operator provided the solution. 'Ambulance then, and the police.' Something of Felicity Corwen's character peeped through. 'Are you all right, sir?'

'Nothing a good malt won't cure,' he said bravely. Then added, 'Poor woman. Her face, you know. Gone through the windscreen. Met the wall.'

'You leave it to the police,' she soothed, 'and go have that malt.'

'Happy to.'

He knew he would get no more sleep tonight. And if he did, after hours of questions and recovery vehicles and the inevitable noise and delay, he would not be dreaming of coral reefs again this night – and probably not for a long time.

THREE

Saturday, 11 March, 9 a.m.

The weekends always seemed to creep towards Martha Gunn, leapfrogging in hops, skips and jumps, so when she awoke on Saturday morning it was invariably with a feeling of surprise. It was always a slight shock to find that she did not have to drive into work or dress in sombre clothes. No, today, she thought with a skip of her heart, was a free day. A day for jeans, boots, a sweater and a long walk through the woods with Bobby, their Heinz 57 Collie cross. The weather men had been optimistic, forecasting sunshine, though, as usual, they were qualifying it with *'may not reach all places until after the weekend'*.

Even that didn't dent Martha's spirits as she showered and slipped into jeans and a sweatshirt. Nothing would, she thought. Sam was playing an away match against Chelsea, which kicked off later today, so that was him accounted for. And Sukey had her new boyfriend, Pomeroy Trainer, known as Pom, to occupy her. So Martha felt very free and practically danced her way into her boots, out of the house and into the woods even under a cloudy grey sky that scowled at her. There was one cloud darker than the rest. The truth was she didn't really like Pom, who had a way of making snide comments usually focused either against Sukey and her acting career, or Sam's enthusiasm for football, or even Martha's cookery skills. Whatever he turned his attention to he seemed to have a knack for finding the vulnerability in one's happiness and could turn even a cosy family supper into something unpleasant, besmirching anyone's pleasure. *'Gosh, isn't this meat tough?'*, *'I don't like your hair like that, Sukey'*, or, with a bored yawn and eye-roll at Sam, *'Do you ever talk about anything other than football?'* He didn't seem to realize how fucking rude he was being.

Martha quickened her pace. Even telling herself that Pom's negativity was probably the result of his insecurity hadn't made her like him.

Bobby scampered ahead as her thoughts reflected back to Sukey's previous boyfriend, the intellectual, quiet, clever William Friedman. She had much preferred the solemn, bespectacled lad who had never made a single derogatory comment in the brief time she'd known him. Actually, she smiled to herself, stepping over a fallen tree, William had kept his views very much to himself, so it was anyone's guess what his private thoughts were. Maybe they were equally negative. Pom, however, was an abrasive, critical character and Martha felt uneasy and inadequate around him. But now the sun was peeping through the trees, dappling the pine-needle path with equal parts sunshine and moving shade. The scent of the trees was strong. A rabbit tempted Bobby into a brief, unfruitful chase. Even thoughts of Pom couldn't swamp the weekend feeling. She extended the walk until way past lunchtime since today she had no one to cook for.

Stoke (and Sam) drew against Chelsea and Pom and Sukey went to the pictures on Saturday night followed by dinner somewhere in town. And Sunday? Recovery for Sam, a lazy day reading *The Sunday Times* from cover to cover for Martha, and Sukey and Pom spent the day with friends in Market Drayton.

Perfect.

She always avoided the local papers or the local radio station over a weekend. If there was tragedy she would learn about it soon enough via her job. And much as she loved her work as coroner, the weekends needed to be death-free.

But this meant she remained unaware of local events.

FOUR

Monday, 13 March, 9 a.m.

The 'after the weekend' prediction of the weather forecasters proved to be true. It was a fine morning, bright sunshine beckoning her towards the town, and as Martha pulled up outside her office she wondered whether the week ahead might, for once, be plain sailing. Sometimes they began that way but got trickier towards the end of the week; other Mondays began with a bang and that continued right through until Friday. Her job was as unpredictable as the grim reaper. She rarely had an entirely quiet week, although just occasionally, usually in summer, she was blessed with nothing more than a few elderly persons dying naturally and peacefully, surrounded by family and with doctors' certificates present.

This proved to be one of the weeks when first thing Monday morning was calm and relatively quiet, and she had a couple of hours to sort through her emails, with coffee provided at regular intervals by Jericho Palfreyman, the coroner's officer.

10 a.m.

Sometimes she learned about a death through Jericho. He had a keen (some might call it nosey) involvement in local events – particularly mopping up bad news via the papers or BBC Radio Shropshire. He considered it a coup if he learned of a death before the coroner. At other times Martha was informed by email or the telephone or simply a new set of notes placed on her desk. But

there were occasions, usually cases of homicide or other violent
or unexpected deaths, when she was informed either by phone or
in person by DI Alex Randall himself. This was one of those
mornings. He arrived, unannounced, a beige folder under his arm,
frowning slightly as he knocked, but when she opened the door
to him the frown was quickly erased and he grinned at her. 'Good
morning, Martha,' he said. Then added with a hint of mischief,
'Hope I'm not disturbing anything?'

She wanted to respond. *You? Disturb? Never.*

But it would have been unwise and a little presumptuous, so she
simply swallowed the words and shook her head. 'Come in, Alex.'

It must be something out of the ordinary to bring him here so
early on a Monday. She was on instant alert.

But he didn't speak straight away. Instead, after a quick glance,
as though asking her permission, he crossed the room and settled
into the armchair in the bay window as he had so many times before.
For a moment he remained silent as he looked around at the room
so familiar, lined with bookshelves, the books a random selection
of titles from gardening to law, from medicine to natural history,
fact to fiction. It was representative of her eclectic mind. He smiled
to himself, thinking of the ragbag of subjects contained somewhere
inside the unruly red hair, peering out from behind those witchy
green eyes. The desk stood alone in the centre of the room, facing
the window as though she kept watch over the town of Shrewsbury.
To him the scent of lemons, roses, lavender, the room itself was all
so familiar, so comfortable, so reassuring. So *her*. He said nothing,
though his eyes, somewhere between hazel and grey, were expressive
in their appreciation as they roamed the space.

It was up to her to begin. 'So,' she said briskly, 'what brings
you here this morning?' She paused, adding, 'Alex?'

He put the folder down on his lap. And in his eyes she now
read pain.

He half smiled. 'I take it you kept to your usual practice of
avoiding any local news over the weekend?'

How well he knew her private life and foibles.

She nodded. 'Absolutely. I have enough death, sadness, grief
and mayhem in the week.' Her eyes rested on the folder and she
raised her eyebrows. 'So?'

'A suicide,' he said, then, knowing her pedantry, he corrected himself. 'It *looks* like a suicide.' And almost to himself, he added, 'I can't see what else it can be.'

He handed the folder to her as he spoke. 'Gina Marconi, thirty-six years old. Successful barrister specializing in criminal law. Divorced seven years ago, from Mr Marconi, due to be married for the second time in September. One son, Terence, aged eight.'

She lifted her gaze from the picture on the front of the file, a picture of a woman in a red T-shirt laughing into the camera, happy with shining dark hair which waved down to just below her shoulders. She looked as though she did not have a care in the world. Dark eyes shone out of the photograph, eyes full of merriment and mischief and fun. Which had disguised . . .?

Martha looked across at DI Randall for explanation and he continued, his eyes on hers.

'Inexplicably she gets out of bed at three a.m., drives north out of town, meets a sharp right-angled bend and doesn't take it. Instead she unbuckles her seat belt – that's if it was on in the first place – and drives her car at sixty miles an hour straight into the brick wall. Multiple injuries, dead more or less instantly. Certainly by the time the paramedics got there.'

'Post-mortem?'

'Sometime this week. Mark Sullivan will let you know.'

She nodded and, still looking at the picture, asked, 'Why suicide? Why not bad driving? Loss of concentration – even loss of consciousness?'

'The imprint of the accelerator was on her shoe. That is before she was ejected through the shattered windscreen.'

She winced at the inevitable mental image the words evoked. 'Was there a note?'

'No.'

'So . . .? Was there a history of depression?'

'No.'

'So why suicide, Alex? The seat belt? Not conclusive. She might just be one of those people who don't buckle up – or sometimes forget.' She was already uneasy. Suicide was one of the verdicts she was always reluctant to give. It had such a knock-on effect on the family. 'Couldn't it have been simple insomnia with disastrous results? Maybe she'd taken something to help her sleep? Alcohol?'

He shook his head.

'Maybe she couldn't sleep because of excitement over her approaching wedding? Then maybe a moment's distraction? A mobile phone call?'

This time it was his turn to shake his head. 'She'd left her mobile at home. On the bedside table.'

'So . . .' She was aware she was running out of options. 'Was anything wrong with the car? Faulty steering? Brake failure?'

Again, he shook his head. 'We've had it looked at. So far they've found nothing wrong with it.'

'But why *would* she commit suicide? You say she had a young son? A fiancée? A wedding planned? Have you talked to her close friends?'

Randall covered a smirk. He was well used to Martha's interest in police work and their line of reasoning often mirrored each other. It was as though they worked together – two police officers rather than coroner and DI. 'Give us time, Martha,' he said gently, tempted to touch her arm to slow her rampant reasoning. 'It's early days yet but my initial instinct tells me Gina Marconi left home that night with no intention of returning.'

'Gina Marconi,' she mused. 'Unusual name. Was she Italian?'

'Her first husband was New York Italian.'

'He is her son's father?'

'Yeah, but as so often happens he's disappeared into the ether. Had very little contact with his son or Gina.'

'Have you spoken to her mother?'

Alex's mouth twisted as it did when he was finding something hard. 'Yes. She's distraught. I can understand it. One minute she's discussing wedding plans, next thing measuring up for a shroud.'

'Oh.' Martha shuddered. 'Don't. Please.'

'Well,' he said, looking around him now and shifting in his chair, always a precursor to leaving. 'You'll be opening an inquest?'

'Yes. I'll speak to Mark Sullivan. Get the post-mortem findings when they're ready and start gathering evidence.'

'Right you are.'

She smiled warmly at him and for an instant, as he rose to his feet, he felt he would like to stay in this warm, sunny room all day until the sun set and then some, seeing Shrewsbury through plate glass rather than the reality.

But he heaved himself out of the chair.

Time to go.

FIVE

When he had gone the room seemed empty, although, as Martha contemplated, Alex was hardly an intrusive personality. He didn't fill the room with loud jokes, a booming voice or a dominant presence. His voice was quiet – she'd rarely heard it raised. And he tended to think carefully before he spoke, hesitating as he searched for the right word or phrase. He was a man of quiet decency and strong convictions. For a while after he left she sat, thinking. Then she picked up the file, and as she read through it she began to see why Alex Randall had come to her to share his concerns.

It was baffling. As Martha read each page and began to form a picture of the dead woman, she began to realize something here was very wrong.

Gina Marconi had been a high-profile, intelligent criminal lawyer and, looking at the photograph again, she had also been beautiful. In a town the size of Shrewsbury, she would have been well known. Martha stared at her photograph for a few seconds, trying to understand what on earth had driven this woman to such a violent act when she had, apparently, so much to live for. She searched her memory. Had she ever met her in real life? In the flesh? She shook her head. But she had been aware of her through pictures in the two local papers, *The Shrewsbury Chronicle* and *The Shropshire Star*, as well as pieces in *Shropshire Life*. Alex had photocopied a couple of them and inserted them into the folder. Martha read through them and studied each one of the accompanying photographs. Gina's vibrancy shone from the pages, a brilliant smile, beautiful teeth, confidence lighting up every single picture. Not a hint of doubt or depression. She had been as photogenic as a supermodel with a huge, white-toothed smile on a perfect face, a curtain of dark, shining hair, a slim figure and confident air. Martha read more. Not many supermodels have an Oxford first degree in law, are articulate as a public speaker and are a partner in a flourishing practice in an affluent town. Gina had been everything a small girl might aspire to. She had both the gifts: beauty and intelligence. She had been admired in and around Shrewsbury, not only for her wit and skill in defending high-profile cases, or even because she was photogenic. The cherry on top of the icing on the cake had been that she'd been engaged to a BBC foreign correspondent who was equally charismatic, except *his* charisma had been augmented by bravery and a certain gung-ho spirit. Julius Zedanski had been filmed facing a Daesh member wielding an AK47 and had not flinched. That image alone would have been enough to ensure his place in the nation's hearts. Don't we all love a hero? Wasn't that what everyone would *like* to have done when in real life their legs would have turned to jelly and their brains to water? But Julius Zedanski had somehow survived this encounter when so many others had not. He had kept his head, literally and metaphorically, continued with his broadcast, practically ignoring the bent arms, the clenched fists and the black flag waving behind him, and had coolly returned to his Jeep and left. Film intact. On another occasion, cameras rolling, he had grabbed a gun from a terrorist in Beirut and brandished it at the cowering and clearly terrified man, but not shot him. Oh, no. Julius Zedanski had handed the man (and the gun) over to the authorities, cameras still rolling. And then, to show his softer side, he had rescued refugee children from the waters around Lesvos, one under each arm. These pictures had given him the romanticism of a Robin Hood, a Black Prince, a defender of the faith. A saviour. He was what we all wanted: a real life superhero. Brave Heart – that was the epithet which had been applied to him.

Brave Heart.

Had Rageh Omaar not already been given the epithet of Stud Missile it could equally have been applied to Julius. He was devastatingly romantic and attractive, and with Gina on his arm they almost outclassed the Clooneys. They were a charmed couple.

In reality Julius Zedanski was a Politics, Philosophy and Economics Oxford graduate of Polish origin with an engaging grin and bright blue eyes. This was Gina Marconi's fiancé. A wedding had been planned for September at St Chad's Church in the centre of Shrewsbury.

Alex was right. This death was odd. Gina had had everything to live for . . . surely?

Martha picked up the phone to speak to Jericho, preparing to set the date for the opening of the inquest, which would be adjourned pending investigations. Monday, 20 March.

Then she connected with the mortuary, only to be told that Dr Sullivan was in the middle of the post-mortem and would ring her back.

Maybe, she thought, he would have some answers. But somehow she doubted it.

She looked at the pictures and articles scattered across her desk. She rarely had so much colour in her cases. Normally she couldn't put flesh on bones or form living pictures because she never met her subjects living, only their ghostly shadows after death illuminated by the accounts of others, family, friends. Sometimes rivals or enemies, people who hated them as well as those who had loved them. She only ever saw the negatives, their imprint, empty footprints without feet or shoes. That is the nature of a coroner's work. All she would have to work with would be the written and submitted statements about them, descriptions seen through others' eyes, and watch the tears shed for them. The detritus of a life and death. Gina had been dead for just a couple of days. One week ago she had been a living, breathing person, with something bad growing inside her. And now the investigations had hardly begun. According to the preliminary police reports and interviews there had been no indication of Gina's intention in recent days.

Martha scanned the statements. According to Gina's traumatized son and her equally traumatized mother this was totally – *totally*, they'd repeated more than once – out of character.

So what was all this about?

She picked up the phone and connected with Alex Randall. 'What do you know about her professional life?'

'Huh. Murky, Martha,' he said. 'She was involved with some high-profile cases and defended some very nasty pieces of work, but if you want more detail you really need to talk to her partner, Julius Zedanski, and her law partner, Curtis Thatcher. They'll know much more.'

'I will.'

She could picture his frown.

'Why are you barking up this tree? She wasn't murdered, you

know. It just isn't possible given the facts. She took her own life which, as you can imagine, means it isn't really a police matter, so it's over to you. None of those idiots she was happily defending would have had the brains to get the better of her.'

'I'm only digging around,' Martha defended. 'Just digging. And her GP?'

There was a pause, probably while Randall looked this one up, finally coming up with: 'A Doctor Milligan.'

'Stuart Milligan.'

'Yes, that's the guy.'

'I know him, or rather I know *of* him. A trusty and experienced Sheffield graduate with years of experience behind him. I've had a few dealings with him.'

'Did you ever meet her, Martha?'

'No.'

As she put the phone down, she knew she had two good starting blocks.

She returned to the file and read through two of Gina's friends' statements, both of whom expressed shock and knew no reason why their friend might have wanted to end her life. No clue there.

She closed the file and caught the picture again. Stared at it, searching for something.

But what she actually felt were the stirrings of guilt, a memory. What she'd told Alex about not knowing Ms Marconi wasn't strictly true. While she hadn't been familiar with her, she *had* met her.

Two Christmases ago Martha had attended a charity ball in aid of the NSPCC. It had been held at the Albrighton Hall Hotel, an upmarket place with lovely grounds to the north of the town, coincidentally within half a mile of the road on which Gina Marconi had decided to kill herself – if that was the truth and there was no other explanation. Martha smiled. She had been with Simon Pendlebury that night – since both were widowed they tended to attend formal occasions together, simply as a way of going at all. They had arrived late, around nine p.m. Simon had been concluding some business deal and had apologized profusely. When they had entered the ball had been well under way – crowded and noisy even in the anteroom but not too noisy to hear, just as she walked in, a loud, earthy laugh. There had been something sparkly about it.

She had searched for the source of the raucous merriment and had seen a woman in a short gold dress standing in the centre of a group of men and women. She had been tossing around her head of long, shining dark hair with its hint of a curl, and her animation and warmth had reached right across the room. She was obviously relating some funny story and had her audience's rapt attention and mirth. The man on her arm, olive-skinned, was also suitably glamorous. Martha had been intrigued.

She'd turned to Simon. 'Some lawyer or other,' he'd said, reading her mind. 'Don't really know her. Not personally, anyway.' And then the evening had gone on and Martha had forgotten the encounter.

Until now.

And this was the same woman who had apparently driven her car straight and deliberately into a brick wall?

SIX

Martha picked up the phone and this time connected successfully with Mark Sullivan. She got straight to the point. 'You've finished the PM on Gina Marconi?'

'Oh,' he groaned. 'That's an awful one.'

'Conclusions?'

'Where do you want me to start? She died from a ruptured aorta and a nasty collection of other injuries, at least five of which could have proved fatal. Other than her injuries she was a perfectly healthy young woman.'

'Any sign of excess alcohol? Drugs?'

'Just the equivalent of a small glass of wine and no evidence of drugs so far. Obviously I'll have to wait for the toxicology but it looks as though there was nothing abnormal except the results of the impact.'

'There isn't any possibility she had a temporary loss of consciousness?'

'The brain was normal apart from the result of the impact.'

There was silence for a moment and she could almost guess his next sentence.

'I'm not trying to tell you your job, Martha, or influence the result of your inquest, but I can't see that there can possibly be any other verdict but suicide.'

It didn't help.

'Tssch, Mark. I'm struggling here.'

'Me too,' Sullivan confessed. 'Me too.' Now it was he who hesitated. 'I hate the term "temporary insanity" but I can't see any other conclusion.'

'Temporary insanity,' she mused. 'I don't think I've ever used that verdict. A bit like you, I've always hated it. It sounds so – well – medieval. But maybe this time I'll be forced into it.'

'I'll keep you up to date with any results or developments and you'll get my full report in a week or so.'

'Right. Thanks.'

She picked up the file again. More than one friend or acquaintance of Gina's had been quoted.

'Gina was really happy.'

'It's inexplicable.'

'She had everything to live for.'

Nothing to die for?

She read through more friends' statements emailed over by Alex. The police were working hard, busily turning over stones, searching for something, anything, crawling underneath the stones if necessary, but so far there was nothing.

No hint of indiscretion either in her private or professional life; no indication that she was anything but Caesar's wife – beyond reproach. Martha suddenly smiled, inexplicably transported back to fourteen years ago, reading *Little Miss Perfect* as a bedtime story for a demanding Sukey.

Was anyone perfect? Really?

She scanned through further, trying to read between the lines. No dirty little rumours or expressed doubts about her forthcoming marriage. She picked up the phone, connected with Alex Randall, and took down Julius Zedanski's mobile telephone number.

It was switched off. She left a message asking him to give her a call.

Then she rang the law practice and spoke to the secretary, explained who she was and requested an interview with Curtis Thatcher, Gina's partner. He too was temporarily unavailable but the secretary assured her he would call back. 'As soon as he's got a minute,' she said, her voice high-pitched and squeaky with a slight lisp. 'We've had so many phone calls with Miss . . .' she paused, then continued, trying to find the words, '. . . with Gina's . . . accident.'

So that was the official line. It would do for now.

Martha forced herself to focus on some of her other cases. Gina Marconi had not been the only person to die over the weekend. And in the sight of the Grim Reaper all deaths are equal.

Ten minutes later the phone rang and Curtis Thatcher introduced himself in a very Patrician accent.

'We're struggling to understand why Gina's accident happened,' Martha said.

'*You're* struggling?' He spoke with a frankness that was as refreshing as a peppermint.

'Had you noticed any change in her lately?'

'She'd been a bit quieter than usual, but she was busy. We both were.'

'Tell me about her work,' she said. 'Detective Inspector Randall hinted that she had dealings with the underworld.'

Thatcher laughed. 'She was a criminal lawyer,' he said. 'Of course she dealt with the underworld.'

'Anyone in particular?'

'Plenty.' He paused, adding, 'You could line them up.'

'Tell me.'

'Well, I suppose the most high-profile was a case that began about five years ago with a fellow called Mosha Steventon. He was accused of money laundering. She got him off, which I thought was amazing considering the evidence and the tightening up of proceeds of crime laws. Anyway, he must have thought so too, because he basically sent all his criminal cronies straight to her. With some she was successful and with others not so. Obviously the ones who paid her fees but still went to prison took it badly.' Again, he stopped speaking as though reflecting. 'Though that might account for say a threat or even at worst an

assault, it hardly explains how these various cases could incite
her to suicide.'

'No,' she agreed.

'The other point here, Mrs Gunn, is that . . .' She could sense
his awkwardness, even over the phone. 'Not to put too fine a point
on it, Mosha was in her debt. He's an evil fellow with a lot of
influence. He's been mixed up with all sorts of stuff – murder,
torture, bribery, organized crime. And Gina was a criminal lawyer
with some very dark clients. If there was any threat to her, Mosha
would have protected her.'

'Did she ever discuss this with you?'

'No. There are some things, as a professional partner in a law
firm, that it is better not to put into words.'

'Quite.' Even knowing she was barking up the wrong tree,
Martha couldn't stop herself from pursuing the point. 'Did she
ever appear nervous, threatened by her clients?'

'Sometimes, but I can't think of anyone in particular,' he said.
'She would sometimes express very private thoughts, say someone
was guilty, that they were better off in prison, that even defending
them put her in a tricky position.'

'I think,' Martha said, having glimpsed into Gina Marconi's
complicated professional life, 'I may want to speak to you again
as we proceed with our enquiries.'

'But she committed suicide,' Thatcher pointed out reasonably.

'Suicides usually either leave a note or show signs of instability
in the time leading up to the act.' She realized she was leaving
the door ajar for some agreement or statement, but none came, so
she continued, 'Perhaps you'll email me the main cases Gina was
involved with up until her death?'

'Of course. But I can't see what any of this could possibly have
to do with her suicide.' He sounded defensive, and she realized
that he was already distancing the law firm from his partner's
death, so she hid behind the blandest of explanations. 'We're
exploring all possibilities, Mr Thatcher.'

'I can't think she had a guilty conscience about something she
did or did not do at work. If she did she never spoke to me about
it. Maybe her mother . . .?'

'I'll be speaking to her.'

She thanked him and the conversation was over, leaving Martha very thoughtful. There was something about the violence of Gina's death that particularly disturbed her. In general, it was men who killed themselves by violent means – knives, guns, high buildings. Women tended to opt for the gentler ways of ending their life – drugs, alcohol. This had been a determined bid for death. She had left her mobile phone at home. So that she could not leave a last message or be contacted?

Added to that, she had not written a suicide note, which left an element of doubt even after such an act. There was no doubt she had planned her escape. And even that word – escape – seemed significant. Escape from what? Escape from whom?

To Martha, the absence of a note meant she had not wanted to explain – not to her son, her mother or her fiancé. She would leave them wondering, even though she must have known questions would roll around in their minds – possibly forever. Was it this? Was it that? Was it something I did or did not do? Gina had given them no answers.

Martha stared down at the facts that she knew so far. What was she missing?

A connection with the criminals she worked with? Had she compromised her professional integrity? Or was it something closer to her?

Terence Marconi, Gina's eight-year-old son, surely could have had nothing to do with his mother's death. And Gina's mother, Bridget, who was originally from Ireland, must be devastated. Preparing for a society wedding, she surely could not have expected her daughter to die.

Martha leafed through the file and picked up on another character. Gina's ex-husband, Terence's father, lived in New York. According to DI Randall's one brief reported telephone conversation with him, the divorce had been amicable. He had had very little to do with either Gina or their son and had not travelled outside the United States of America in the last five years. Contact with his ex-wife was minimal, limited to money paid into her bank account for the upkeep of their son. And that was really her close family.

Julius Zedanski, Martha felt, would be much more interesting. Perhaps her fiancé, who would have known her best, might have some explanation?

SEVEN

Wednesday, 15 March, 8.45 a.m.

J ulius Zedanski finally rang her early on the Wednesday morning, apologizing very politely for the delay.

'I've been travelling,' he said in a hoarse voice. 'I was . . . away when the news broke. I'm sorry. It must seem impolite.'

Martha was swift to assure him that there was no problem. 'I take it you'll be wanting to attend the inquest, Mr Zedanski?'

'Yes. Yes – of course. I'll be there.'

'This is a shocking business.'

Silence on the other end. Martha sensed Julius Zedanski was reining in his emotions very tightly. 'I could do with talking to you face-to-face before then,' Martha said gently. 'One or two things are puzzling me about this tragedy.'

He gave a sour laugh. 'One or two things, Mrs Gunn? Puzzling? The whole bloody thing doesn't make any sense. No sense at all.'

She ignored the bitterness and the anger and continued smoothly. 'You're in this country?'

'Yes. I got back as soon as I heard.'

'Shall we say three o'clock this afternoon then? Can you get here for then?'

'Yes. I'm staying with my . . .' A pause. 'Mother-in-law.'

'You know where my office is?'

'I'll find it,' he said shortly, and the conversation was at an end.

Speaking to Gina's fiancé had set Martha's mind whirring again and she rang the GP.

Stuart Milligan was an elderly doctor with whom Martha had had dealings on numerous previous occasions. He was a traditionalist who put his patients first and spent as little time as he dared on targets, directives and flow charts. 'Instinct,' he'd barked once down the phone. 'Instinct and experience. They're what count in General Practice.' But she saw a different side to him today. He

responded to Martha's questions with quiet, thoughtful answers
and she heard real sadness behind his responses.

'I was shocked when I heard. She was the last person I'd have
expected to kill herself.'

He continued almost without a break, answering all her questions
in one go. 'No, Mrs Gunn. She wasn't a drinker; she didn't do
drugs. She wasn't depressed. She was happy.'

Martha swallowed the retort that happy people don't leave their
beds at three a.m. to drive their cars into a wall at sixty miles an
hour.

He was as puzzled as she was. 'It doesn't make any sense, Mrs
Gunn. She had *everything* to live for. She'd found love again. She
was marrying a wonderful man with integrity, a world-class jour-
nalist. She had a big heart. The warmest heart and the kindest
nature. She had a career she loved and was brilliant at. A man she
loved. A son she loved. A mother she loved. So many people she
would hurt that she *couldn't* have wanted to kill herself. She
couldn't have wanted to hurt *them*.'

But she had. Deliberately.

A thought flitted through Martha's mind. *Unless she thought or
believed that by living she would hurt them more.*

The thought struck home with some resonance, tumbling around
in her mind as Dr Milligan continued, 'She was an open, friendly,
intelligent, beautiful young woman. It makes no sense, Mrs Gunn.
When I heard about the tragedy I thought they must be referring
to someone else. It couldn't be her. It wasn't her.'

This phrase also resonated with Martha and it would continue
to bounce around inside her head. *It wasn't her*. But it was. She
had been identified by the mother she had virtually destroyed by
her action.

Dr Milligan was still speaking. 'She had no money worries.
She was beautiful. I cannot, *cannot* understand it.' He sounded
personally confounded.

And Martha too was floundering. 'She'd not been on anti-
depressants or . . .' And now she was stuck for words, questions,
avenues to explore. Sensing all of them led to a blind alley.

'Absolutely not.' He was vehement, but then something must
have snagged his mind. 'Although . . .'

It was the first chink of light, the first hint that maybe, just maybe all was not as it appeared. Martha held her breath – and was disappointed.

'Hearsay,' Dr Milligan said quickly. 'Just gossip.'

'That's what I'm interested in, Doctor Milligan.'

According to DI Randall there was nothing in the public domain.

He had his answer ready then. 'Not if it isn't the truth, Mrs Gunn.'

She bit her lip. She didn't want clouds covering even this tiny glimpse of veracity. She skipped around his hesitance. 'She was looking forward to her wedding?'

'Oh, yes, excited about it.' A pause. 'Have you met Julius Zedanski?'

'No. Not yet. I've spoken to him on the phone but we haven't met face-to-face. He's coming here this afternoon.'

'He's quite a chap.' The doctor's admiration shone through. 'I've met him once or twice. He's very, umm . . .' The doctor sounded embarrassed. 'Charismatic.'

'And her mother?'

'Lovely woman. Highly competent. Intelligent. Ex-teacher. Widowed. A character. A personality. You could see where Gina got it from.'

'Her father?'

'Died some years ago, I believe.'

'Her son?'

'Ah, yes, young Terence. Good chap. They had his name down for Shrewsbury School. Good runner, I think. Sporty boy.'

This woman had a Teflon life, Martha reflected. Everything perfect? One big bed of roses? Did she have none of life's little frustrations and anomalies? She dug again.

'What about her ex-husband? Is he on the scene? Even for the boy?'

'To be honest I don't know. I never heard her mention him. I think he was an American – as far as I remember. They were divorced years ago. Long before I took her on as a patient.'

Which backed up Alex's version and sealed off that line of enquiry. Gina's personal life appeared flawless. A carefully constructed fable, or the truth?

'There's nothing more you can add?'

'No.'

She sensed the doctor was dying to put the phone down – she could hear voices in the background, heard a door open and close and a whispered response. Reluctantly she ended the conversation.

She moved to other work, but Gina Marconi's suicide was never far from her thoughts.

Jericho rang through at three o'clock to say Julius Zedanski had arrived, ready to talk to her. A punctual man.

Strange, she reflected, how we all feel a frisson at meeting someone famous, whatever the circumstances. She was excited, feeling like a teenager about to meet her superhero, her pop idol, her favourite film star. She even found herself checking her appearance in the wall mirror, trying to damp down her unruly red hair, checking her eyes for mascara smudges and trying to cool her cheeks down.

She shook her head at her reflection and, by the time Jericho had ushered him in, she had composed herself.

Like many celebrities only ever seen on television or screen, he was smaller than she had imagined, thinner, and he looked older, unless that was the result of his grief or a lack of TV make-up. But his features were familiar. He had an olive complexion, an angular, bony face, hooked nose and lovely teeth, but his smile today was cynical, twisted into an expression which was almost painful and his eyes, dark as jet, were pained and restless as though he too searched for an explanation. As she shook his hand Martha reflected that this recent tragedy would forever be nailed to his cross. Or maybe painful cynicism was his habitual expression. Journalists were well known for their objectivity. It was a necessary part of the job. When broadcasting from some war-torn hotspot Martha guessed viewers wouldn't see much of that lovely smile, even twisted as it was today. She had watched his war reports many times on the television but reality was not quite the same. His eyes were just as dark and unfathomable, his presence commanding, and yet she had the feeling he was also capable of merging into the background rather than standing out. She'd seen pictures of him in camouflage with the military, desert fatigues in Iraq and Iran, a djellaba in Morocco, a suit in London and country tweeds. Today he wore beige chinos and an open-neck shirt.

What she hadn't realized from the flat screen in her sitting room was that Julius Zedanski exuded a hot charisma. He was positively sexy. He fixed his eyes on her, held out his hand and gave hers a firm handshake. Very precise and, under the circumstances, businesslike.

'I'm glad to have the opportunity to talk to you about Gina,' he said in a low voice, not the authoritative tone he used when broadcasting. His accent wasn't quite English. Maybe the Polish roots weren't quite so far removed as she'd thought.

She invited him to sit down, asked Jericho to bring tea and sat opposite him, in the bay with the long sash windows which over-looked the spires and town of Shrewsbury. But the view had a disadvantage she hadn't considered. From this angle it was impos-sible not to recognize the dome of St Chad's where their wedding would have been, soon to be the venue for Gina's funeral when the body was released. Zedanski saw it too as his eyes swept the view. His mouth hardened and his eyes screwed up. He jerked his head away from the window and angled his chair away from the view, even though one's natural instinct would be to embrace it. On a shining day like today it was lovely. The town of Shrewsbury rises on a small hill enveloped by an oxbow in the River Severn. It looked exactly what it was, the modern-day version of a medieval stronghold, a safe refuge within the river's hug, although in the past the river had done its mischief too, cutting the town off by flooding its access routes and swamping both main bridges, the Welsh Bridge to the north-west and the English Bridge to the south.

She turned towards him and got straight down to business. 'You've had a few days since Gina's death,' she said gently. 'Have you thought about it?'

His mouth distorted even more. 'I've thought of nothing else,' he said, 'but I suspect that isn't what you mean.'

She shook her head and he nodded.

'You mean have I thought of any reason why Gina chose to die?'

She waited.

But he shook his head, eyes flickering away. 'Nothing that makes any sense,' he said, his bony face and eyes burning with intensity. 'I . . .' He screwed his face up to try and suppress his grief, but it didn't work. It spilled out of him, shockingly raw, like guts spilling out of a Hara-Kiri slash. His eyes were hot, hurt and angry, squeezing out boiling tears. 'I . . .' He seemed to choke then and was unable to speak.

She leaned forward, put a hand on his shoulder and waited. Sometimes silence is more eloquent than any words in the English language, or any other language in the world, a little space needed for grief to burst. He put his hands over his face and groaned.

Finally he looked up. 'I . . .' It was a mammoth effort for him to continue. Someone who had seen all the horrors of a hostile world paraded in front of his eyes, someone who took those horrors, sanitized them and presented them to the 'civilized' world.

His next sentence confirmed this. 'I've worked in war zones in practically every continent.' He licked his lips and continued.

'I've seen people – good people, nice people, people I've just interviewed, soldiers I've got drunk with, colleagues I've swapped stories with, children I've picked up out of the dirt, given sweets to – I've seen them all blown to bits, maimed, screaming with pain, terrified. I've seen people starve to death in front of my eyes, too weak to speak and others too emaciated to unwrap the chocolate bar I've just given them. I thought I'd seen it all.' He frowned and rubbed his forehead. 'I thought I was immune to suffering.' He looked at her directly then. 'The life Gina and I planned together would have been a balm for all that, but instead . . .' His eyes were on her. 'Gone. All gone, Mrs Gunn.' His voice and expression were bleak. 'I thought when I came home from one of these places that I would have a home to return to. A loving wife. A son. Perhaps more children. And now . . .' His hands fluttered.

'She was . . .' He couldn't find the words and simply shook his head as though trying to shake off the memory. 'She was a light in the darkness.'

'And you can think of no reason why . . .?'

He shook his head but she pressed him.

'You must have asked yourself this, Mr Zedanski. What did you come up with? Why did she do it?'

'I don't know.' He ran his fingers through his dark and silky hair. 'I don't know,' he said again, calmer now. 'She had everything to live for. A career, a son. We loved each other. We had a life planned. A wedding. We'd planned to have more children. We both wanted a family. I loved her.' He looked at her, an angry fire burning now in his eyes. 'If something was wrong, why didn't she just confide in me? Tell me? I would have helped her. We would have worked it out. But now?' He held his hands out wide, letting in this empty future. 'Now?' He answered his own question. 'Nothing,' he said bitterly. 'Nothing.'

She remained quiet. There is no need to fill every silence with sound. She let him think.

He did and reached his own unsatisfactory conclusion. 'The only thing I can think of,' he said slowly, echoing Mark Sullivan's words, 'is temporary madness.' It was almost a hopeful suggestion but it was an empty cliché – nothing more. And in this case it was not the answer.

'Anything else?'

His face screwed up tightly again and Martha waited. But he continued down the road of the life they would have had.

'We had plans for the house – Terence had decided he would board at school when he was thirteen. He was excited at the prospect. He'd be home for some of the weekends. It's only a couple of miles up the road. Bridget – Gina's mum – had a bungalow in the grounds. We have a couple of acres. We're halfway through doing up the house.'

For a split second she realized he had forgotten. His face had changed, softened. Still angular but the angles were less sharp.

'We planned to landscape the grounds – make part into a nature reserve, a meadow, apple trees, beehives, owl boxes. A patch of Little England.' He looked around him, cruelly waking now. 'That was our dream. How could she destroy it?' His anger was surfacing. Another stage in grief. 'Why? And why now?' He scratched his head in bemusement. 'I have a flat in London. I'll be going back there. My life is destroyed. It isn't just *her* life she's buggered up. It's mine too. And Terence's and Bridget's. If she had a problem, why didn't she confide in me? Why put her nearest and dearest – the people she loved and the people who loved *her* – through this? Our lives will never be whole again.'

And now, for the first time, Martha almost smelt his stinging fury against the woman who had constructed so much before destroying it so completely. Anger is part of grief. But it is the selfish part of grief, the *look what you've done to me* part of grief. And riding on its wings comes an ugly emotion – self-pity.

She sensed that now this had kicked in she would learn no more from Mr Zedanski. He looked up, smiled, slightly sheepish now but engaging her with a frank stare. 'I suppose,' he said, with a hint of bravery, 'I may as well put the house on the market and return to some far-flung war-torn part of the world. There's nothing for me here.'

What could she say, except, 'And young Terence?'

'I can't pick that up,' he said, his eyes full on her. '*She* was the thread that would have bound us together. It's no good now.'

So the boy would lose a hero-father as well as his mother. And for what?

She saw him to the door, closed it behind him and sat down to think.

Even though Julius had gone he'd left behind a room full of turbulence, anger, anguish, pain. She threw open the windows and welcomed in the fresh, clean, cold blast of air. No answers yet.

But ten minutes after he'd left and the turbulence had settled, her mind travelled a different track, somehow bound up with her own daughter, Sukey. Some men are so busy with their aspirations that their partners are dragged along in their wake. Was it possible that Julius's powerful persona had made Gina feel her own personality was drowned?

EIGHT

Wednesday, 15 March, 4 p.m.

Terence Marconi came in with his grandmother. He was a quiet, contained, thin boy with a strange, shadowy presence, almost sliding into the room after Bridget, a set expression on his face, eyes fixed on the floor, determined not to cry. Martha picked up on a wary, watchful child with a guarded demeanour. Whatever he knew he was not going to share. Martha recognized his stance. The boy had his defences up. He had his mother's dark hair and was not unlike the stepfather he would not now have.

Bridget, Gina's mother, looked like a bag of sagging, empty, pale skin, as though the personality Dr Milligan had described had had the life sucked out of it. She was tidily dressed in a dark woollen jacket over black trousers and was surprisingly short. Her

hair was salt and pepper, cut neat and framed a face that was alert
and, before this incident, would probably have looked lively – even
merry. Not now. Like her prospective son-in-law, she too must
have lost weight over the last few days. Her clothes were loose,
the skin on her neck saggy. She had a pleasantly quiet and polite
manner, a soft voice with only the tiniest hint of an Irish brogue.
Gina's voice had been louder, more commanding, but she had also
been easy to listen to, judging by the crowd of listeners at the
ball. It had been a voice that would lull the court into agreeing
with her. Maybe that was one of the reasons for her success as a
criminal lawyer – a pleasant voice must be an asset to persuade
a jury of your client's innocence.

Even if he was guilty? Perhaps Gina's voice had been instru-
mental in freeing felons.

'Thank you so much for seeing us,' Bridget opened with as
though *they* had been the ones to request the meeting. Polite and
charming; her daughter had been the same.

Martha responded in neutral gear, simply nodding. 'I generally
do,' she said, 'in cases which are tragic and unusual.' Her eyes
were on both of them, detecting, picking up on anything that passed
between them, anything that would give her a clue. She spent the
next few minutes running through the procedure of an inquest and
preparing them for the sequence of events.

The boy's eyes lifted and flickered over her, briefly appraising
before dropping back to the floor. She had the uncomfortable feeling
he'd been sizing her up. Wondering whether to confide in her?

Bridget continued. 'Needless to say, we're . . .' She waited a
long time before selecting her word. 'Confused,' she finally settled
on, faded blue eyes bearing out her statement.

Martha probed gently. 'I'm sure you've tried to come up with
a reason why your daughter . . . why Gina . . .'

The boy's eyes definitely *were* challenging her now, warning
her not to trespass into forbidden country, not to use the words
though they hovered in the air like a cloud of poisonous gas.
Committed suicide.

Martha chose a neutral word. 'Died.'

'It doesn't make any sense.' Bridget leaned forward to give her
words some weight. Her tone had turned steely and vaguely hostile.
Her defences were up too. There was no doubt she was defending

her daughter. 'She had everything to live for. She was successful and beautiful.'

To her shock Martha read scorn in the boy's eyes as he glanced across at his grandmother. He was mocking her for believing this fable. He knew something. But he was eight years old. A minor. Martha felt suddenly uncomfortable. How much could an eight-year-old know and how much would he understand? She met his eyes and read something else there. The boy was holding his breath, watchful and waiting, wondering whether she would pick up on something. What, for goodness' sake? She turned all her attention on to him.

'Terence,' she said gently, then with a brighter smile, she tried to win his confidence by spending some time on safer ground. 'Do you like to be called Terence or Terry?'

'Terence,' he said steadily, adding very politely, 'if you don't mind.' His private school education was paying off.

'I'm sorry about your mummy.'

His eyes dropped quickly. Deliberately hiding his expression.

She continued to address the boy. 'I wonder . . .' Granny Bridget's hand was tight on his arm. Restraint? Warning?

Martha continued anyway. 'I wonder if you thought your mummy had seemed . . .' She rejected the words 'distracted' or 'depressed', substituting instead, 'Sad? Different. Lately.'

The boy opened his mouth ready to speak but his grandmother's grip tightened. He dropped his eyes, shaking his head. Martha felt frustrated.

If there was a truth behind this, Grandma Bridget didn't want it to come out. So there was little point continuing the interview. Neither would speak in front of the other. Access to the child without a responsible adult was not possible, or in fact legal, and the obvious responsible adult was his grandmother – the grandmother who would not speak in front of the child. Both were bound to silence by the other. Hands tied behind their backs.

Bridget Shannon made an attempt to cheer up the boy. 'At least we didn't have to find the body,' she said.

It was such a small consolation that Martha didn't respond immediately, instead focusing on the interview. 'Mrs Shannon,' she said gently, 'shall we have a chat on our own? Jericho, my assistant, can keep an eye on Terence.'

Bridget knew exactly what was coming. Defeated, she nodded.

Jericho came when summoned and led the boy away, closing the door very carefully and deliberately behind him. It was time to stop chasing around the bush.

'Mrs Shannon,' she said, 'there must be something behind your daughter's suicide.'

The woman's eyelids flew open at the word but Martha remained steadily on course. 'I don't inevitably find the verdict suicide unless there is a note or incontrovertible evidence. Understand?'

Bridget nodded, eyes wary, hands gripping each other as though left would support right and vice versa.

She looked far beyond the window, perhaps seeing her daughter's face in happier times hovering over the dome of the church.

'At least I didn't have to find her body. She spared me that. But I feel so guilty that I didn't pick up on it.'

Martha murmured something neutral.

'I don't know any details,' Bridget added quickly, getting that out of the way, 'but a month or two ago, sometime over the winter, something happened. Gina was always a very happy person. Always happy with her place and status in life. My daughter,' she said, 'had a very strong sense of right and wrong. And then six or eight weeks ago I found her sitting in her lounge, lights turned off, just staring into space. It was so unlike her that I felt cold, almost frightened. You know that saying "someone just walked over my grave" – well, it was as though someone had just walked over *her* grave. Understand?'

'Yes, I do. What did you think it was?'

'That's the trouble. I don't know. She said to me then: "If anything happens to me you'll look after Terence, won't you?"' Bridget's face froze, her eyes screwed up against tears. 'I was really frightened. I thought she must have cancer or something.'

'I've spoken to Doctor Milligan,' Martha responded. 'There was nothing like that. Gina was in perfect health.'

Bridget nodded. 'Yes – she assured me she was well, she was fine, but I knew there was something.' She halted so abruptly it was as though a thought had just hit her. 'Mrs Gunn . . .'

Martha anticipated her question. 'Anything you say to me,' she said, 'will be kept in the strictest confidence. Nothing need come out into the public domain unless you want it to.'

Bridget let out a breath. 'I saw it in her eyes. A look I've never seen before. She was ashamed of something.'

'To do with her personal life? Julius?'

'Oh, no.' The denial came sharp, hot and strong. 'Julius is a saint. A lovely boy. We adore him, Terence too. No, whatever it was I don't think it was anything to do with Julius.'

'Then her work? Someone she was maybe defending?'

Bridget's face, turned towards her now, was pitiful, ageing in front of her eyes, collapsing in on itself. 'I just don't know.'

'Does Terence know?'

'I don't know that either. We're finding it difficult to talk.'

Martha was silent for a moment, absorbing this. Then, 'I've spoken to Julius Zedanski,' she said thoughtfully. 'He doesn't seem to know anything, so what are we left with, Mrs Shannon? Her professional life? She dealt with some . . .' She recalled Alex's words.

Nasty people.

'That's what I'm afraid of.'

'Do you know anything about the cases she was involved in?'

Bridget shook her head. 'She didn't tend to talk about it that much. To be honest, most of the time we were together lately we were discussing the wedding. It was going to be . . .' And then she did lose it, shoulders heaving with sobs.

Martha had seen tears before – too many, truth be told. She'd learned to put a wall between herself and her professional role. In this job it was essential to preserve her sanity. But the abject misery confronting her now was so raw it affected her.

She asked Jericho to bring in a cup of tea for Gina's mother and Terence returned, putting his arms around his grandmother, comforting her as though he was a fully grown man.

The boy was intriguing her. Martha met his dark eyes and assessed him as he returned her gaze. Mature beyond his years with an almost adult understanding. Perhaps even beyond adult. She felt that he had a better handle on his mother's state of mind than poor Bridget, who was distraught.

Ten minutes later, they had discussed the release of the body, which could go ahead now the cause of death was not in any doubt. Gina had died of a high-impact vehicular incident. That was the easy bit. The difficult part was why.

Bridget told her of the plans for the funeral. Heartbreakingly Martha's instinct had been correct. St Chad's Church, a distinctive landmark with its round shape and high tower standing over the quarry, which was the town's play and recreational area and site of the famous annual flower show.

It was only once the pair had left and the room returned to its usual stillness that something Bridget had said assumed a new significance.

At least I didn't have to find her body.

Could this be the reason behind the manner and place of Gina's suicide? Had she thought that carefully about location and planned to spare her mother or her son from making the discovery?

NINE

Gina's partner's email arrived late in the afternoon and Martha scanned through it. Gina had been a busy woman. And she saw immediately what Curtis Thatcher had meant.

After her brilliant defence of Mosha Steventon, the floodgates to the criminal world had swung wide open. There were numerous cases of petty crime, burglary, theft, assault, Actual Bodily Harm and Grievous Bodily Harm but some stood out from the rest. Gina's current case load consisted of a few more interesting cases.

There was a Joel Tansey, appealing against a seven-year sentence for fraud. He'd been importing car parts, avoiding paying the VAT but claiming it back from the government. Gina was appealing against his sentence, citing new evidence, but scanning through the detail, Martha couldn't see anything that would have convinced her that he was not guilty. The fact was he had not paid the VAT and had claimed it back. He had gone to prison and Gina was handling an appeal. But Tansey was currently banged up in HMP Wakefield and she couldn't see how he could have got to her. Her visits to the prison would have been watched if not listened to by prison officers. And his access to the outside world would have been limited. According to Curtis Thatcher, the prison governor had stated that there was nothing untoward in their contact. But Tansey was smarter than most of her other clients. The trail of bookwork, claims and counter claims was dizzyingly complicated.

There was a Lenny Khan. Now Khan might have been interesting, particularly with Gina's connection to Zedanski. Khan was a Pakistani accused of terrorism offences but, according to Thatcher's comments, Gina had read through some of the police notes and stated that it looked a flimsy case to her – nothing more than an order over the internet for ingredients which weren't necessarily solely used for making explosives, a few phone contacts who had bad reputations, a holiday in Turkey and some questionable friends. A lawyer like Gina Marconi would have made short work of this. And she had. The case had been thrown out of court, although Martha would have been very surprised if MI6 hadn't kept a watch over him.

Perhaps the nastiest creature was Pete Lewinski. He was currently accused of a road rage stabbing. Gina had claimed provocation, that the man who had been stabbed had been weaving in and out of traffic and slammed his brakes on, causing Lewinski to hit him, and then the man, a Bill Truman, had punched him. So where, Martha wondered, had the knife come from? She scanned Curtis Thatcher's notes but couldn't see that this very important question had been asked. Gina, it appeared, was not above defending the worst of villains. So how, Martha wondered, had she felt about releasing these offenders back on to the streets? Had she lacked a conscience, or had the guilt caught up with her? Goaded her to self-hatred? Had her defence of Steventon caught her in a sticky spider's web? Was that the reason she had felt unable to marry Zedanski? But Gina had been a criminal lawyer. This would have been the nature of her work. Martha tried to focus back on the case. She was no lawyer but she sensed that Lewinski was one of Alex's *nasty pieces of work* and the knife had been conveniently in the glove compartment of his car, ready to be used. Mr Bill Truman, Lewinski's victim, had survived the assault, but his survival probably owed more to medical skill than Lewinski's tale of simple self-defence. The knife had pierced his lung and missed his heart by just one centimetre.

Last of all in this list of villains was a guy named Jack Silver who was a fence for stolen goods and had been caught with antique jewellery, the result of a violent crime. Gina's defence had consisted of the fact that he was a fence, not a violent thief. She had placed him far away from the robbery, which had consisted of threats, violence, torture and the rape of the homeowner's wife. But Gina's involvement in the case had been futile. She didn't always win. The jury had been unconvinced. Silver was currently awaiting a similar sentence to the gang who had committed the crime. Thatcher had added his comment. *Silver feels very aggrieved.*

But surely even this involvement with the dregs of the human race wouldn't have driven her to take her own life when so much lay ahead? Martha spent some time staring at the names and the crimes – hoping for what? Inspiration?

She rang Alex Randall and shared with him her information about Gina's workload. He sounded buoyant. 'Yeah,' he said. 'Mixed bag or what? But I don't see what any of this bunch of beauties can possibly have had over Gina. She was way above all that.'

She felt a twinge. So . . . Alex had a high opinion of the dead woman?

'You knew her?'

'Vaguely,' he said, and she heard a teasing note in his voice. He'd picked up on her little green-eyed monster.

'She was, after all, a *criminal* barrister,' he reminded her gently. 'Yes, we were usually on opposite sides of the court, but she was a very charismatic woman.'

He'd used the word deliberately. She felt cheated.

'And that caused you to change your evidence?'

'No, Martha, it didn't.' His voice was steady and uncompromising. 'A criminal act is a criminal act. It was up to us to anticipate her questions and try and fend them off so the jury wouldn't be taken in by her. But she was adept at finding a chink of light. She caused us a few nasty moments and there are people walking the streets who in my opinion shouldn't be, but in general, yes, I respected her. She was good at her job.' He paused. 'Even if sometimes she used her feminine wiles a little too audaciously.'

'Well, that's given me a much clearer picture of our dead woman.'

'It was out of character for her to commit suicide,' he said, 'but it isn't really a police matter.' She knew he was smiling with his next sentence. 'More a job for an inquisitive coroner.'

'Well, thank you for that,' she said drily.

'But under the circumstances, Martha – and I've visited the site – I can't see how it can have been anything but a planned and deliberate act.'

'Then she must have been driven to it.'

He paused before repeating himself with, 'It isn't a police matter.'

And she had to leave it at that.

TEN

Martha spent what remained of the week preparing for the opening of Gina's inquest which would be on the Monday. It would be a brief affair. Adjourned pending enquiries. Mainly hers, from what Alex had said.

But Gina was not her only case. Her desk was full, her in-tray piled high with cases less interesting but which still demanded her attention.

The weekend went as planned – or rather, expected – an away win for Sam against Watford: 2–0. A triumph for Stoke City. Her little hero didn't actually score but was as exuberant as ever when he rang to ask for a lift back from the ground.

'We're really on the way up, Mum.'

It would have been too much of a spoiler to comment that what goes up can also go down. But, as always, when Sam was such a presence, she knew she would feel his absence keenly when he left home. What would she do when he had gone, apart from miss him, miss him, miss him?

Sukey had turned up on Saturday lunchtime, her boyfriend Pomeroy in tow, mouthing off about her driving. Sukey simply looked pale, thin and exhausted. Unhappy. Almost defeated. Ill. But then life with Pom would never be a picnic. What, Martha wondered, was his family like? Had he got this depressingly critical outlook from his mother? His father? Or had it formed inside him like an abscess which would infect those who surrounded him? Or was it Sukey herself that brought out this mean streak in him? Sukey, clever and beautiful? Was he jealous of her successes? The real question was: why the hell did Sukey put up with it so sheepishly? Why was she letting him destroy her? Martha had never before seen her daughter like this. She had changed. And she wasn't happy. Sukey was at university studying drama. Martha had had little doubt that her daughter's career as an actress would be as successful as her twin brother's career as a footballer, but Pom was dissuading her from following what had been her destiny since she had been able to walk and talk.

Mother-like, Martha kept schtum, put a meal in the oven for them, turned the heating up and lit the log burner. A bitter wind seemed to be howling right through the house. She smiled, remembering her mother's mantra for March. *In like a lion and out like a lamb.* Or else, *In like a lamb and out like a lion.* The March winds had certainly found them.

Then she drove to the Britannia Stadium to pick up Sam and Tom Dempsey, his friend who also played for Stoke City. And even her football-playing son who usually noticed absolutely nothing unless it was between two goal posts seemed to have picked up on something of his twin sister's mood.

'Mum,' he said halfway home after non-stop football chat with Tom, which included game plans and discussion of form, criticism of a player who'd committed the obvious offence of diving and whom they both agreed should have been sent off as a warning, and a complete analysis of every single move all of the players both Watford and Stoke had made or failed to make. Finally they ran out of conversation and he looked across at her. 'Do you think Suks is all right, Mum?'

She wanted to clap. He'd noticed something off the pitch? Yay!

She turned to look at him. While Sukey had all the gifts – straight teeth, fine blonde hair, big baby-blue eyes and the most slender of figures, her brother was the diametric opposite. Not one of his teeth was straight and he now wore a brace to try and correct what nature must have flung at him on an off day. His hair was wiry and ginger. It didn't even have his twin sister's faint hint of red-gold but, like his mother's, it stuck out all over the place. But this odd little collection of cells which made up her son and had been flung together, much of it courtesy of both her own genes and Martin's, had this most wonderful gift. Sam Gunn could dribble a ball as effectively as though it was attached to his feet with invisible elastic. He could shoot that same ball straight, guide it to the place his mind had set for it, curl it right under the goalie's nose just under the bar. She'd watched his own particular kind of magic and, like watching her daughter pour herself into another part and not so much act as *become* that person, speaking, thinking, moving differently, she was in awe of them both, these gifted children who were twins but whose gifts could not have been at farther ends of the spectrum, and she watched and marvelled as each had glued themselves to their ambition.

'Not really, Sam,' she answered. 'I don't think Sukey is very happy but there's not a lot we can do about it except sit it out.'

Her son settled back in his seat, thoughtful.

And she continued with her own thoughts. Pomeroy Trainer – the nasty big fly in the ointment. As she dropped Tom off and turned back on to the main road she smiled to herself. It wasn't fair to be prejudiced against someone for their name but just hearing 'Pom' spoken in her daughter's flutey little voice made her wince.

Unfair.

She could almost hear Martin's voice scold her for her attitude as he would have done. Always calm, always reasoned. Predictable. A keel for her boat which invariably floated on choppy seas.

ELEVEN

Monday, 20 March, 11 a.m.

After the sensational circumstances of her death, Gina's inquest could not have been less dramatic. It was quiet, subdued and orderly. Coroners' courts are not backdrops for drama but a civilized, rational setting for a verdict.

Martha began with the almost-forgotten Graham Skander, first on the scene, still more concerned about his damaged wall than a woman's death, a woman who, after all, he'd never known in life. He gave his evidence in brisk, unemotional fashion.

'I was . . . asleep. I heard a loud bang.' He hesitated, frowning. 'I think it was about three a.m. I knew instantly what it was. It wasn't the first time a car had hit my wall.' He couldn't quite obliterate the note of severity from his voice. His eyes skittered along the floor. 'The police have suggested I have some chevrons put there. But . . .' His frown deepened as though he now felt in some way responsible. And who did not feel responsibility in this crowded courtroom? Martha glanced around the faces, Bridget, Julius, Curtis Thatcher – not Terence, thank goodness. She homed in on Julius Zedanski, who was sitting in a dark grey suit, eyes half closed. What was he thinking?

Alex and a couple of his officers sat in a stiff row near the back. She would only be calling the officer who had been first on the scene, PC Gethin Roberts, a young officer who had the knack of turning up almost whenever there was a dramatic event. As she understood it wedding bells were about to ring for the PC.

Mark Sullivan, the pathologist, sat in front, watching everyone, listening intently. He looked very alert. It was his way to absorb all the information that surfaced. She smiled inwardly. She had a great fondness for the pathologist and respected and admired his work. He had had a drink problem in the past caused, she believed, by a bitter and unhappy marriage, but an internet date with a divorcee with three children appeared to have cured him of alcoholism. And the medical pathology department had benefitted as a result.

And Alex? As always, Alex's legs appeared too long for the seating. They stretched out in front of him. Their eyes met for an instant and she felt the connection as physical as if there was an invisible line of silken thread that attached them unseen by anyone but themselves. He grinned at her and, in spite of the surroundings and the circumstances, she felt warm and relaxed.

She turned her attention back to Graham Skander. She could guess what he was about to say. 'Carry on,' she prompted gently.

'I, umm. My house . . .' His voice was confrontational, slightly aggressive, defensive. 'It's over three hundred years old. Built way before cars came careering around the corner. I have had the wall rebuilt numerous times. The council have offered to have markers put there to draw attention to the sharp bend. They've already erected road signs. But I don't want some brightly coloured chevrons right outside my house. They would be out of character for what is a Georgian building.' Like Zedanski, he too half closed his eyes then, hiding his emotions behind hooded lids. 'But I suppose,' he conceded. 'Maybe.' He squared his shoulders and pulled his face into a tight frown. 'I think maybe, under the circumstances, I should reconsider.'

Said with admirable dignity. A little wave of appreciation rippled around the room. There is nothing people like better than for good to result from bad.

Bridget and Zedanski were sitting next to each other and now they leaned in very close. Bridget had her hand on his forearm. What a shame, Martha thought. They would have got on like a house on fire. Terence too. The family unit would have worked so well. But now there was this black hole right in its centre. Like a sink hole they would all tumble in. And the three people most affected by tragedy would inevitably drift apart, like planets after an explosion finding their own new orbits.

Graham Skander finished his statement sympathetically. 'Poor woman. I think she was already dead when I reached the car.' And then, addressing both Bridget and Zedanski directly, he finished with a gruff, 'I'm so sorry.'

Almost, Martha thought, as though his wall had been the villain here.

'Thank you.' She dismissed him gently.

And then she heard the testimony of Zedanski, spoken in a quiet, dignified voice, that they had been planning to marry and he knew of no reason why Gina would want to take her own life.

Bridget added her response to this, as did Dr Milligan and Curtis Thatcher.

All spoke of Gina as being happy, clever, beautiful, vivacious with everything to live for. These were the words spoken in tribute. But it could not be true. She might have had everything to live for but, if her mother's observation had been correct, maybe she'd also had something to die for.

The emergency ambulance team of paramedics and the police were factual. They gave no opinion but simply reported their findings. No pulse. Not breathing. Not conscious. Pronounced dead at the scene by the police. An attempt at CPR had proved futile. Life extinct had been pronounced at 04.27 a.m. Body transferred to the mortuary for the post-mortem.

And then over to Mark Sullivan who related his PM findings, the long list of injuries. Broken bones, torn blood vessels, catastrophic haemorrhage, head injury, brain trauma.

Martha closed her eyes. A textbook example of multiple injuries due to high-speed vehicular impact.

She could have uttered the verdict of suicide then, but something was holding her back. She looked at the waiting faces and knew something was missing here. There was that part of the story that Bridget had picked up on. Until she had that missing piece she would adjourn the inquest pending enquiries. When she said this she felt a shiver of relief in the room.

It wasn't over yet. She set a date for a review and set the case aside.

Alex was waiting for her outside and he agreed with her. 'Yes,' he said in response, 'we know only part of the story. There's something behind this. I have the feeling Gina was cornered. Someone else is involved. I'll make gentle, tentative enquiries, keep an eye on what's going on and . . .' He grinned. 'Report back to you.'

'Thank you.'

His eyes were far away now. He was somewhere else. 'I think,' he said, 'the brick wall she drove into is almost an analogy for where her life was. No escape.'

Something about his tone and the abstraction in his eyes sent a shiver up her spine. He wasn't talking about Gina Marconi's death. She knew his home circumstances were not happy. She put her hand on his as a gesture of friendship. 'You're being very deep today, Alex.'

But the moment had passed. His face lightened and he smiled at her. He met her eyes without flinching or looking away. 'This suicide,' he said, 'feels like it is the beginning of something. Oh.' He scolded himself. 'Take no notice. I'm just being fanciful.'

Which was not like him. He was the pedantic police officer. It was she who sometimes took flights of imagination. He turned to leave and she watched him stride out of the building in a firm, even step, soon joined by DS Paul Talith and, trailing behind them, the gangly frame of PC Gethin Roberts.

But his words had left her wondering.

So what, she wondered, was the back story? Would she ever know it? And if Alex was right and this was the beginning of something, what was it the beginning of?

TWELVE

Tuesday, 28 March, 8.45 a.m.

She didn't have to wait long to find out.

The irony of it all was that the day had started so well.

Martha had sprung out of bed and thrown back the curtains to let in sunshine. It seemed like the first day of spring – the first really hopeful day of the year after a miserably soggy winter when homes had been flooded just in time for Christmas and the temperatures kept warm enough to harbour the most persistent of colds and influenza. Everyone had seemed to be coughing or sniffing or sneezing into tissues. People felt they had been robbed of winter's purifying frosts and seasonal traditions: sledging and bracing walks in ice-cold sunshine, skating on ponds. That was what winter was about – not this country drowning in mud. There had been something too reminiscent of WWI in the mud, something equally dreary and dismal about the perma-dull skies and the ever-present sound of rain hammering down on roofs. Added to that the people of Shrewsbury had worried and watched the River Severn swell almost to bursting only to be held back by the flimsy-looking flood defences. Their beloved town was safe and dry but they couldn't rid themselves of a tinge of guilt about the swell of water now passing downstream, to other towns and villages: Bridgnorth and Ironbridge, even as far down as Upton-upon-Severn. However, Martha was putting all this behind her that morning as she drove to her office. Her spirits under the canopy of a blue sky were high enough to hum a tune she was finding it hard to forget. Goodness knew why.

'I just called to say I love you.'

Stevie Wonder. She laughed at herself. Maybe it wasn't just young men whose thoughts turned to love when spring beckoned.

Right now, had she been a bird she would have been sitting at the top of a bush, beak wide open, trilling a welcome to the warmer days ahead.

11.45 a.m.

They'd been to visit their daughter who had just had a baby at the maternity hospital in Birmingham. The birth had been uncomplicated. 'A normal delivery,' Stella had announced proudly. She was due to be discharged later that day. And now, thinking of baby powder, nappies and breast milk, they were heading home. They'd travelled along the M54 and had hit the A5. Initially they were happy and relaxed, both dreaming of the little girl and her future. Radio 2 was playing old songs. Eileen was humming along to an old Elvis ballad that took her right back to her courting days. She turned to smile at Felton, her husband, wondering if he too recalled the moments.

Afterwards she could never again hear 'Wooden Heart' without a shudder and a bubble of nausea, but at the time she was smiling, lulled by the sunshine streaming in through the windscreen, the vision of their exhausted daughter, enveloped in her loving husband's arms, and the tiny wrinkled face of their new grandchild who was to be called Kate. Not Catherine or Katerina, Cathy or Katy. 'Just Kate,' Stella had said firmly, brooking no argument or objection. But they wouldn't have said anything even if she'd chosen to call the baby Muriel.

Even when they first saw the boy standing up there on the bridge they had still felt happy, excited.

The sky was blue that morning, practically cloudless, which made visibility just about perfect. But that, cruelly, made subsequent events all the more vivid. The day was warm for the month – another curse – the A5 was not that busy and they were in no great hurry. They were meandering, both of them still breathing in that soft, sweet-milk baby scent.

'Kate,' she murmured and they both smiled. They had their separate dreams. He was already constructing a dolls' house. In his mind he was beginning to plan tiny rooms, a staircase, battery-operated chandeliers. Pictures. While she was equally busily dressing the little girl in pink with lace and ribbons – no, not ribbons. They get caught with dreadful results. She snatched back the ribbons and proceeded to imagine knitting something pink. Stella hadn't wanted to know the sex of the child before it was born. 'It'd be like opening your presents before Christmas,' she'd said and her husband, besotted both with his wife and the image of fatherhood, agreed. So all Eileen's knitting so far had been white or lemon. The layette would soon be augmented with pink.

They expected to arrive home in less than half an hour and planned to tidy up the garden after the recent storms. Afterwards they would separately estimate their speed as having been sixty miles per hour, or thereabouts. Eileen's eyes were lazily scanning the road ahead, watching the sporadic shadows of other vehicles chase and then pass them. She looked up at the dazzling sky then along the verge where some unfortunate was waiting for the breakdown services. *At least it isn't raining on him*, she thought before she tutted at the litter. How could people just chuck things out of their car, making the countryside filthy?

And then.

Her eyes drifted upwards to the bridge in the distance, seeing the silhouette of the child who had climbed the barrier. He seemed to be looking along the A5. At them. Now he was standing on the top rail. Balancing. *He shouldn't be there*, she thought. Afterwards she would remember details. He was alone, wearing a red anorak and a blue beanie. But as she looked upwards, dumb and mute with horror, he seemed to raise his arms up, like Christ in Rio, almost in blessing. Then he toppled and fell through the air, spread-eagled like a sky diver, landing in a horrible crunching, swerving, skidding blur, thumping down on their bonnet before being tossed into the road. The breath that came out of her was a scream, her thoughts tumbling out.

Make it a dream. Make it a nightmare. Make it not real.

Then she started to shake. 'Felton?' Her husband had somehow, God knew how, managed to brake and put his hazards on, but all around them was mounting chaos, drivers, taken unawares by the sudden drama, unable to process the information quickly enough, failing to stop, slewing across the lanes, banging into one another like huge metal dominos, while a few vehicles, drivers intent on their journey, or perhaps not processing what had just happened, looped around them and carried on, slipping past the chaos and mounting pandemonium, screams, shouts, noise. It seemed to take forever for the whole scene to come to a crazy, slewing stop, and then there was a deadly quiet and brief stillness except for cars braking and skidding far behind them. And something was happening on the opposite carriageway as drivers heading east knew *something* was happening and were slowing to see what. Eileen, still belted into her seat, scrabbled around but she couldn't find her bag, couldn't find her mobile phone. Couldn't stop her hands from shaking. She felt waves of dizziness and sickness as her eyes and then her brain initially tried to reject the dreadful image of the child thumping down on their bonnet but then, peering through the windscreen at the bloody dent, feeling and hearing the impact again and again and again, they both knew it had been for real. People were getting out of their cars to look. Look? She couldn't look, not to the side, to the front or behind her. She couldn't move. She wanted to shut her eyes, shut it out. She didn't want to see his broken body because she knew it was there – somewhere in that confusion of vehicles all at the wrong angle to each other and the road. And if she saw it she knew it would stay in her mind forever. Whenever she closed her eyes, in the future, it would be pasted to the inside of her lids. When she slept it would invade her dreams. And worst of all, when she held her new beautiful little granddaughter, Kate, she would remember this boy in the red anorak and blue hat who had died (because he must be dead) on the very day that Kate had been born.

And so she focused only on her husband. 'Felton.' She tried her voice cautiously. 'That was,' she began to say, watching the colour drain from his face as it must already have done from her own. 'It was . . .'

They both knew what it was.

Now the cars were stopped, the A5 blocked, it was quiet. The people standing on the road seemed like zombies, mute, not quite knowing what to do. They looked at each other, shocked into silence. And after the silence came a noise from a distance, softly approaching at first but increasingly strident. It was the noise of approaching rescue, of normality, of order, of the authorities.

Police, ambulance. Even a fire engine screaming towards them along the hard shoulder. Eileen felt a sense of relief. These were the people who could return the scene to normal, make sense out of madness. Someone must have made the call and summoned them. And now the sirens were closer, screaming all around them. More were joining them. Louder and louder. Lights brighter and brighter. Relief had arrived, people who knew exactly what to do in such a situation. The peaceful scene had been shattered in the blink of an eye. From beginning to end was less than eight minutes.

THIRTEEN

Tuesday, 28 March, 5 p.m.

Alex rang her as the afternoon was drawing to a close. For Martha it had been a peaceful, pleasant day. She had eaten her lunch while still working, to Jericho's disapproval, but she'd cleared a backlog of form filling and felt the usual satisfaction when you've completed a mundane task. She was just wondering what to cook for tea when the phone rang.

Jericho had got used to the fact that though he fended off all the coroner's calls, somehow DI Alex Randall had become an exception. So when he picked up the phone and recognized the voice he didn't even ask but put the call straight through.

'Martha.' She immediately picked up on the sense of foreboding in the detective's voice.

'Alex?'

'Remember my saying that this felt like the beginning of something . . .' He hesitated, not wanting to use too melodramatic a word. 'That it felt like there was something dark about Gina Marconi's death?'

'Yes.' She wondered what on earth was coming next.

'There's been another death . . .'

Afterwards she would toss those two words around: *another death*. Why, she would wonder later, was he linking the two together? Even in sparsely populated, generally healthy Shropshire, people died every day. 'What – another car accident?'

'No. A young lad. A boy called Patrick Elson jumped off an A5 bridge this morning. We found his schoolbag on the bridge over the dual carriageway.'

'Another suicide?'

'It looks like it. A couple driving in the Shrewsbury direction saw him standing on the parapet over the road. They saw him jump and he hit their car . . .' He hesitated before adding: 'And others.'

'I take it he's—'

'Yes, multiple injuries again. The boy's mother—'

She interrupted. 'How old?'

'Twelve.' He resumed his story. 'The boy's mother can't understand it. He should have been at school. He wasn't in any trouble. According to his mother he wasn't depressed or ill. He didn't take drugs.'

They all say that.

'So could it have been an accident?'

'Even if it was, his mother says it would be out of character for him not to be at school and he wasn't exactly a daredevil sort of boy. If anything, he was a swot.'

'So what was he doing there in the first place? Why was he *there* instead of at school?'

'We don't know. He was pronounced dead at the scene. Pretty horrendous injuries. Mark says he can fit in the PM in the morning. Mother has identified him.'

'Right. I'll need to speak to her and anyone who witnessed the boy on the bridge.'

'Plenty of those,' he said, with cynicism, 'but the main witnesses are the couple who were driving back to Shrewsbury after visiting their daughter. She'd just had a baby, apparently. Anyway they were returning home along the A5. The woman, a Mrs Eileen Tinsley, saw the boy climb up on to the top rung and fling himself off. Those were the words she used.'

'Fling himself off – like flying?'

'That's what she said.'

Twelve years old, she was thinking. Drugs? They made you believe you could fly through the air, even off a bridge over a busy dual carriageway, and come to no harm. 'We'll need a full toxicology screen.'

'Yes.'

She just needed to check on a detail. 'Could it have been an accident and he fell? Is it possible someone dared him and he either overbalanced or was pushed?'

'The couple said he was alone. They didn't see anyone anywhere near him.' He finished with, '*Now* do you see why I link the two together?'

'I'm beginning to. I'd better talk to the boy's mother. Is she in a fit state to . . .'

'I think you would be the best person.' He sounded relieved.

FOURTEEN

Wednesday, 29 March, 10 a.m.

Martha felt it would be politic to be certain of the known facts so she left it until the next day before contacting Eileen Tinsley and her husband, Felton. The poor woman would have been in shock on the Tuesday. But as she had analysed the sketchy facts between the two apparent suicides she began to draw parallels between them and see why Alex Randall had linked the two deaths. Though there were obvious differences – sex, age, background – there were also apparent similarities. Two violent and inexplicable suicides in such a short time?

She needed to learn more facts about these two disparate people, delve into their backgrounds, not just focus on their deaths. And she mentally warned herself against jumping too far in her conclusions. It was too easy to make connections where there were none, spot ghosts hiding in shadows, imagine circumstances which simply didn't exist.

Begin by learning the facts.

Her first call was to a very shaken Eileen Tinsley. She could hear the waver in her voice, particularly when she explained who she was.

She began by apologizing for the intrusion, using her tried and tested phrases, 'at this difficult time', and so on. She explained her position and role and the purpose of her call.

Eileen Tinsley still sounded shocked. 'It'll stay with me, Mrs Gunn,' she said, 'possibly for all my life.'

Again Martha used well-worn phrases. 'Counselling will be made available, Mrs Tinsley, but for some people the images just naturally fade and that's the way they deal with it. Now all I want is this. Simply the facts.'

'OK.'

Martha's calm manner appeared to be having an effect.

'We were returning from Birmingham. My daughter had just given birth. We didn't stay long. She was tired and wanted to be alone with her husband and little Kate.'

'Yes.'

'The weather was just gorgeous. We were both dreaming, I suppose, thinking about the little girl, making plans. You know?'

'Yes,' Martha said again.

'We were going at an average speed. About sixty. The radio was on . . .' She paused. 'Elvis. Some cars were going faster than us. Someone had broken down on the hard shoulder. I remember thinking, *Lucky it's not raining*. And then I looked up and the boy was standing on the rung halfway up the railing on the side of the bridge. He was looking down. It seemed as though he was looking down at us. Before I knew it, he was balancing on the top rail and then he flung his arms out and launched himself into the air. And then . . .' Her voice tailed away.

'Did you see anyone else on the bridge with him?'

'No. He was on his own.'

'Did it seem like a deliberate act or possibly a daredevil stunt? A stunt gone wrong?'

For a brief second there was no response. Then Mrs Tinsley said quietly, 'He knew what he was doing, Mrs Gunn. He was looking straight at us.'

'And your husband?'

'We talked about it last night,' she said. 'He was focused on the road so he didn't quite see what I did. But he did look up at one point and said he saw the boy with his arms outstretched. The boy didn't look as though he toppled. No. He was more like a diver on a board – poised, in control, balanced. It's an awful thought but he was quite graceful as he fell.'

The image was painfully graphic. 'The boy's name,' Martha said slowly, 'was Patrick Elson. He was twelve years old. He lives – lived – in Shrewsbury with his mother.'

'The poor woman.'

Martha thanked her for her help, asked that she contact her if she or her husband thought of anything else that might help them understand Patrick's death. She said that her officer would be in touch to give her the details of the inquest, which she would be expected to attend. She reassured her that her statement would not need to be more than she had just delivered.

She finished with another platitude. 'And I hope that your love and care for your new little granddaughter will help dispel these dreadful images. I'm sure there is some sad story behind Patrick's death.'

Eileen Tinsley muttered her thanks and Martha put the phone down. Alone in her room she could think. Plan, work this one out and wonder.

She looked down at the folder she was amassing on the boy's death. Alex had emailed through some pictures taken at the scene. And according to the local news website, flowers had already been strewn on the A5 hard shoulder, which would soon be cleared by the police as they were a 'driver distraction'. A few more bunches had been tied to the railings of the fateful A5 bridge. The pictures had zoomed in on one or two of them so Martha could read a few of the scrawls. Messages of affection and the ubiquitous: *Why?*

She read through Alex's email a second time, detailing the facts the police were gathering.

Patrick had been twelve years old, his mother's only child. According to Amanda Elson he had had no contact with his father; she had brought him up alone, but he'd had adoring maternal grandparents and a vast collection of aunts, uncles and cousins. According to the statements so far he had been a happy, intelligent, sensitive boy with a small circle of friends. *A bit of a geek*, according to one or two social media tributes. His teachers and schoolmates had echoed this sentiment. He was more than bright. One or two of his relatives had called him brilliant. A few more had commented: 'Really clever'. His mother described him as always top of the class.

She took a good look at the photographs sent over to her. Patrick Elson had a thin, sensitive face, bright and eager. Clear blue eyes, looking straight at her, open and friendly. He had big teeth, an engaging smile. No hint of trouble or unhappiness. The picture had been taken at the beginning of the last term, just after Christmas, three short months ago, and Patrick was neat in his school uniform. So what, she wondered, had turned this fresh-faced boy into someone who dived off a bridge on to a dual carriageway and certain death? She looked back at other observations. He had been small for his age but intelligent beyond his years, fond of reading and of science projects. In particular, one teacher had commented, he had been interested in space. The teacher's name was Freddie Trimble. For the first time that morning, Martha smiled. The name evoked Dickens. She would try and contact him herself. Of all the statements, she felt he would be the one to provide more detail to the picture of the dead boy.

Next she leafed through the police photographs taken of his bedroom walls papered with pictures of the planets and the International Space Station. Again, according to Freddie Trimble, Patrick had followed Tim Peake's progress every second that the astronaut had been up in space and he had wanted to be an astronaut too. OK, Patrick, she thought, it was a long shot. But now it would be an unfulfilled ambition. He would never even get the chance.

And then Martha peered deeper at the next part of the report.

Recently, she read, friends and family had said that in the month before his death he had become quieter, more reserved. 'Perhaps frightened of somebody or something,' his best friend, another geek, Saul Matthews, had suggested, but when questioned by the police, he had said he had no idea who or what was troubling his friend. In fact, no one could give any reason why Patrick had done what he had. He should have been at school that day. His completed homework had been found in his schoolbag as though he had intended going to school but for some reason had detoured. Piecing together CCTV and witness statements, Patrick had taken the bus into town and instead of walking up the hill to the school gates he had walked the two miles to the bridge, carrying his schoolbag heavy and full of books including the completed homework. At the bridge he had apparently stood for around twenty minutes, according to other passers-by, a couple of cyclists, some drivers and minutes of CCTV footage. Initial police investigation indicated that Patrick had been hit by a total of five cars and a lorry. Martha looked at the CCTV footage. Patrick was facing east, into the oncoming traffic heading west. His features were hazy except for an outline. He had hefted his schoolbag from his shoulder, dropping it down to the pavement. Zooming in, his manner appeared resolute but sad. His shoulders sagged. At one point he stopped and put his hands to his face. He appeared to watch the traffic for some minutes before climbing on to the first rung. There he had bided his time. Then he had stepped up to the second rung, reached the top rail, balanced for a second before stretching his arms out and dropping on to the carriageway. The footage bore out Eileen Tinsley's statement. There was no sound to the film, which gave it an eerie, silent movie quality, but the pictures were good and clear. She could even see him bounce off the bonnet of the Tinsleys' car, see it swerve, the body tossed, and then the consequences, cars careering into one another. One lorry driver three vehicles behind the Tinsleys had had a dash cam fitted. Martha switched to this. You could see the car lose control, the boy's body tossed back into the air, frantic attempts to brake and hear the lorry driver's expletive.

Sickened, she switched it off.

She would never show this film to his mother. Neither would she share with her the details of the boy's injuries as reported by Mark Sullivan when he rang later that day.

'Traumatic below-knee amputation of the right leg, multiple fractures, five ribs broken, a torn subclavian artery, skull fractures . . . Take your pick, Martha. I could go on. Skull injuries, eye sockets. The bloody lot really. There wasn't much of his body left without something broken, damaged.'

She could hear the catch in his voice and knew this postmortem would be one that would stay with him. 'There was one finding that was more unexpected and not anything to do with the vehicular impact.'

'Go on.'

'Anal dilatation and some tears. Fairly recent. Could be the result of constipation, Martha. The trouble is if you ask his close family whether he suffered from constipation they'll know full well what the implication is.'

'He was underdeveloped for a twelve-year-old.'

'Oh, yes, nowhere near puberty. But you never know. Anyway, you'll get my full report in a day or two.' He chuckled grimly. 'When my lazy secretary gets her head out of the clouds.'

'Lisa?'

'Yeah – fallen in love.'

She couldn't resist it. 'Rather like somebody else in the mortuary.' She could pick up on his embarrassment even in the brief, 'Hmm.'

'So how is Nancy?'

'She's great. Thanks for asking.'

'Mark, I'm glad.'

'Thank you.'

He returned to the subject of the phone call. 'Anyway, the poor boy died instantly. Difficult to say categorically which injury was the fatal one but at a guess I would say head injury plus shock from haemorrhage from the subclavian artery and the leg injury.' He couldn't resist tacking on one of his mantras: 'Bodies and cars are a lethal combination when speed is involved.'

'Quite.'

She was thoughtful when the conversation ended. Like Gina Marconi, there could be no doubt that Patrick Elson's death had been suicide. There had been no one else in those pictures. No one near enough to have touched him.

She rang Alex and caught up with events. 'Nothing so far,' he said tersely. 'We're digging as hard and as deep as we can, but so far nothing. He had a pay-as-you-go mobile phone but there was nothing on that either. Texts to and from school friends, plenty to Saul Matthews, but mainly comments on schoolwork. Messages to his mother were almost all about times he would be home. Nothing else.'

'What about the fact that he'd appeared . . .' She thumbed back through her report. 'Quieter, more reserved, in the last month or so?'

'Some people say that,' he said, 'but others deny it. You know as well as I do, Martha, that after the event people imagine all sorts of things.'

'Mark Sullivan picked up on some anal trauma.'

'Yes, we're aware of that, but Mark said it could be the result of constipation. It wasn't necessarily that he had been sexually abused.'

'It's something to bear in mind though, Alex.'

'Yes.'

She dipped her big toe in the water. 'I thought I might have a word with one of Patrick's teachers.'

'Thought you might.'

Even though the issues were serious she could still sense the mischief behind his response and the challenge in his voice. He knew her. Martha did not like mysteries. She said goodbye, put the phone down and her green eyes narrowed. She preferred explanations. She preferred to understand.

She hadn't forgotten about Gina Marconi's death. It was still there occupying the back of her mind. She wouldn't let go until she understood a little more about that case. But at the moment she would focus on Patrick Elson's death. And for that she needed to speak to his mother.

Jericho arranged a meeting for the following day at noon.

Amanda Elson, Patrick's mother, was a slim woman of medium height. She had pale, perfect skin, shoulder-length brown hair, wore little make-up and was dressed in a grey suit. Work clothes, probably. She worked in an office in the town. She was accompanied by her sister, Melanie. Melanie was an altogether flashier affair in a short denim skirt and dark blue faux-leather jacket. But she too looked pale and shaken with grief, dabbing at her eyes with a floral tissue. She said nothing.

Amanda looked as though she had been hollowed out. And though it had been Martha who had requested the meeting, she held out her hand. 'Thank you, Mrs Gunn,' she said quietly, 'for seeing us.'

Her sister, following in her wake, said nothing but met her eyes briefly and nodded, adding her thanks to her sister's.

Martha guided them to the armchairs in the bay window and they sat down gingerly, eyes watchful. She knew that look. They were apprehensive, worried about what she might say, frightened they might find out more horrible detail about the death of the boy they had loved.

Martha began, as she had with Gina's mother and with all bereaved relatives who walked through the door, by explaining the formalities of death and the purpose of an inquest. So many people wanted her to point the finger, express their anger. On more than one occasion she had interviewed the perpetrator of the very crime she was investigating. But she treated them all the same – villain or victim. An inquest was a formal process of the law to answer the questions: Who? Why? How? When? And she was its mouthpiece.

She began by asking them both whether they had formed any theory as to why Patrick had . . . she deliberately avoided the words 'committed suicide' or describing too graphically the sequence of events.

When possible she tried to spare the family, minimize their grief. They already knew enough detail. So her question was, 'Have you any idea why this happened?'

'We can't understand it.' Melanie spoke for her sister who was looking even paler – a bit stunned. Martha eyed her and was worried she was about to faint.

The sisters exchanged glances.

'I take it Patrick didn't leave a note?'

Both shook their heads. Martha frowned. Was she imagining it, that there had been something furtive about that look that had passed between them?

It made her slightly less cautious.

'Do you know why Patrick didn't go to school that morning?'

Then it burst out. 'No.' Amanda spoke now with real force. 'It made no sense. The first lessons were double science. He was brilliant at it. He was a really clever boy.' And then she lost it completely as she contemplated a lost future. 'Even the teachers commented. Said he'd be a candidate for Oxbridge. They could see he was brilliant. He was way ahead of his years. I'd even started putting a bit by towards his student costs – just ten pounds a week. It wouldn't have gone very far . . .' She jerked her head, eyes wild now. 'My boy,' she said. 'My boy. All I had.'

Her sister put her arm around her, patted her head, said nothing.

'Why?' It burst out of Patrick's mother as huge as a tsunami, sweeping away everything in front of her. University, student life, loans, relationships, career. 'What's the point of my working, eating, saving, planning?'

To still the turbulent waters, Martha said, 'Tell me about your son.'

They both looked now at the photograph in Martha's hand, the school photograph, the one the papers had used. This was the image of Patrick Elson that would remain in the public consciousness. Big teeth, school tie, huge grin.

But Martha held another picture in her mind. The pictures the police had taken of the accident scene on the A5, taken after his fall: the sweep of the bridge, the chaos, traffic facing this way and that, bemused and shocked motorists standing outside their cars, Eileen Tinsley's voice squeaking as she recalled events. There was no need for them to see what she had, see those post-mortem pictures of his smashed face, smashed body, distorted broken limbs. There was no need for them to see any of that.

Amanda's chest was heaving.

And then the stories spilled out, of him reciting *The Lion and Albert*, 'with actions', when he was just six years old, the shock when he had worked out complicated equations on the back of his schoolbooks, the fact that he was surfing the internet looking at space exploration, already picking up on NASA's tweets. Martha's ears pricked up at the mention of the internet. She would check with Alex whether they had looked at Patrick Elson's computer.

She approached the subject delicately. 'He had his own computer?'

Amanda nodded. 'The police have taken it away,' she said, and Martha relaxed. She should have known this would be one of the first things Alex Randall would do.

Melanie chipped in. 'Patrick had a mischievous sense of humour,' she said, able to smile. 'Remember that Christmas he wrapped up this enormous present for you, Manda?'

It produced a smile through tears. 'Yeah. I kept unwrapping it. It got smaller and smaller. In the end it was a pair of earrings. Imagine that. As big as a telly the box was.'

Martha smiled. 'A sense of humour then.'

Both women dropped their faces into their hands.

'What did he do with his free time?'

Amanda shrugged. 'Same as other kids really, went out with

his mates, played endless computer games, kept up with his school-work. The police have been to the school and spoken to his mates.'

Martha waited but Amanda shook her head. 'Nothing,' she said. 'Just nothing. Everyone says the same thing, that Pat was well liked, kept himself to himself. He was a good boy.' She stopped herself. 'A good son.' There was something defiant in both her words and her hard stare. 'He would never have done anything he was ashamed of.'

As with Gina's mother's observation that *at least she hadn't had to find the body* the phrase held some resonance in Martha's mind. Later she would roll it around her head.

He would never have done anything he was ashamed of.

But for now she decided to shift her emphasis. 'One of the teachers said that Patrick had been unusually quiet lately. This change in his manner – his behaviour – did you have any idea what the cause was?'

The two women exchanged another glance. 'Umm.' It was Melanie who made the response. 'Pat *had* been a bit quieter,' she said. 'A bit less chatty . . . more thoughtful.' Another look passed between them. 'He'd lost some shoes,' Amanda finally said reluctantly. 'They were expensive ones. Christ,' she said, 'money's tight, you know. I was angry and he just didn't seem to care. They'd cost a week's wages. I said money didn't grow on trees. And for the first time it was as though he was shutting me out of something. He seemed to want to close the subject. When I asked him about them he got quite defensive. Surly. Only that. It wasn't like him. I put it down to him just growing up.'

Martha nodded but it was the first sign that everything in the garden was, perhaps, not quite so rosy.

She leaned forward. 'Is there anything in particular you'd like me to mention at the inquest?'

'Describe him as happy and clever. Kind and full of life,' Amanda said, leaning forward, eyes pleading with her. 'Without him I don't have any point to *my* life.' She looked away then. 'If I had an answer – any answer – it would make things easier, I think. If I could only understand *why* it would help.' But then her eyes slid away.

Martha nodded.

*   *   *

As soon as the two women had left Martha rang Alex Randall again and detailed the points that had been made. 'They thought he'd been a bit quieter lately, a bit more thoughtful,' she said. 'Was there anything on his computer?'

'We're having a real problem there,' he said. 'Clever little lad had wiped out all his browsing history.'

'When?'

'The morning he jumped.'

FIFTEEN

Friday, 31 March, 5 p.m.

The morning began with another phone call from DI Randall. It was as though he had spent the last twenty-four hours chewing over the facts of these two violent but incontrovertible suicides.

'How many suicides are there in a year in Shropshire, Martha?' Her mind had been tracking along the same path so she had her answers ready.

'About fifty.'

'And how many of those are elderly, bereaved, divorced, alcoholic, have a history of mental illness?'

'Practically all of them.'

'So suicide is rarely completely out of the blue?'

Her professionalism made her cautious. 'It's unusual, yes.'

'And now we have two, within a month, both from Shrewsbury – one town – and a town that does not have a particularly bad track record as far as suicide rates go.'

'Correct.' Still she was cautious. 'But you can get clumping. A few together and then none for the rest of the year.'

DI Randall agreed. 'I know that.'

And then she was curious. 'You're linking them together? A twelve-year-old boy with a professional woman in her thirties, when there's no evidence they even knew each other? I don't understand your thinking.'

'Surely you can see some similarities?'

'Yes and no. Incontrovertible self-destruction, apparently no notes left. No explanations. Both appeared to have much to live for. Both suicides appeared to be planned but also came out of the blue. Yes, Alex, I can see similarities, but I can also see big disparities too.'

'Well . . . you're the logical one,' he said. 'And I should be the one to use the bare facts.'

'Are you serious that you think someone is picking on random people and somehow tipping them into suicide?'

That brought him down to earth. 'Hmm,' he said, 'put like that it does sound a bit far-fetched.'

'Yes, it does.'

'Even so, I think there is something here. I'm almost waiting for the next one. And if there is some sort of link, who will be the next victim?'

'You're putting shivers up my spine, Alex,' she said. 'Stop it. You're spooking me.'

He was silent and she didn't know quite what to say next, but the silence between them wasn't awkward.

Eventually he broke it. 'I need to let you get on with your weekend,' he said. 'Have you anything planned?'

'Sam's playing away,' she said with the touch of maternal pride that usually clung to her somewhere. 'And I think Sukey's coming home with her boyfriend.'

'How I envy you,' he said, his mood patently lifting. 'Though do I take it from the sucked-a-lemon sound that you're not especially fond of Sukey's boyfriend?'

'Oh, no. Is it that obvious?'

'To me, yes.'

'Without going into detail, Alex,' she said, 'he's a singularly unpleasant young man who appears to believe that the world owes him a living – and acting parts.'

Martha would have liked to ask the DI what *his* plans were for the weekend – if he wasn't working – but she had learned to be circumspect and skip around a subject she knew he found both excruciatingly embarrassing and distasteful. His personal life? If anything, he tried to pretend it didn't exist, and so that was the plan she fell in with.

SIXTEEN

The weekend passed peacefully. Even Pom seemed to have simmered down for the occasion. In fact, he was a little quiet. Rain didn't stop play and Sam seemed particularly pleased with a couple of passes he'd made and had even taken a shot at goal – which hit the post and bounced back on to the pitch. Martha celebrated the team's draw with a Sunday roast – lamb and rosemary with accoutrements, followed by rhubarb and ginger crumble with custard which Sam and his friend Tom, Sukey and Pom all wolfed down with the silent appreciation that goes with a good dinner and hungry youngsters. They all helped her load the dishwasher afterwards, which was a bit counterproductive. Each passing a plate, stacking and restacking was actually not very efficient – she'd have been twice as quick doing it all by herself – but hey ho. They were trying to help and there was something about the jolly comradeship which felt like the family they should be.

She and the entire family went to bed with a glow of happiness which lasted right up until she walked through her office door on Monday morning.

Monday, 3 April, 8.50 a.m.

She could tell instantly that Jericho had news to 'impart' – a rather pompous word, in her opinion, that he was over fond of using. He was standing in the middle of the hallway, waiting for her, a spare frame, not tall, rounded shoulders, leaning forward, eyes focused in mock humility on the floor, where he looked in times of trouble. His mouth was pursed, his straggly grey hair almost quivering in anticipation. Bad news then. Jericho's speciality. She could read all the signs. Sometimes she thought he had deliberately chosen a career as coroner's assistant because it would give his macabre, almost ghoulish character a chance to blossom – like deadly nightshade.

Martha greeted him, passed him and entered her office, closing
the door gently behind her. She knew better than to prompt her
officer. He would 'impart' soon enough. In fact, wild horses
couldn't have persuaded him to keep news to himself. He could
have got a job as town crier. All she had to do was wait. Seconds
stretched into a minute or more. But the troubling thing was that
when he finally knocked on the door and she called him in, instead
of blurting out his news he couldn't even meet her eyes. And this
puzzled her. Jericho was a person who *loved* passing on bad news.
It was practically a hobby of his. And this patently wasn't good
news or he would have passed it on already and wouldn't have
looked so – she ran her eyes up his face – apprehensive. She knew
the drill so well. With news to *impart*, his eyes would light up,
his mouth drop slightly open so she could see those sharp lower
teeth. He'd shake his unfashionably long grey hair as though
mimicking a rather disapproving Dickensian character – maybe
the *'ever so 'umble'* Uriah Heep. He'd offer her coffee and chocolate biscuits if the news was harrowing or, he imagined, would
prove particularly distressing to her – the death of a child, a
motorway pile-up, a wife beaten to death by a husband, a murder,
a suicide, a cot death, a house fire with tragic consequences. The
list was endless. She'd heard them all from him first. All *these*
events would send him into sympathetic mode. So working in a
coroner's office was the ideal place for him. His mournful
demeanour and looks suited his role to perfection.

Had he been given the part by a casting director, Martha would
have applauded the choice. *Clap clap clap.* But today, here, on
this early indication that spring – the season of optimism and warm
promise, the season when a young man's fancy was supposed to
turn to love, maybe a middle-aged woman's too – would finally
arrive, she was pulled up short by a feeling of dread as though
someone had dropped a black velvet curtain in front of the window
that looked out over that lovely town and those blue skies, blocking
out the view and replacing it with a shrouded nothing. What could
this news be that was so awful he could hardly bear to pass it on?

Yet he would.

She waited, still observing. And picked up on something even
more disturbing. On this bright, beautiful morning there was something even more worrying than usual, something foreign, some

emotion she'd never read before. There was, deep in his grey eyes, when he finally looked up at her, a touch of sympathy. And now Martha was more than curious. She was apprehensive. *He* was sorry for *her*? Anxious now, she spoke. Quietly.

'Jericho?'

'Mrs Gunn . . .'

The elongated pause worried her even further – almost frightening her.

She was going to have to prompt him.

'Jericho?' She kept her voice soft and gentle, inviting his confidence.

He was looking past her, towards the still half-open door as though he expected someone or something to walk through it. Trouble.

'Jericho,' she prompted again, trying to stem the anxiety that was rising.

He gulped. 'Mrs Gunn,' he began, then wet his lips and his frown deepened, scoring his forehead with deep, unhappy lines. 'You haven't heard.' It was a statement – not a question.

'Jericho,' she said again, gently prompting. 'Heard what?'

'About Inspector Randall's wife.'

And that stopped her breathing. Now she was puzzled. Alex's wife? Erica Randall? The woman whom he claimed was mentally and physically unstable? The woman he claimed was a blight on his life?

It was as though a black crow had entered through that door and now it flapped, unwelcome, around the room, cawing its harsh message and perching on her shoulder, claws embedded too firmly in her flesh for her to shake it free. And even if she opened the door it would not fly away.

She kept her voice steady. 'Heard *what* about Mrs Randall?' It was taking a gargantuan effort to keep the panic out of her voice.

'She's died,' Jericho said bluntly. 'She fell down the stairs and died. Saturday night. Late.' Now he'd begun, the words were accelerating, spilling out of his mouth uncontrolled. 'The circumstances, Mrs Gunn.' There was a note of accusation in his tone – or was she imagining it? 'The circumstances are very suspicious. Even now they are questioning DI Randall down at the station. Detective Sergeant Talith wants to speak to you as soon as you arrive.'

That was when her thoughts and vision turned into a tumbling, dizzying black screen, everything out of focus, waves of orange flickering in front of her eyes. She blinked, trying to control the picture throbbing, trying to return to the familiar room. She needed to sit down. She needed air.

And so found herself sinking into a chair, head drooping into her lap, Jericho handing her a glass of water, his eyes carefully, neutrally blank, but she could read the emotion behind it. He pitied her. It was a new experience.

Jericho knew she and the inspector were friends. More than friends. Much more than colleagues or simply acquaintances. They were close. Much closer than was right and proper for a widowed coroner and a married policeman, even if he claimed his marriage had been less than happy. *Especially* as he claimed his marriage had been – frankly – unhappy.

Oh, yes, Jericho knew all right as he drove the dagger home with his next sentence.

'They're treating it as a suspicious death. It's been referred to you, Mrs Gunn.'

SEVENTEEN

Monday, 3 April, 10 a.m.

Monkmoor Police Station, Shrewsbury, is buried away in a large housing estate on the eastern side of the town. The station itself is a typical sixties cheap and ugly building. But it houses a largely happy force who cope with government cuts with a certain dogged acceptance and resilience.

It was a building now so familiar to DI Alex Randall that he could have found his way around it in a blackout. But never like this. Never from this angle.

It was a strange feeling, being on this side of the questioning. It felt unreal, this role reversal, this nightmare. He scooped in some long, slow breaths and listened to Sergeant Paul Talith almost with disbelief. 'Just confirm your name, sir.'

You already bloody well know it.

He swallowed the words. 'Alex Fergus Randall.'

It was all very well responding as honestly and politely as he could to his own detective sergeant, but the penetration of his home life, the home life he had struggled so hard to keep secret from his colleagues, was painful. And when Martha learned the sordid details . . . Anticipating her response, DI Alex Randall winced. He was paying the price for having dared to dream the fool's dream.

His heart felt as heavy as the millstone that had hung around his neck for the last few years. That's what Erica had been. Heavy, dragging, depressing. But, paradoxically, now he was freed from the millstone, he felt the burden had grown heavier. Perhaps it was because it hadn't really sunk in that she was dead, but privately he knew it wasn't that at all. It was the ambiguous circumstances surrounding his wife's death that would form a cloud of suspicion over him, a permanently poisonous miasma. Like the sulphurous cloud that sits over a volcanic pool, it would cling to him, possibly forever. That was why, relieved of her physical presence, the cloud she had left behind seemed more menacing and harder to free himself from. He felt no lighter because he could see all too clearly into his own future. And it was even uglier than his past.

DS Paul Talith cleared his throat and apologized again. 'I'm so sorry about this, sir,' he said. 'You understand we just need to know what happened.' He gave a noisy, embarrassed scrape of his throat. 'Fact finding, you know? In your own words.'

DI Randall responded wearily, 'It's all right, Talith,' he said, 'I understand completely.'

His mind right-angled, unexpectedly finding a track of its own, recalling Erica as she had once been before life and something else, nameless and terrible – something heavy and grey as a winter's sky – had destroyed it, her own and his. In this memory she was still alive, not twisted and dying at the bottom of the stairs, eyes pleading into his. It was as though, in those final moments, she had become herself again. He drew in a deep breath and felt trapped in this dreadful position. He closed his eyes and saw her, the Erica of years ago. She was dancing and singing, humming and twirling, hands on pregnant belly, right in front of his eyes, tempting, unpredictable and oddly bewitching.

Bewitching? His mind, always prosaic, objected to the word. Who did he think she was? Blaming events on witchcraft? She wasn't a witch. But she had been a woman damaged by life's events and in those last few months the damage had seemed to compound. Unpredictable since that one terrible day when their son had been born dreadfully, morbidly damaged, happiness had become a stranger to him and her, never visiting their home again except for the briefest of moments. The odd second when they could both forget. Little more than blinks of an eye. And lately she had been worse – bordering on violent. Unpredictable, sometimes looking almost mad, like the women who stared out of the windows of Victorian bedlam. She had almost frightened him, so he had taken to locking his bedroom door at night fearing that her threats of violence would come true and he would be found one morning, a knife sticking out of him. But, in the end, it wasn't he who had been found dead but Erica herself. And, as far as he could tell, it hadn't been during one of her violent, vindictive acts but a simple accident. The trouble was he could never prove it.

And it had ended in this.

He knew the procedure only too well. There would inevitably be a lengthy inquiry which he feared would lead nowhere except to leave a dirty residue. A permanent stain on him. A tide mark of scum. A question mark hanging over his head that he was powerless to remove. How could he? There had been no witnesses. Just the two of them. Neighbours would have heard screams and shouts, as they must have done on numerous occasions before. Randall was a realistic man, not given to bouts of self-pity or despair, but now he felt swamped by both.

And he was brave enough to face that it could even mean he would have to resign from the police force. Everything that could have planted happiness in his life was drifting away downstream, moving farther and farther away, and he could not swim after it to retrieve it. He was man enough to face the facts, look upstream to the long river of his future and prepare himself for it as he now met DS Paul Talith's eyes and recognized the sympathy that beamed out of them. He wanted to get this over with. And at the same time, as he folded his arms, he knew it never would be 'over with'. It would always be a noose of loose rope lying around his neck waiting for the opportunity when someone would tug hard and unexpectedly. And then what? Oblivion.

Inadvertently he put his hand around his neck as though to check whether the rope was already there.

It was not.

Talith prompted him. 'In your own words, sir. In your own time.'

10.28 a.m.

Martha eyed the phone, knowing that, inevitably, it would ring.

Any minute now.

Soon.

DS Paul Talith had waited until she would have been in her office for well over an hour. He was dreading it. His boss and the coroner had what might be called a cordial working relationship. He hadn't even worked out how he was going to put this, but the call had to be made. Someone was dead. She was the coroner and as such had to be informed. It was the law. As he dialled the number reluctantly, he was hoping that inspiration would come and he would be able to speak his part.

EIGHTEEN

Jericho put him straight through to Martha, which told him the jungle drums had already beaten out their grim message. DS Talith hadn't told the coroner's officer what the call was about and Jericho hadn't asked. He hadn't needed to.

DS Talith knew Palfreyman, the coroner's assistant, ears to the ground, would already have known. Somehow he knew everything. As he waited for her to pick up the phone he had never felt more awkward.

Martha eyed the phone and knew this was it. But she had had time to recover at least some of her equilibrium and she trusted she would deal with this professionally. As Talith stammered out his request she sensed his difficulty and spoke briskly, dispassionately, hoping her voice was leaking none of the emotions tossing around in her brain.

She cued him in.

'Jericho has only given me the fact that DI Randall's wife has died in . . .' That was when she paused, the word 'suspicious' sticking in her throat like dry bread, so she substituted with, 'Apparently unexplained circumstances.' Surely DS Paul Talith could not possibly know that as she spoke she was clenching and unclenching her fists. She continued in the same brisk, businesslike voice. 'So you'd better fill me in on the details, Talith.'

She was trying to make this job easier for him. There is nothing worse than an internal investigation, looking around the faces of your colleagues and reading suspicion and doubt.

Talith cleared his throat. 'Right then. The DI lives in Church Stretton, ma'am. In a semi-detached house in a small cul-de-sac. Apparently Mrs Randall – Erica, her name is – and the DI, ma'am . . .' By every word he was selecting so carefully but oh, so clumsily, she could tell how hard he was finding this.

'They didn't have the most . . .' And now Talith felt defeated. This was the home life his inspector had defended so tightly. This was too difficult, but he still pushed on: 'Amicable of relationships.' He got the words out quickly. This was toe-cringingly awful.

'Mrs Randall was apparently . . .' And now his words were slowing as though they were being dragged out of him under threat of torture. They were failing him. 'They used to argue a lot, ma'am. She was, according to the neighbours, a strange and difficult woman. Unwell. There had been trouble before.'

Martha heard the words. *Unwell. Trouble.*

Get on with it, she wanted to say. *Give me the details. I need to know.* But Talith was still hedging. 'She had a history of unpredictable behaviour. Last night, apparently, they were arguing again and to cut a long story short . . .'

Please do.

'To cut a long story short, Mrs Randall, Erica, she fell down the stairs. Her neck was broken, according to the medical examiner. She died quick. No one really knows . . .'

But Martha had already jumped ahead. Falling down stairs. Her heart sank. Unless you find string tied around the top step, how do you *ever* prove whether someone fell or was pushed? It is impossible. *Accident, murder, suicide?* The words tossed around in her head like a dinghy in a force-ten gale. *Deliberate, homicide, suicide.* With no witnesses no one can *ever* be sure what happened. It could be the result of a fit of anger, attention seeking, a trip, a drunken fall or even a bit of all four. Did Erica drink? Martha didn't even know that. A small push, a pique of fury, a hysterical woman and from the little Martha knew about Alex's wife she was that. She was also unhappy. Unhappy people do not care what happens to them, whether they live or die. There is a carelessness in abject misery. And as for unpredictable behaviour, Alex had told her that his wife had a history of arson, of petty crime, ever since the tragic event in their past.

DS Paul Talith's voice cut in. 'She would have died more or less instantly according to the police surgeon.'

Martha *hated* herself for asking, but if she didn't others would. 'Were there any signs of *other* injuries?'

He knew exactly what she was asking. *Is it possible that Detective Inspector Alex Randall, your boss and my friend, is a killer?*

And he answered as honestly as he could. 'We don't know, ma'am. They haven't done the post-mortem yet but so far the pathologist says—'

Her turn to interrupt. 'The pathologist?'

'Yes, ma'am. Doctor Sullivan.'

To herself she nodded. Mark Sullivan would not get it wrong. He would not let friendship or even sympathy for a colleague stand in the way of the truth. His presence was a relief. This situation needed clarity, honesty and he would deliver both.

'So far Doctor Sullivan says that Mrs Randall's injuries were consistent with an accidental fall.'

Satisfactory yet strangely unsatisfactory. The statement answered no questions. The word *consistent* is weak and uncommitted.

'Paul.'

'Ma'am?'

'You understand I can't investigate Mrs Randall's death.'

Silence from the other end.

'I shall have to ask a colleague to take over the case. I'm . . . I wouldn't . . . I couldn't be entirely impartial. It would be unprofessional as well as open to question. And it wouldn't be fair to Inspector Randall. Or to Mrs Randall.'

'Ma'am?'

'I'll ask a coroner from a neighbouring area to take over, probably David Steadman from South Shropshire. I'll speak to him today and get back to you. In the meantime, it would be a good thing for Doctor Sullivan to continue with the post-mortem. I'll, umm . . .'

Courage, Martha.

'I'll authorise it and let him know about the change of coroner.'

'Thank you, ma'am.'

Talith put the phone down and sat for a moment, thinking.

This was awkward and it was definitely not in his life plan. He liked working in Shrewsbury. It was a pleasant, peaceful town. His wife, Diana, was about to give birth to their first child and he wanted to focus on that. Truth was he was hugely excited and awed by the whole concept of becoming a father, whether it was a boy or a little girl. To allow for his new role he'd hoped for an easy ride for the next few months, working in a civilized town under an inspector who was fair and generous, and he felt would have been sympathetic to his altered circumstances. Now it looked as though that happy era might be drawing to an end. If there were any grounds for suspicion that his inspector had had a hand in his wife's death, Talith knew it would be the end of Randall's career. This was beyond a DS's remit and he would be referring the case upwards and upwards until it reached the very top. He could hardly bear to think of the consequences. He'd had a vain hope that the coroner would deal with it and the entire event would be swept under the carpet, but the very fact that she had side-stepped the case told him all. These were dangerous and murky waters.

He returned to the interview room.

His inspector was sitting motionless, lost in some thought of his own. His face was pale and strained. Talith sat down opposite him. Whether he liked it or not, he had to do this. It was his job and better *he* did it, a sympathetic colleague and friend, than someone from a neighbouring force who wouldn't treat DI Randall with the same respect and understanding.

Buying time before he had to look into his DI's face, he glanced at his notes. 'Neighbours say . . .' He cleared his throat. He knew just how much his boss had kept his wife and home circumstances far away from his position here. And now he was beginning to learn why.

He swallowed. 'Sir,' he began. 'A neighbour has come forward to say that she heard voices.'

Alex didn't respond. He couldn't meet Paul Talith's eyes either. Both men were finding this harder than they could ever have imagined.

Even Talith had his doubts now. He pressed on. 'Arguing, sir?' This was at least as difficult for him as for his superior. They were going to have to bring in some top notch officers if this investigation was going to escalate.

He met the inspector's eyes. 'Do you want to tell me what happened, sir? In your own words?'

'All right.' DI Randall lifted his eyes, squared his shoulders. 'My wife was not an easy woman. She's been extremely unpredictable ever since our son was born six years ago.'

'I didn't know you had a—'

Randall cut in. 'I don't. He died.'

His clipped tone should have warned Talith.

Randall continued. 'He was born with a condition known as anencephaly. That means he was born without a head. At least without a cranium, a brain, et cetera, et cetera. The condition is incompatible with life. He barely breathed and was dead within an hour.' Randall lifted his eyes with the faintest of smiles. 'A blessing, the doctors called it. It turned out to be more of a curse. Within weeks of his death Erica began to show signs of mental instability. She . . .' He frowned. 'Do you really need to know all this?'

Talith was uncomfortable. 'Not really. I'm not sure. It depends. Sir.' He appealed, 'This is difficult for me too.'

'I know.'

11.30 a.m.

Martha was already on the phone to Mark Sullivan, the Home Office pathologist with whom she had worked on numerous cases. He sounded jaunty and untroubled, as though he had no great concerns over performing his colleague's wife's post-mortem or doubt in Randall's role in her death. Or perhaps, Martha mused, his new relationship was going so well and Nancy, an internet date with three children, was proving such a good swap for his alcoholic ex that Sullivan's mental state was permanently optimistic and undamaged by others' problems. He certainly sounded ebullient and unconcerned.

'You've heard about Alex's wife, I take it?'

'Yeah. Nasty situation, Martha. Poor Alex. Trouble is . . .'

She knew exactly what the trouble was.

'In these sorts of cases, I mean, falling downstairs, it can be hard to piece together the exact sequence of events. I've got some background information but it doesn't make things any easier and it's possible the post-mortem won't shed much light on the circumstances surrounding her fall.'

'You know she was mentally unstable?'

'Yeah. I've already had a word with Alex and with her GP. She'd had problems for a few years. Alex must have had a very difficult home life.'

She could tell from Sullivan's tone that he had no suspicion that she felt emotionally involved or that this was anything other than an unhappy accident. He – and she – were simply discussing a colleague's situation. That was all. No dark background.

She tried to ascertain at least some facts. 'I don't know whether she was a drinker.'

'We'll be running through all the usual tests. We'll do a blood alcohol test as routine drug screening.'

'You've been out to his house?'

'No. Not yet. Might do if the PM looks a bit ambiguous. So far I've just seen the photographs of the accident scene. It's a fairly average semi.'

She breathed out softly before continuing. 'Mark, I won't be handling the inquest. I don't feel I could be impartial.'

'Surely it's going to be accidental?' He sounded surprised and unsuspicious. Was it only she who had a mind open to a darker possibility?

'I can't – I can't make that decision.'

And that was when something must have clicked in the pathologist's mind, a cog finding its ratchet. His manner changed, partly stiff, partly sympathetic, and now definitely detached and distanced.

'OK, Martha,' he said slowly, digesting this piece of information.

'I thought I'd refer it to David Steadman. He's a decent enough chap.'

'You still want *me* to proceed with the PM?' Definitely guarded now.

'Oh, yes, I think so. There's going to have to be one and I can't think of a pathologist I'd trust more.'

'You don't doubt *my* impartiality?' She could feel the gap between them widening by the second. Everything she said seemed to be making it wider.

'*Your* impartiality? No.'

'So. Tomorrow?'

'OK.'

'I can do Erica Randall's PM in the afternoon. I'll keep my eye out for any further injuries, Martha, that might have contributed to her fall.' There was a pause before he finished with, 'I'll do a thorough job, but I can tell you Alex Randall is not a man to have pushed his wife down stairs even in a fit of anger. It isn't in his nature.'

She couldn't believe it. *He* was defending Alex to *her*?

She tried to respond with a laugh but it sounded hollow and insincere. 'Sure you're not deciding the result before you've even done the PM, Mark?'

'No.' Mark Sullivan's tone was deadly serious. 'But in this case I know the man.'

It stopped her in her tracks. *Did he? Better than she?*

And he hadn't finished but was scolding her now. 'Goodness me, Martha, he's the most controlled person I have ever met.'

And that was what frightened her. *What happened when that control snapped?*

'OK. Thanks.' Training over the years had taught her to regulate her voice as well as her manner as well as her clothes. In fact, her whole persona. Only Martin and then Alex had been able to peer beneath the surface.

'Well, I suggest you proceed with the PM then. David Steadman will, I'm sure, be in touch with you shortly. OK?'

'Yeah.'

'Good. Thank you. And Mark . . .'

'Yes?'

'As far as the results of Patrick Elson's post-mortem go, I think I'd prefer it if we kept the suspicion of anal interference back for the moment. We don't know it has any bearing on his suicide and it'll only distress his family further.'

'I agree.'

She put the phone down with a feeling of relief and warmth, but it was tinged with a bitter regret. She'd always liked Mark Sullivan and had felt unhappy at the way his life had appeared to be heading – an alcoholic wife, a drink problem himself which had threatened his career, manifesting itself with shaky hands and equally shaky judgements. But now he was through to the other side and she was glad. She trusted him. If only her own life could work out similarly neatly.

She made her second call.

David Steadman was coroner in the next jurisdiction. They knew each other – not well, but well enough to respect each other and, more importantly, well enough for her to be partly honest with her explanation. She got straight to the point. 'I wonder if you'll help me out, David?'

He wasn't her favourite person in the world – pompous, snobbish and arrogant – but one thing she did know about him was that he possessed absolute integrity. No one could buy him or persuade him. He knew the law and stuck to the absolute letter of it. He was one of those people who seem born honest, unable to lie or deceive. Maybe that was what made him so sure of himself, perhaps a little smug. She may not like him but she didn't have to. She only needed to trust him. And that she did.

She was well known for her independent streak. She could picture his face, gleeful at her having to ask him for help, blowing out his plump pink cheeks in pleasure at her plight. But underneath she also knew he would listen to every word she spoke and weigh it up, evaluate it, think, plan and act. Honestly and carefully.

This was why she had turned to South Shropshire for his help.

He got to the heart of the matter in one slick move. 'Why do you need my help?'

Only the truth would suffice. 'I've worked with DI Randall over a number of cases. I feel we're friends as well as colleagues. To be honest, David, I would find it hard to be completely impartial in his wife's death.'

His response was a noisy blowing out of his cheeks. A moist-sounding *harrumph.*

'And I'm sure you can appreciate that his wife's falling down stairs is hardly a clear-cut case?'

'Hmm.'

'I've authorised a post-mortem.'

'Who's the pathologist?'

'Mark Sullivan.'

'Good. He'll do a thorough job without resorting to the usual play-acting and conjecture.'

Martha smiled to herself. David Steadman and she might not agree on many points, but this was one they were in perfect harmony with.

'I don't know the full facts, David' (she could have added *yet,* confided in him that while she might be handing the case officially to him she would be continuing with unofficial investigations of her own), 'but I understand that his wife died some time on Saturday night slash early Sunday morning following a fall down the stairs. I know nothing more than that. Jericho said her neck was broken but I think we'll wait for radiological confirmation before we decide on that.'

She heard him snigger at Jericho's diagnosis. 'What do you know of his home circumstances?'

She knew his antennae were already up, twitching in her direction, picking up electrical signals like aerials. Steadman was astute enough to have picked up on the vibes she could hardly stop herself from giving out – even over the phone.

'I understand it wasn't terribly happy.'

'How much do you want to be kept in the picture?'

'I don't know.' The question was unanswerable but Steadman seemed to understand.

'OK, Martha.'

She felt she needed to add something more. 'There will inevitably be a police investigation alongside the inquest. I'm anxious that the truth is not hidden behind spurious facts.'

His response was sharp. 'Spurious facts?'

'Rumours, David. Hearsay. Malicious gossip.'

There was a long pause, then he asked the hundred-thousand-dollar question. 'Is there any possibility of homicide here?'

Homicide? A possibility? She recalled an afternoon spent last summer in the quarry, a warm, sunny day they had shared and the words that had burst out of him. *I hate her. I hate her. I wish she was dead.* Martha wished he had not spoken them but had kept that to himself. And if he had needed to say the words, she wished she had not heard them. But now she needed to know the truth as far as it could be uncovered. And so her response was blunt and honest. 'I don't think so. I don't think DI Randall is capable of murder, but I don't know the full facts. Please, David. That's why I'm asking you.'

Something in him must have melted. 'Of course I'll take over the case, Martha.' Said with real warmth and friendship now. Maybe she needed to revise her harsh judgement of him.

And as she thanked him again he said with an even gentler note in his voice. 'I take it you would like me to keep you informed?'

And now she felt she could afford to be honest. 'That would be really kind, David. Thank you.'

'My pleasure, my dear. Just tell them to refer the case to me and I'll take over. I'll be happy to help you out.'

Yet again she thanked him – profusely, told him she owed him one and knew he wasn't going to forget that anyway.

And so that was that. She had detached from the case. Cut free. It was not her responsibility any more. She need not learn all the dirty sordid details, each quarrel and spat, reports of late-night arguments and other tittle tattle. As she put the phone down she stared at her hands, at the small diamond engagement ring and the gold wedding ring she still wore almost twenty years after Martin had died. She'd worn it longer for a dead man than when he had been alive. Time to move on, Martha Gunn, she thought. But it isn't as easy as all that. Moving on is a cliché. It does not reflect real life. People do not move on. They move to a different place dragging their baggage behind them like wheelie suitcases and bearing their scars. Martin was a distant memory now, a memory kept alive by her own recollections and his two children – Sam in particular, who had a look of his father about him and a certain pensiveness that evoked Martin.

But the fact was that since he had died she had not really felt anything for another man. She had had a few dates, dinners and even days out, but they had always felt strange, wrong, a betrayal, and she had bolted her front door behind her, glad to be alone again. Both her mother and her mother–in-law urged her to marry again, find someone else, but it just hadn't happened – until DI Alex Randall had inched into her life, invaded her mind and stolen her affection.

There – she'd said it now. *Affection.*

It took an immense effort to focus on her other cases. Back to the two suicides. And Patrick Elson's inquest was due to take place soon. Focus on that, Martha, and Gina's death too. You owe it to them and it is your job.

And Alex? *Out of your hands.*

There was a soft knock on the door. It was Jericho with a cup of strong coffee and two chocolate biscuits. She eyed him speculatively. Jericho Palfreyman, coroner's assistant, was famously nosey. He knew everything about everyone and revelled in that knowledge. How he acquired so much she didn't know but suspected that he didn't quite close the door when she was conversing with relatives or colleagues, whether it was on the phone or in person, and that he lingered just outside, picking up on crumbs of details and squirrelling them away in his sharp little brain. However, in this case she could use that inquisitiveness to advantage. 'Close the door, Jericho,' she invited. Eyes bright and alert, he did just that and then stood, waiting.

'Tell me what you know about Mrs Randall's death.'

He started to say, 'Just hearsay,' before realizing that she already knew this. She wanted this hearsay so she could make her own judgement.

'Apparently on Saturday night, or rather in the early hours of Sunday morning, Mrs Randall, the inspector's wife . . .' She resisted the temptation to respond with an impatient, *I know who Mrs Randall is*, merely pressing her lips together and listening to Jericho's halting account.

'People heard them rowing late into the night.'

She couldn't resist a little skip of joy in her heart, a trickle of honey.

'They heard her screaming. Then silence and a *bump, bump, bump* and then nothing.'

How on earth did he know these things?

Jericho stopped before continuing. 'He called for an ambulance, but she was dead at the foot of the stairs. Her neck was broken according to the police doctor. That's all I know so far, Mrs Gunn.'

Her mind started to work furiously. 'His house is . . .?'

'Just on the outskirts of Church Stretton – a semi. The neighbours said they heard the noise through the walls. And not for the first time.'

Church Stretton was a well-known beauty spot, the Stretton Hills made famous by Malcolm Saville and the town which had a character and unique identity of its own. There was something mysterious about the place, bordered by myth and legend and sporting its very own Devil's Chair. It was quiet, off the beaten track. Yes, that was exactly where Alex *would* live, in an anonymous house with the wife he was ashamed of.

'I understand that they're questioning him down at the station now.'

It was normal procedure but Martha felt unnerved. The thought of Alex being questioned at his own police station by his colleagues . . . And there was nothing useful she could do. She could not help him. She drew in a deep breath. 'Anything else?'

Jericho Palfreyman shook his head sadly. He would have loved to have the whole story to lay at her feet. But . . .

Even he could only go so far at stretching the truth like a piece of elastic.

'Umm,' she began, wondering how best to put this. 'Jericho. I'm not going to be handling Mrs Randall's case myself. I've asked David Steadman to hear it instead. He'll keep me . . .' She corrected herself. 'He'll keep *us* informed.'

'Oh, right you are then.' It was his only response and casual, almost gleeful at that, but she felt she should further justify her decision. 'I know Inspector Randall too well. It wouldn't be right for me to hold the inquest. I could be accused of a lack of impartiality.' She met his eyes and realized he understood this only too well. She continued, 'I am, however, interested in the outcome, any facts that you find out, and in the result of the post-mortem. If you can just keep me informed?' She felt she needed to add some justification and found it. 'I consider DI Randall a friend. A good friend.'

By the gleam in Jericho's eyes he was getting this completely. 'I'll keep you informed if I hear anything, ma'am,' he said.

'And Jericho.'

He turned. 'Ma'am?'

'Thank you for the biscuits.'

He gave a watery smile and left.

She had work to do, other troubling cases. She needed to prepare her statements and format for the morning's inquest. Her hand brushed on the two sets of notes which she had been reluctant to file.

Patrick Elson and his jump from the A5 bridge. He had died instantly but in the resulting mayhem and pile-up four other people had been injured, none seriously, and taken to hospital. All four had been discharged later that day. It had been an unexpected consequence of the suicide, unlike Gina Marconi's death, which had only had a physical impact on Graham Skander's wall.

What, she wondered, had led this boy to commit such a violent act? Was it sexual assault?

Her hand found the second set. Gina Marconi.

Like Patrick, another violent suicide, certainly not the overused cliché of *a cry for help*. Rather it had been a determined scream for death, at sixty miles per hour and with her seat belt unbuckled driving straight into a wall. Neither Gina nor Patrick had had any intention of surviving. Unless Gina had simply missed the corner? Leaving her bed, her mobile phone and asking her mother to look after Terence should anything happen to her? Unlikely but not impossible. She made a mental note to visit the scene of the crash.

She drank her coffee, munched abstractedly on the chocolate biscuits and flicked on to the website of the Royal College of Psychiatrists, searching through suicides.

There were numerous papers published on the subject, lots of theories, talk about signs of depression, of the leaving of the note, of the mode and time, of the feelings of guilt in those left behind, of the denial of any knowledge that anything was wrong. Then there were anecdotes of the health care professionals who had had earlier contact with the deceased. The bottom line was that in most cases there were signs that something was wrong but both professionals and family had not realized the severity of the condition. In very few was there no hint that something was building up. Interestingly this applied in particular to violent and

determined suicides which both Patrick's and Gina's were. They
had both left behind a cluster of bewildered family and friends
who had thought nothing was wrong.

In Gina's case this had extended to her fiancée. But, Martha
reasoned, something *had* been wrong. Something *must* have been.

And Erica Randall?

Plenty of signs there that something had been wrong. But in
Erica's case suicide was unlikely. People who really want to die do
not throw themselves down a staircase. Far too unreliable. Besides,
Erica's mental collapse had always been blamed on the birth of
Christopher Randall, their little boy born without a head, without a
chance of life.

She worried now. Who knew what evidence Mark Sullivan's
post-mortem would expose – drugs, alcohol, medication?
Statements from family, friends, GP, psychiatrist? What would
David Steadman unearth, now she'd passed the baton over to
him? What facts would he bury deep and lay to rest and what
would he expose? How much would Alex have to go through?
What would the final verdict be?

She tried to guess . . .

Homicide? Martha shook her head. Unlikely without proof. A
little like a suicide attempt, pushing someone down a flight of
stairs is equally unreliable as a form of murder. But nevertheless,
a push, a shove, in the heat of an argument can result in
manslaughter. Alex was surely not capable of deliberate violent
assault. But a push? In a moment of frustration? She had glimpsed
his feeling of powerlessness against his circumstances, witnessed
his frustration with life, his wife, his marriage, his envy for her
own children, her precious twins. People would gossip. The
gossip would smoulder. For a moment she allowed herself to
dream. If or when Alex Randall had another relationship the
flames of gossip would be fanned. Particularly if that person (that
lucky person) was the coroner who had tried the case of his wife.
No, no that would never do. Whatever happened in the future
she had done the right thing in handing the case over to Steadman.

So without corroborative evidence, what would be his final verdict?

Probably 'unexplained', the verdict that leaves the door wide
open for endless accusations and gossip. And a verdict which
covers a few more scenarios, a fall, a trip, a push, a dive?

And then her mind took an unexpected turn. Was it possible that Erica's death was, in reality, another suicide?

She spent a minute or two considering this option from a coroner's point of view and shook her head. Given the documented state of Erica's mind a suicide verdict was very unlikely. No, her instinct was that it would be the worst verdict of all, for everyone concerned – the woolly, unsatisfactory *unexplained*. A permanent question mark, sands that would shift like the tide, ebbing and flowing as rumour found a voice and died or proliferated. Martha knew how it was. You stick a label on someone. She could hear the voice. *Oh, him? The one who most likely* (said behind a fluttering hand) *killed his wife and went on to . . .*

And would the post-mortem prove anything? Probably not. No. There would be no happy ending for her and Alex. Neither of them could afford for their names to be linked in anything but a professional scenario.

NINETEEN

Monday, 3 April. 3 p.m.

She looked at her watch. At this very moment Mark Sullivan would be performing the post-mortem on Erica Randall.

At 3.15 she dialled the police station, telling herself that she was ringing to inform the Shrewsbury force that she would not be dealing with the death of Mrs Randall. Any reports, queries or arrangements should be directed at her colleague. Luckily the call was answered by PC Gary Coleman, whose head was so full of thoughts of his upcoming wedding that he was hardly likely to wonder why the coroner was taking an interest in this case if she had handed it over to a colleague.

'Gary,' she said brightly, 'how are the wedding plans going?'

'Wonderful.' His voice was bright with enthusiasm. 'All set for the summer.' He couldn't resist adding in some detail. 'We've even chosen the wine.'

Martha smiled. This was one of the things she liked about PC Coleman. Most men's responses when you ask them how their wedding plans are going is ignorance or boredom. They're leaving it all to the wife and/or the impending mother-in-law. Guests, dress, wine, food, church. The groom just does his duty, turns up sober and on time on the day wearing the specified cravat, waistcoat and morning suit, makes nothing but complimentary comments in his speech and pays for the honeymoon.

But not Gary Coleman. He was full of it. The venue, the cake, the dress (not that he'd seen it of course, Mrs Gunn!). And then halfway through he remembered who he was speaking to. 'Mrs Gunn, I'm so sorry. Who did you want to speak to?'

She made a stab at who would be the SIO now that Alex was out of the running. 'DS Talith?'

'He's, ummm . . .' Acute embarrassment. She could almost feel the warmth of his blush over the wire and guess at its cause.

Gary Coleman confirmed her suspicions. 'He's just with the inspector at the moment. Can I get him to call you back?'

'No.' She kept her voice steady. 'Just tell him I've arranged for David Steadman, the coroner for South Shropshire, to hold the inquest for Mrs Randall.'

'Right.' The awkwardness was still there.

She couldn't resist it. 'That isn't to say,' she added crisply, 'that I wouldn't want to be kept informed.'

'Oh. Right you are. All right, Mrs Gunn.'

'Do you have the result of the post-mortem?'

'Not yet, Mrs Gunn.'

'Right. I'll be interested in the result.'

'Of course.'

'I may not be handling the case, PC Coleman, but I would like to be kept in the loop.' It was as far as she dared go.

His response was politely predictable. 'Yes, of course, Mrs Gunn.'

And that was that. She'd shot her bolt, done what she ought. Now it was up to Alex's colleagues to investigate, Mark Sullivan for the medical forensic evidence, the scene-of-crime analysers and, of course, David Steadman, her appointed deputy as coroner.

They said their goodbyes and hung up.

3.30 p.m.

In the mortuary, Mark Sullivan was conducting the post-mortem on Erica Randall.

Peter, the mortician, had begun with the basic measurements. Weight: 10 stone – 63 kilograms. Height: 167 centimetres – 5 feet, 6 inches.

In good health. Erica's body was stripped naked and scrutinized for external injuries. There were a few bruises on her limbs consistent with the fall. Sullivan ran his hands down her arms and legs searching for distorted limbs which would warrant an X-ray. There were none. He was being videoed as he worked and took his own notes. Some observations he kept to himself. Ragged nails, unkempt hair, grey and undyed. The clothes that had been taken off were shapeless cheap garments. Erica had patently not been a woman who had taken pride in her appearance. Her hands were roughened. But once . . . Mark Sullivan studied her face in true repose. Once she might have been a beauty. Or she might not. She had a good complexion but her face was scored with lines of unhappiness.

He and the mortician used the Stryker saw to open her cranium and he worked for over an hour on her head and neck searching for answers.

Martha had been waiting for a call but at four thirty she was too fidgety to remain in her office.

She stood up and caught sight of herself in the mirror. We are all at our best when faced with a challenge, and the gleam in her eyes plus a certain alertness in her stance told her everything. She would do her bit for her friend. She slipped her jacket on, determined now. Whatever it cost, if the truth was out there she would find it. She owed it to him.

She left her office and went over to Jericho's desk. 'Do you know DI Randall's home address?'

TWENTY

She already knew that Alex lived in Church Stretton, a small town at the foothills of the Long Mynd and Stiperstones, large lumpy hills in the Shropshire countryside. Church Stretton itself was a quaint town with a large antiques centre, the ubiquitous Co-op and some individual shops. Full of legend and folklore, the Stretton hills were a popular destination for mountain bikers, hikers and people wanting wide open spaces and views that did, literally, take your breath away. To get to the top was a stiff climb.

The town itself nestled in the foothills. And Alex's house sat on the southern edge of the main street. At the end of a cluster of ex-council houses was a small, tucked-away estate consisting largely of 1940s semis, sturdily stone built, with generous double garages, small front gardens and space for parking. She turned into the road and parked, looked up and down. There was no one around. The estate looked quietly deserted, the street sunny, backing on to fields, and between two of the properties there was a narrow footpath whose sign promised a park and ultimately a duck pond. It all looked quiet and innocent. No one would believe the drama that had taken place here a few nights ago, but she could picture it. Blue lights strafing the sky, open doors, panic and consultation. It had all melted away now as though it had never been.

Martha locked her car and walked up the street looking for signs of life – anyone who might have witnessed something – but the houses were all neat and quiet with parking space for two cars at the front, most of which were currently empty. Everyone was out at work or inside having their tea, watching TV. It looked deserted.

Alex's house was at the top, much as she would have expected it, as tucked away as it could manage. It looked uninviting, innocent, anonymous and also soulless. There was no sign of individuality or personality. Nothing. If a house could manage to look sad then this one did. It looked as unloved as a stray animal. He had told her it was not a happy home, but nothing could have prepared her for this blank sheet or the feeling of depression that seemed to emanate from its walls. No love had been poured into it or seeped out of it. No little touches, draped curtains in the bedroom windows or rose bushes in the front patch. It was in a good state of repair but there were no flowerpots, no house name, no sign of affection. The downstairs curtains were drawn, shielding the interior from curious stares or the paparazzi. There was no sign of the recent drama either – no forensic van parked outside, no officer on guard, no police tape. No notice on the door. Nothing. That was a good sign. It meant the investigation had not been escalated and was still currently low key. Waiting for the post-mortem results, at a guess. But that was where things could change. One bruise in the wrong place, an injury or sign of other assault and the police vans would soon come chasing, DI or not. But the post-mortem would almost certainly prove nothing. Seeing a Ford in the drive – Alex's, Erica's? – Martha did not dare linger but walked back down the road and returned to her office. So that was *chez* Alex. She felt a bit sad. What had she hoped to achieve by driving down here? To speak to him? Find out the true story behind his wife's death? She didn't even know that. How had her being there helped?

Well, she had other work to do. Jericho handed her a couple of sets of notes. People are dying all the time. So she forced herself to do the job she was paid to do.

And now that included two files. Two suicides, and Erica who was not her responsibility. Her instincts, as coroner, were telling her that there was something different about two of the deaths, and she couldn't work out why she bracketed Erica Randall's sad little accident in with two violent suicides. On the surface and beneath the surface there was nothing to link them. Maybe, she decided, it was only that they had all happened in the last few weeks and all were unusual for one reason or another. Somewhere behind these tragedies there would be explanations, but she might never learn them.

Erica Randall might not be her responsibility but she was of personal interest.

It was the other two cases, the boy Patrick Elson and the woman Gina Marconi, which *were* her responsibility, and she shouldn't be diverted from doing her job. She was the one who should speak for them. But how could she when she did not know their stories?

Her years of experience as a coroner had taught her much. If she was unhappy about a case, at some point, maybe far into the future, there would be an explanation. Events happen for a reason. It is the way of life. Experience builds up instinct. And her instincts were screaming and crying at the same time. Something was pulling at her. Trouble was she didn't know in what direction.

But she knew children. Twelve-year-old boys don't just hurl themselves off bridges into the path of oncoming traffic and an inevitably ugly, terrifying, painful death; neither do successful professional women with a fiancé and young son kill themselves.

The two cases were linked somehow by an invisible thread. Both were violent, determined and successful suicide bids.

And Erica Randall? Probably an accident. At the same time two things burrowed into her mind. The first: why was her mind stubbornly linking Erica's death with the two suicides?

Had she picked up on something that made her believe Erica Randall had deliberately hurled herself down the stairs? Was that why she was bracketing them together? She knew Alex's wife had been unhappy. He had described her as 'tortured'. Tortured was one way to describe a pre-suicidal mental state. Throwing oneself downstairs could be accidental, a trip, or it could have been an act of desperation. David Steadman would be the one to unravel Erica's story. And it was up to her to do the same for Patrick and Gina. She had studied their photographs, willing them to speak to her. Patrick a slim, earnest-looking boy who wore thick glasses and had what her mother would have called buck teeth. Maybe they would have been straightened when he was older. Gina was a confident, radiant-looking beauty with a dazzling smile, thick dark hair, big eyes and a wide mouth. And Erica? She did not know what Erica looked like. Alex had never described his wife and she had never met her or seen a photograph. So what *had* she looked like? And now Martha was curious. Had Alex's wife been a beauty or plain? Was she fat or thin? Did she habitually hold an anxious, haunted look? That was how Martha had always pictured her. Or had she smothered her anxieties with a pleasant smile and polite expression? And so . . . Had this faceless woman hurled herself down the stairs just as Patrick had sky-dived off the A5 bridge and Gina had pressed her foot down on the accelerator having released her seat belt? *If* she had it on in the first place.

Did that link them – a desire for death? Just that?

Riding on these thoughts was a worry. What exactly was Alex Randall saying down at the station?

Or – and this was the worry that gnawed at her – was he saying nothing and yet not at liberty to leave? Were they keeping him there? Were they considering charging him?

TWENTY-ONE

Monday, 3 April, 6 p.m.

Two and a half miles away, at Monkmoor Police Station, the interview was ongoing but DS Talith was going easy on his boss. He knew the DI had made every attempt to keep his home life a closed zone. The pain this exposure was causing him was just as bad as being blatantly accused of murdering his wife.

Which Talith had no intention of doing.

'Just give me the events, sir.' Talith was determined for his boss to maintain his position and dignity, something which DI Randall picked up on. He flashed his sergeant a look of gratitude.

He cleared his throat and prepared to lay bare his private life. 'Erica, as you know, was not a well woman. She was extremely unpredictable.' Randall's eyes flicked across the room to the recording light. Off.

Another reason for gratitude. If it didn't need to be shared then it would stay within these walls and his sergeant's head.

'Her habit was to watch television fairly solidly in the evening. She'd flick through programmes.'

'And you, sir?'

'I used to sit in the front room. I preferred to read – or look at stuff on the computer.'

Talith frowned. *Oh, shit.* 'What sort of stuff, sir?' Both men were well aware they had not seized the DI's computer.

But Randall laughed it off. 'Oh, just stuff on iPlayer, you know. Radio plays, serials I'd missed.' There was not a trace of embarrassment. All looked honest and true. As one would expect.

Talith cleared his throat. 'Go on, sir.'

'Well, round about eleven I heard Erica switch the TV off. It was the normal time for her to go to bed.' His face changed then to a look of anguish, embarrassment and something else which Talith thought he could read. The inspector and his wife didn't sleep together.

'She took . . .' Randall drew in a deep breath. 'She took quite a lot of prescription pills. Anti-depressants and some tranquilizers.'

'We'll be speaking to her doctor, sir.'

Randall showed the first leak of irritation. 'I know that, Talith. I'm just explaining about that night.' He continued. 'She would take them and then settle down to go to sleep.' His good humour had returned. 'They seemed to do the trick. Usually she'd be out like a light until morning.'

Talith waited, wanting to prompt the DI with a, *But?*

'I stayed downstairs.' DI Randall's tone was clipped, his gaze abstracted, far away. 'I was listening to "From Our Own Correspondent" on iPlayer.' He smiled briefly. 'It's one of my favourite radio programmes. But then I heard the noise. *Bump, bump, bump*. I knew what it was.'

Talith asked his first question. 'So you were downstairs, you say?'

Again, Randall's response was terse. He'd picked up on the sergeant's doubt. 'Yes, Talith, I do say.'

Talith moved on quickly. 'She'd fallen before?'

His inspector's eyes seemed to bore into him. 'No,' he responded, irritation bubbling up. 'She hadn't. If she had we would have moved to a bungalow. But the sound of someone falling down a flight of stairs is quite distinctive.'

'Did she cry out?'

Randall squeezed his eyes shut. 'A sort of strangled scream. I ran out but she'd hit her head on the corner of the wall and wasn't moving.' He was frowning now. 'Her head was at a strange angle. I thought it best not to move her in case her neck was broken.' He couldn't hold back a shudder as he spoke. Maybe the thought of a mad paraplegic wife would, finally, have been too much for him. 'I dialled the emergency services.' A wisp of humour. 'I would think you know better than I the exact sequence of subsequent events.'

Talith did. He'd heard the transcript. Once the call had been documented the wheels and recorders had been set in motion. The

999 team had logged his call at 12.15 a.m. His wife had fallen downstairs. She wasn't breathing; she wasn't bleeding. He thought her neck was broken. They had sent an ambulance crew plus the police.

Alex Randall leaned forward, his eyes locked on to his sergeant's. 'Talith,' he said, and knew there was something his sergeant was holding back. 'Talith?'

But the sergeant's eyes flickered away.

6.30 p.m.

Mark Sullivan had finished the post-mortem. He stood back. 'Well,' he said, ripping off his gloves. 'Now that *is* interesting.' He spoke to his assistant. 'Get those samples off to the lab. I don't want to start speculating until we're sure.'

Peter Williams grinned. He knew the ways of the pathologist only too well. They'd worked together for years.

'We'll keep this under our hats for now. Eh?'

Mark Sullivan was rarely a hundred per cent certain of the events which had led up to a person's death. Pathology can be an inexact science. Usually he simply gave the facts, sometimes adding in an opinion. This time he was ninety-nine per cent certain he had an answer.

TWENTY-TWO

Wednesday, 5 April, 9.45 am.

Martha was motionless, as she had been since she had arrived at work that morning.

Hit by a sledgehammer of inactivity. She needed to remind herself: Erica Randall was not her responsibility. She needed to do her job. And so, in a determined mood, she picked up the file on Gina Marconi and read it through again, searching for some explanation.

She didn't need to dwell on the injuries detailed by Mark Sullivan

in the post-mortem. Multiple injuries were the inevitable consequence of a high-impact crash and no seat belt. She wanted to
find answers and the only way would be to approach Gina's mother,
her son Terence, or Julius Zedanski. One of those would surely
give her a clue.

She needed to formulate a plan. Some structure.

She would also visit the scene of the crash to at least get a
clearer picture of the geography. It might help her to be more
certain whether this had been premeditated or a spontaneous
impulse. Crash scene investigators had estimated her speed had
been around sixty miles per hour. Bloody fast to go flying into a
wall, Martha muttered. She knew that road out of Shrewsbury and
had braked round that very same corner. Going at sixty round that
bend was suicidally fast. She'd had a narrow miss when she had
hit a patch of black ice late one night when she had been driving
home from a night out in Ellesmere. Even so, if Gina's seat belt
had been on she would almost certainly have survived the impact.
Unbuckling her seat belt – or leaving it off – had surely been the
clearest indication as to her intention. Unbuckling it had removed
any chance she would survive.

Martha started by listing the indisputable facts: it had happened
at three a.m. No witnesses.

Next, she leafed through the forensic report of the car.

Gina had, it seemed, driven straight and true. The damage to the
car – and to the wall – had been symmetrical. There was no sign she
had braked. There had been no brake pedal marks on the sole of her
left foot. And Martha knew in high impact the brake pedal patterned
the sole if the person had his or her foot on the brake pedal.

The only mark on Gina's sole was on the right shoe, the clear
imprint of the accelerator which had likewise mirrored the sole of
the shoe. Everything pointed to suicide – except there had been
no note and no indication that anything was wrong. In fact, the
reverse was true. All the evidence and statements indicated Gina
had been going through a happy period in her life.

Martha was thoughtful and disturbed. Before finding the verdict
she needed to satisfy herself that this had been a deliberate suicide.
And she realized that meant asking twin questions. Not only *why*,
but also *why not?* Not just why a beautiful and talented woman
with a future ahead of her wanted to kill herself, but why had she

not left her nearest and dearest some explanation? Why leave them to forever wonder and suffer?

Gina had been a barrister – a profession that articulated actions in terms clear enough to convince a judge and jury. This obfuscation just didn't fit, which meant she should consider an alternative. Was there the remotest possibility that she had been unable to sleep, had been heading somewhere, ended up impacting the wall by accident? As coroner, this was Martha's job. Her decision. Could she honestly find an accidental verdict? Duck the issue by finding the death unexplained? All her instincts screamed at suicide and yet she would not find that verdict unless . . . She could not be a hundred per cent sure without that note, without some stark reason, some benefit, some sign that Gina's Teflon life was not quite as it seemed. She needed to find that 'not quite'. Was it possible that, unable to sleep, perhaps fizzed up at the thought of her impending wedding, she had by some godawful chance found herself fatally distracted and *bang*? So why no seat belt? Was it possible her distraction had extended to that? It was all most unsatisfactory.

She picked up yet another report. Toxicology. Gina's blood alcohol level was 10 milligrams per 100 millilitres of blood – less than the equivalent of one small glass of wine. Well under the legal limit. Hardly pissed. 'Don't tell me that would have impaired her judgement,' Martha muttered, her mind taking an unexpected left turn. It wouldn't even have softened the impact. She had not taken the cowards' way out, anaesthetizing herself first with a bottle of whisky, but had suffered the full impact. Punishing herself, leaving no way out. She had left her mobile phone at home, carefully placed on the bedside table. Martha needed to be sure and Gina wasn't helping her. She took a look at the photograph and recalled the laugh she had heard ringing that night.

She read through the police description of the scene. One hundred feet behind the wall was a neat and symmetrical Georgian house. The owner slept in a front bedroom and had heard the impact, felt a shudder in the house, heard the bang, the crashing of glass, the tearing of metal, the dreadful sound of violent impact, the sound of death. No scream. Though he must have realized this was a catastrophic impact, he had initially peered through the curtains and, when he'd seen the carnage, had wasted no time in dialling 999. The ambulance had arrived first to a dead woman trapped half in and half out of a crushed car, radiator steam still puffing out, headlights angled into the night sky. The fire engine had arrived with cutting equipment and then, with the police, had removed the body straight into a body bag. There was no need for a police surgeon to confirm death. These days a senior policeman could do it just as well.

The scene had been sealed off and the wheels of forensic investigation began.

She sighed and returned to her train of thought. Leaving her phone behind meant no *Where are you?* phone call or text, as well as no fatal distraction. But no phone could also mean something else: no chance for a last-minute funk or goodbye message. More than ever Martha wished Alex was here, by her side, so they could comb through the facts together as they usually did and try and come up with some rational explanation. Having someone to test her ideas on, bounce around various scenarios, had been more useful than she had realized. Truth was, she was missing him.

It was strange to think that only a few days ago he had been here, in this room, so familiar with its beige carpet, cream walls, bookshelves. Her eyes drifted towards the bay window and the armchairs close to them. He had been sitting in that very chair, long bony frame, legs stretched out in front of him, that familiar frown as he tried to work something out, that particular mixture he held of angst and relaxation, of reassurance and provoking questions, at the same time asking and answering them. It was he who had coloured in the picture made from observation at the scene, that Gina had initially gone to bed that night. His theory was that she had made the decision only minutes before she had left the house.

And yet she must have staked out the spot.

It had been Alex who had further painted the picture of her bedroom. The covers had been thrown back, the phone placed squarely on the bedside cabinet (a mark of determination), but the nightdress tossed on the bed. He had accompanied this comment with a sly glance at her. 'An expensive garment,' he'd said, and when he'd noticed the curse of the redhead – a deep blush on her cheeks – he had described it further. 'Purple satin trimmed with real lace.'

She had made the only response she could. 'Really?'
Which had provoked a wide grin quickly smothered.
He had gone on to describe the contrast in Gina's heavily
bloodstained apparel. 'Jogging bottoms and a sweatshirt with
trainers. No socks, no knickers, no bra.' And the hint of boudoir
had been blown away. They were clothes one would pull on
hurriedly if unable to sleep, clothes you would wear to creep out
of your house, leaving your eight-year-old son asleep, your mother
safe in her bungalow and leave the house to kill yourself. So, DI
Randall had surmised, and she had agreed with him, Gina had
gone to bed and been unable to sleep. Troubled by thoughts,
perhaps? She had come to a decision and then, agitated, she had
got up, dressed and left the house, apparently without leaving a
suicide note.

Martha had interjected then. 'Only one in six suicides do leave
a note, Alex.'

But both had come to the same conclusion – that Gina Marconi
was a lawyer. She would have wanted to leave things neat and tidy.

Or perhaps that was the subtlety of a lawyer's mind. Leave them
wondering, why don't you? Martha started to plan. She had some
ideas.

She wanted to interview Bridget Shannon again and, with
her permission, Terence. But she had to be realistic. If Gina's
mother had known nothing, what did she think an eight-year-
old could possibly know? Was she inferring Terence was more
perceptive than his grandmother? Maybe. It was not impossible.
Sometimes children are. Sometimes they see things others do
not. Sometimes they blurt out statements or observations that
adults would hide.

Martha frowned. To have any insight into this case she needed
to escape her office and visit the scene of the crash, preferably
with a police escort. That brought her up short. Admit it, Martha,
you're really missing him. You want to know how Alex is.

She stood up, tossed the papers aside, picked up the phone,
connected with Monkmoor Police Station and asked if someone
could drive her out to the crash site.

TWENTY-THREE

Forty minutes later PC Gethin Roberts arrived. She liked the young PC, his gawky manner, his huge feet, his obvious pride in the job only equalled by his ability to introduce the subject of his adored Flora into every conversation, though not so much recently, she'd noticed. Roberts was an endearing sort of fellow, an oversized, clumsy, *Some-Mothers-Do-'Ave-'Em* sort of guy, always bumping into things, knocking his head, stubbing the great toe on the end of his size elevens. But lately, even Alex had commented, as PC Gary Coleman had become increasingly excited over his impending nuptials, Roberts had done the opposite. Something of his spark seemed to have been extinguished. The bouncy exuberance that had marked him out had all but abandoned him, but she didn't know why.

She glanced across at the young officer's face. 'You all right, Roberts?'

He nodded, didn't look at her, his face set and focusing hard on the road ahead. He wasn't talking so she changed subjects, putting forward one of her weaker theories. 'Do you think it's possible Ms Marconi couldn't sleep, went for a drive, was distracted?'

He still kept his eyes on the road, hands steady on the wheel, frowned and shook his head. 'Not a chance, Mrs Gunn.'

'And you say further checks on the car turned up nothing? Brakes OK?'

'Yeah. So far they've found nothing wrong with the car.' He took a swift glance at her, opened his mouth then clamped it shut again.

She would have loved to be able to ask Roberts what the trouble was, but it wouldn't be appropriate. And he probably wouldn't confide in her anyway. And now she couldn't even discuss it with Alex, so she said nothing.

But she continued her musings in silence.

Maybe Flora had dumped him.

Maybe he no longer wanted to get married to her.

Maybe he'd just *fallen out of love* with her.

Surely not. They were one of those simple couples who meet, fall in love, stay in love, get married, have children, grow old together.

The crash site was a silent ten-minute drive from her office and about the same distance from Gina Marconi's home. Fifteen if she'd been driving slowly. But according to the one image they had captured on CCTV she had been doing fifty miles an hour even through the centre of the town.

As a few spots of rain leaked out of the sky they reached the spot, still marked nearly a month later. Police warning signs, weathered now, had been erected along with an appeal for witnesses. None had come forward so far except the unlucky Graham Skander. His wall was still reduced to a pile of bricks. Obviously the insurance company hadn't settled yet.

On a mossy triangle beyond the crash site there was still a bank of flowers, most well past their best, in sodden cellophane wrapping, raindrops looking like tears shed for the dead woman, silky ribbons dirty and sopping wet. Life and flowers do not last. Traffic cones shielded the narrow pavement and the demolished wall behind.

Roberts parked the car in a lay-by fifty yards beyond, switched his blue light to flash and together they walked back to the scene. The pavement was narrow, not wide enough for them to walk side by side, so she went first. The police tape that marked off the area was a flimsy, ineffectual barrier. The wall was ahead of you when you manoeuvred the right-hand bend. She'd forgotten how sharp the corner was, and how the uncompromising wall confronted you. Skid marks were still clearly visible, marked and measured by the crash investigators. Debris also marked the spot: splinters of glass, and silver paint marks on the scattered bricks, even a few dark splashes of blood. There was the usual road kill to the side. A grey squirrel, a blackbird, eyes already picked out by hungry crows. The kerbstone was low. Easy for an out-of-control car to mount. Martha peered over the stones at Graham Skander's house. Very nice, she thought. Mellow Georgian brick with the pleasing symmetry of the late eighteenth century. And the bricks that lay on the ground looked old too. No wonder he was so angry at it being destroyed again. Had this been her house, she reflected, and her problem, she would have accepted the council's offer of bollards to protect the wall. But Skander had struck her as a stubborn man.

The car and its driver had come off worse than the wall. *It* could be rebuilt but not them. Gina and the four-month-old Mercedes had been written off. She looked around carefully, committing the scene to memory. Sometimes visiting the scene of an incident provided answers. At others there was no sense of death or drama. And here? It reflected the Americans' description of what the English call a 'car accident'. The Americans call it a 'car wreck'. At her side, in his clumsy way, Roberts tried to help. 'She went at it at sixty, Mrs Gunn,' he said. 'Straight at it. Never turned the wheel to even try and take the corner. Straight in.' There was almost a note of admiration in his voice. She turned to look at him, read the bleak unhappiness that made his comical features even more misshapen, his nose appear larger, his eyes droopy and bloodhound-like, his forehead creased with lines of anxiety, his hands great big agitated spatulas by his side. The rain came down harder.

She stood there as the traffic, cautioned by the police signs, crept past, drivers peering nosily out of windscreens now rain-soaked, wiper blades trying to swoosh the water away and give clear visibility. Sometimes the weather matched the mood so perfectly it intensified the emotion. But, in spite of the rain, Martha stood still, trying to transport her mind backwards, trying to insert herself into Gina Marconi's desperate state, and from there to imagine the scene moments later when the owner of the house and the wall – Mr Graham Skander, retired civil servant – had peered through his curtains, rung the emergency services and, with typical propriety, put his dressing gown on and run outside. So he had been the first to see the scene of devastation, the car crushed and embedded into the wall, the woman collapsed at the wheel, the radiator steaming into the night air. According to his statement the woman had been unresponsive when he had shouted, with dreadful hindsight and cruel irony, 'Are you all right?'

And yet, Martha realized, it is what we all do. She had once been first on the scene of a fatal accident where an elderly lady had suffered a traumatic amputation of her leg. Her question had been the same: *Are you all right?* Knowing, hoping, that the woman was already dead rather than suffering.

She'd read Skander's statement. The police with typical pedantic stoicism had asked Mr Skander whether Gina had made any response, recording his answer with the same stolid literalism.

'Not a flicker,' he'd said. And so any explanation Gina might have given had died with her.

But something of the civil servant remained. Graham Skander had not abandoned the dead woman or the crash scene but had waited stoically, not leaving her side for eight long minutes, while police, ambulance and fire engines sliced through the night with flashing blue lights and muted sirens.

Over an hour later, finally freed from the wreckage, Gina had finally been pronounced dead at the scene. Under recent legislation the SIO, quick on the scene even at that unearthly hour, had authorized her removal to the mortuary and on Monday morning Martha had been informed and it had been arranged for the car to be removed on a low loader ready for a forensic inspection. End of story and the beginning of the investigation.

But however hard she focused, closed her eyes and tried to absorb the scene, Martha was no nearer the truth.

She would not find answers here, at this bleak roadside, where bright, beautiful and clever Gina Marconi had died. 'Come on, Roberts,' she said, tempted to pat his big, unhappy shoulder, 'let's go back to Shrewsbury.'

She headed back to the car, Roberts in her wake. What had she expected anyway, she thought dejectedly. All she had achieved was that every time she travelled along this stretch of road she would remember. And then she stopped in her tracks.

She glanced across at Roberts, who looked, if anything, even more dejected. She had the feeling that he too was glad to abandon the scene. He certainly marched very smartly, holding the car door open for her with a grin that didn't fool her for a moment. Just before she climbed into the passenger seat she paused, again tempted to ask him what the problem was but, held back by protocol, she climbed in with no more than a nod. Once or twice during the journey home Roberts did glance across, even opening his mouth as though to ask her something or confide in her, but it was only as they turned into the car park of her office that he asked his one and only question.

'Mrs Gunn,' he said hesitantly, turning to face her, 'do you have to be a doctor as well as a lawyer to be a coroner?'

'These days it's preferable,' she responded gently, wondering whether – heavens above – this was the boy's ambition? If so he had a long way to climb. A levels, medical school, pre-registration trial by sleeplessness.

'When I started you could be either.'

'So you're a doctor?'

'I am.'

At that he shot out of the car, whisked around and opened the door for her with surprising grace for PC Roberts. Without banging his knees, arms or head.

She thanked him.

Back in her office, a message from DS Paul Talith was waiting for her on her answerphone.

TWENTY-FOUR

'Just to let you know, ma'am – I thought you'd *want* to know – DI Randall's just left. We don't need to hold him. We know where he lives.' *That sounded sinister, almost a threat.*

He'd hesitated, unsure how far to go. 'According to his statement his wife was . . .' another pause. 'Upset.'

'The post-mortem,' he began again, having trouble finding the words. 'Post-mortem,' he repeated slowly, '. . . Doctor Sullivan. He's waiting for results before he'll commit himself.' This last sentence came out in a rush.

Had he been there on the end of the line she would have questioned him sharply: *What results?*

After a noisy clearing of the throat he finished with, 'Thank you, Mrs Gunn.'

After absorbing the message she rang him back. 'Thank you for keeping me informed, Sergeant Talith. It must have been difficult for you, interviewing a colleague.'

'Yes, but . . . I knew he couldn't have done anything. He can't have, surely?' His very tone suggested that he was not sure.

She too wished she could be certain. 'I take it you've let Mr Steadman know as *he's* the coroner in charge?' She realized as the words came out that she hadn't quite erased a tacit criticism from the slight emphasis to the word. As though she wanted to distance herself.

Talith was quick to respond. 'Yes, ma'am. Of course we have. He just wants to wait for a few other tests and the post-mortem results and then he'll set a date for the inquest. He said it was almost certainly accidental and once he's got the results back . . .'

Ah, yes – the results. She waited but Talith wasn't sharing.

'Once he's got the results back he'll be absolutely sure.'

'Good.' This was good news. But as she put the phone down she acknowledged it wasn't – not really. The truth may not be quite as clear cut as the optimistic DS and her colleague from South Shropshire might imply – and probably wanted to believe. It was that one word that had alerted her – *almost.*

In the end curiosity got the better of her and she picked up the phone again, this time to connect with Mark Sullivan's mobile. At least she had a bona fide reason for wanting to speak to the pathologist.

'I understand the post-mortem on Alex's wife has now taken place?'

'Yeah,' he said, suspecting nothing. 'And I understand *he's* been brought in for questioning.'

'Yes. And released, I believe . . .' But she worried now that she had shown her hand, defended him a little too quickly while knowing exactly what she was up to. Trying to influence outcomes. Strictly forbidden – if not downright illegal. It could cost her her job. Coroners are expected to be impartial. How do you do that, she challenged, when a friend and colleague is involved?

She couldn't continue doing this, skipping across boundaries, in and out of a case. Getting involved was too risky and ultimately would not help Alex anyway. Mark Sullivan was far too intelligent a man and doctor not to know exactly what she was doing – and guess the reason why. And Steadman would not be bought or influenced, but . . .

Sullivan gave a long sigh. 'I don't really want to say anything, Martha, not until I'm sure.'

'Was the PM conclusive?' She just couldn't stop fishing.

Sullivan chuckled. 'When are they?'

She didn't even try to answer this one. It would be skipping through a minefield.

'But in this case I think I've a pretty good idea. It could answer questions. Just be patient and I'll be in touch with Mr Steadman.'

It was a rebuke and she wriggled out.

'Well,' she continued briskly, 'I didn't really ring you about Mrs Randall anyway. I wondered if you'd had any further thoughts about the Gina Marconi case?'

'Not really. I mean, my role was simply to connect her injuries with the impact. I don't step outside the box, Martha, you know that. You've seen my full report?'

'Yes. Yes.'

He paused but, if she had moved on, he hadn't.

'Do you want a full report on the results of the PM on Erica Randall?'

'Umm. I don't know, Mark.' Lucky he was a friend. 'I'm in a difficult position. That's why I asked David to manage the case.'

'I'll give Jericho a call,' he said gently. 'Let him know. Is that OK?'

'Yes. Thank you, Mark. I appreciate it.'

As she put the phone down she was already working through her own list of people who might be able to answer questions. Erica Randall aside, she could not rid herself of the feeling that there was a link between the two suicides she was dealing with. She might be able to deflect Gina's death, even explain it, but she was aware that there was nothing to connect two such disparate people. They could not possibly have met. Different ages, different social class. Only the determination behind their final acts connected them. Was there something more? Something she was missing?

TWENTY-FIVE

Martha didn't need to go over the facts again. She knew them all off by heart. And yet she was still missing something. Probably staring right at it.

Sitting quietly in her office with no distractions, Martha was able to dig deep into her experience as a coroner and focus on this one case, revise what she believed. Gina Marconi had loved her mother, her son and her fiancé, and she would have spared them from this pain if she had been able. Perhaps Gina's personal life really had been as perfect as it appeared. Happy and comfortable.

But what about her professional life? She was a lawyer who had mingled with dark forces. What was it Curtis Thatcher had said?

'She dealt with the underworld.'

Martha nodded and recalled something else Thatcher had said.

'Not to put too fine a point on it, Mosha was in her debt. He's an evil fellow with a lot of influence. There have been some very dark rumours of murder, torture, bribery, organized crime. If these are true he would have protected her.'

From threats made by other criminals? From blackmail?

'They were better off in prison.' Better off? For whom? For them? Had he meant safer on the inside than on the outside? And then his next comment: *'That even defending them put her in a tricky position.'*

Tricky in this instance meant vulnerable. Was there something there? Something Gina had not quite handled right? Had one of her villainous clients a score to settle? And somehow exposed or threatened to expose some anomaly? Martha shifted in her chair. It would have to have been under Mosha Steventon's radar or he would have avenged her. Who could have known about this? Obviously her partner, Curtis Thatcher. How much would he have known about Gina's cases? How much had she shared? Did they work together? Even as she wondered about him too she started planning her next move. It seemed a promising area to begin with.

She kept the notes on her desk. The trouble was her link with the police – her mole, Alex, was no longer active. He had his own problems to deal with and was suspended or on 'gardening leave' or 'enforced holiday' or whatever it was called these days, so she would be restricted to formal channels. Enter by the front door. And tread very gently.

But before events had removed him she and Alex had talked about these two cases and agreed on a few facts. He had been just as wary and dissatisfied with the lack of explanation as she was and he had been aware that she would dig deeper. Alex had helped up to a point, but mobile phone records had revealed little, mainly calls to family and friends. And nothing conclusive had been unearthed during interviews. Colleagues at work (her secretary and the cleaner) had said she had appeared distracted recently. But they always say that after the event and there was no detail. Her secretary had added she had seemed a bit dreamy.

What imminent bride is not?

Martha cupped her chin in her hand and dreamed herself. Dreamy, distracted. She made a silent apology – *Forgive me for being a romantic* – but didn't that sound just like a woman anticipating a wedding to a heroic character?

But if you factor in a suicide with someone appearing dreamy or distracted prior to her wedding the picture forming starts to look rather different. Had Gina been having second thoughts? Had Gina let herself down? Was she about to let Julius down? Her mother and son too, who had formed such a close bond with him?

Only one way to find out.

She picked up the phone and asked Jericho to make further appointments with Gina Marconi's mother, her fiancé and her son. Feeling she was fumbling her way forward in understanding Gina's death she put her notes to one side and picked up Patrick Elson's file.

Her other mystery.

A little like Gina Marconi's, his life had appeared on the surface clean and untroubled. Yes, he was being brought up by a lone mum and there was little evidence of a father figure, but Patrick had been part of a huge extended and loving family. He had grandparents, aunts, uncles, cousins. The Elsons had been a large, rumbustious, supportive family and financially sound – not wealthy, but they had managed. Amanda Elson had a part-time job as a support teacher. Martha picked up the school photograph of the boy, looked at his confident, freckled face, his big grin. It could have been Sam, her own son, footballer, wannabe teacher. She imagined how she would feel if he too had jumped off a bridge on to a road and into the path of fast-moving traffic. Her heart almost stopped at the thought. It was too awful. She suppressed the urge to ring him. Right now. Check he was OK.

She glanced at her watch. He would be in training.

So instead, when she picked up the phone she asked Jericho to make another appointment with Amanda Elson. Now she had her distractions. Adding the two cases to her routine work would keep her busy; her next few days spoken for. It would make it easier for her to hold back on her instinct to try and find out the truth behind Erica Randall's death.

She could leave that to the police, David Steadman and Dr Mark Sullivan. It was their job. Not hers.

TWENTY-SIX

Friday, 7 April, 11 a.m.

Martha had been fidgety all morning, knowing that Mark Sullivan was probably getting the answers to Erica Randall's death. It was a curious sensation. She had no feelings for the woman – she'd never met her – but she'd attended enough post-mortems to know exactly what assaults her body had been subjected to. The body which Alex must once have loved. She left her desk, agitated now, and moved to the bay window. Perhaps the view of the town would calm her. But no. The spire of St Chad's Church only reminded her of death. She tried to block out the vision of Sullivan's fingers teasing out a dead person's story, slicing up specimens, probing with fingers and scalpel, measuring contusions and abrasions, finding out the story, re-enacting sequences of events by piecing together physical signs. Exploration of the brain, the sternal split, analysis of each and every single bruise and injury, specimens for chemical analysis. Someone else peering down a microscope, preparation of slides, centrifuging bloods, chemical analysis. She knew the processes off by heart. What had he found? Had Alex any hand in his wife's death? Even the slightest pressure between the shoulder blades as she stood at the top of the stairs?

She looked at the phone once or twice, fought the temptation to pick it up, make that call, but at the same time knowing she couldn't. She did ring through to Jericho, but just the once to ask if any messages had been left and almost congratulated herself on her restraint. There were messages – plenty of them – but not the ones she had hoped for.

So she waited for Patrick's mother and aunt. Jericho had persuaded them to attend at two o'clock that afternoon.

The two women were bang on time and entered, clutching each other tightly. Amanda looked panicky while her sister supported her with a hand on her forearm.

'We've fixed a date for Patrick's inquest,' Martha opened with the blunt fact. 'Wednesday the nineteenth. It will be held at Shirehall in Abbey Foregate at ten a.m. If you want anyone to speak for your son let my officer, Jericho, know. We will accommodate anyone you feel might have something to contribute.'

Amanda nodded, her grip on her sister's hand tightening.

For the briefest of seconds the two women exchanged glances. And Martha picked up that there was something conspiratorial in the look. Her antennae quivered. She could sense conflict between these two women, who up until now had appeared close sisters.

The look they exchanged spelt out: *Do we tell her or not?*

And she sensed they had a conflict, a question they dared not ask. But she had a question too. Why had Patrick trailed two miles to the bridge over a fast section of the A5, lugging his schoolbag, his homework completed? Why, on that particular morning, had he committed suicide in that very public fashion? As though he wanted the world to see, to bear witness. As though . . . Martha fumbled with the thought. As though he had wanted the headline.

And, as she studied Amanda Elson's face, a phrase that Gina's mother, Bridget, had used swam into her mind. *At least I didn't have to find her body.* Was this the way Patrick's mind had worked? Or had he considered the thought that his mother might find him halfway through an attempt – before he was dead – and bring him round? Tablets, slashed wrists, car exhaust fumes were notoriously easy to intervene.

She looked from one to the other and waited, hoping her silence might flush out the sisters' secret. Then she caught the slightest shake of Amanda's head, little more than a shiver in her hair.

No.

Their decision. But she was finding it hard to be excluded from whatever secret they were hiding and so, after a pause to give them the opportunity to enlarge, she pushed. 'Have you thought of any reason why Patrick was driven to this?'

Melanie looked startled and even Martha didn't quite know why she had chosen that particular phrase. *Driven to this.* Unfortunate analogy, but more than that – if he had been driven, who had done the driving?

Melanie was looking again at her sister with an unmistakable message: *Tell her*. And at that point Amanda Elson's shoulders crumpled as she bent down and reached for her handbag. It was large, capacious, brown plastic, an ugly object. She lifted it on to her lap, unzipped it, reached inside and pulled out a brown A4 envelope.

She handed it to Martha, indicated with a dip of her chin that she should look inside.

And Martha knew.

She kept her gaze steady on the two women as she pulled out a couple of poor-quality pictures, fuzzy and indistinct, obviously printed from an iPhone. She fanned them out on top of her desk then studied each one without comment. The contents turned her stomach. The first one was of the child, Patrick. He was naked, hunkered down, sobbing, hands half covering a distraught face. Martha turned the picture over to look at the back.

Cry Baby Elson. Want these to go viral?

In the background a china lady danced, red skirts swirling in front of net curtains looped back.

The second picture was of the same boy. She could tell by his mop-cut hair, the same shining brown as his mother's. Patrick, trousers down, bottom bare, bending over. The worst of it was that he could have been bending down for a thrashing or for sex or simply obedience. You couldn't see his face but in the hunching of his shoulders and hands on knees, head as low as he could, she sensed the child was terrified and humiliated. A man was on the edge of the picture and he looked as though he was about to . . .

Martha turned it over. On the back was written another mocking message in the same childish writing. *Waiting for it, Pat?*

She looked up. The pictures were horrible. To that boy's mother and aunt they were dreadful; to a twelve-year-old they would have been devastating. Destroying.

She met the two women's eyes, read the anguish in them. Melanie spoke up for her sister. 'We found these afterwards.' She swallowed. 'We think Patrick wanted us to find them.'

Martha nodded. 'You should have taken these to the police,' she said softly. 'They're evidence.'

'Of what?' Again, it was Melanie who spoke. She didn't have her sister's soft voice nor the submissive tone. She was challenging. Feisty.

'But this is obviously why . . .'

In a panic, Amanda was already stuffing the pictures back into the envelope. 'Mrs Gunn,' she said, 'my boy died so these would not be made public. So no one would know except us. I'm not going to go against that.'

Martha was temporarily stumped. She always put relatives' wishes first, unless they clashed with the police investigation. But they had a point. Patrick had died because he didn't want the shame of these pictures being seen.

'But someone is responsible.' She spoke slowly, feeling her way along a wall in the dark. 'Whoever it is might do something like this again. Your son, Amanda, was underage. This is an imprisonable offence. A police matter.' Again, she wished she could share these with Alex who would, she felt certain, have dealt with it better. She leaned forward. 'There might be another boy.'

She recalled Bridget's words once more. *At least I didn't have to find her body.*

It spoke of consideration, forethought. Planning. Both Patrick and Gina had wanted to protect their loved ones from further upset. But Patrick had left behind this clue for his mother to find.

She dropped her eyes to the photographs. 'He left these for a reason.'

Amanda supplied the answer quickly. 'To tell us we weren't to blame. To explain.'

Martha sat back and wondered. Had something similar been the trigger to Gina's suicide too? Even possibly Erica Randall's? Or was she stretching the elastic too far?

If Erica had deliberately thrown herself down the stairs there would be no physical evidence to find, nothing except Alex's testimony. That was the way these things worked. And she would be in the same dreadful limbo land where Gina's mother, son and fiancé were. Never able to find the answer. At least Amanda Elson and her sister had an explanation for Patrick's anguish and death. They would always feel they'd failed him but they did have an answer. Her eyes slid back to the envelope. Out there she sensed someone malicious enough to want to destroy lives. Someone with one thing in mind? Destruction?

She stopped breathing for a moment and recalled the traumatized Eileen Tinsley's description of the boy standing on the bridge, arms outstretched, the similarity to Landowski's statue of Christ in Rio de Janeiro, the brief hesitation and then the fall she had described apologetically as graceful but which had ended up in such carnage, tearing into that otherwise beautiful spring morning. Martha felt fury rip through her too. Someone had engineered this. Planned it, felt the hatred, photographed the boy in the most humiliating position conceivable. A grown man had . . .

It had awoken the monster inside her, which reared up now, releasing the Devil so far only hinted at by her red hair and sparkling eyes. She wanted to find the sick person who found this sort of thing entertaining. Who mocked. And as she knew a man was present, she also knew the writing on the back was a minor's hand. She wanted to destroy him just as they had destroyed not only Patrick's life but also Gina Marconi's. And then sensible coroner mode kicked in.

Wait a minute before jumping to conclusions, Martha. What evidence apart from your so-called Irish intuition do you have for connecting Gina Marconi's death with Patrick's – and come to that Erica Randall's, an even bigger stretch of the imagination? You don't even know the circumstances surrounding Erica Randall's death, except that it could have been a leap into oblivion, not into a wall or on to a busy road but down a flight of stairs. So what are you doing – stringing the row of beads together to form a necklace? There is no necklace. You have strung the beads together. You have seen just one set of photographs so far. And there is nothing in those that involves Gina or Alex's wife.

And then she began to respond to her own doubts. *You've already put your finger on it, haven't you? Intuition.* She'd always sensed the similarity in these two suicides.

The two women were watching her, waiting for *her* to make the next move without realizing it was they who should speak.

Martha's eyes were on them but her inner voice was still speaking. *So what are you going to do about it, Coroner?* She mentally answered her own question. *Something. That's for sure. Not nothing. That is not an option.*

And now she put her hand over the envelope, spanning the fingers to cover as much of it as they could, and asked the question quietly. 'What do you want me to do with these?'

'We don't want them being made public.'

'Absolutely not. They will not come out in court. I quite understand that.' She didn't point out the obvious, that there would be
electronic copies – somewhere.

'Perhaps I should keep them for now?'

The sisters looked at each other, obviously confused by the
request. They had not expected this and they were not certain it
was proper. They were right, of course. It was not, strictly speaking.
There was probably something in the rule book to prevent this,
Martha reflected. But as neither woman would have read the rule
book she continued to meet their eyes with an air of confidence.
She accompanied this with a vague smile intended to reassure them,
convey the fact that they were on the same side – that they were
together in this, side by side, standing against the sick person
who . . . Side by side.

The phrase caught her. Her hand shifted slightly, inching the
envelope millimetres towards her. 'Surely,' she appealed, 'you want
this person found before . . .'

Both women finally nodded.

Martha's toes had grown cold and she knew why they had
capitulated. It was that one word. *Before* . . . Before what? Another
one? Please God no. Out of nowhere she felt vulnerable and
couldn't understand why. Why did that possibility seem so dreadful
and also so personal? This could be nothing to do with her. But
at the back of her mind she recalled Gina's confident manner and
loud laugh. There was one word that linked them.

Status.

Gina had had a lot to lose, as did she. Martha frowned and
shook her head to the bemusement of the sisters.

But now Amanda's hand was also on the envelope, to stop it
shifting further in either direction. 'You promise . . .' she reminded
her. Then it turned into a question wanting confirmation. 'You
promise?'

Martha nodded. 'I promise. I will share these with the police
and no one else. They will not be in the public domain, neither
will they be published in the press. But if we can find this person,
stop them ever doing this horrible crime again, your son's death
will not have been in vain.' She hesitated before her next sentence
but knew she must expose this possibility. 'We can hope that with
Patrick's death these pictures will not surface on social media.'

She didn't add that it was a vain hope but hurried on. 'It's possible there have been other victims in the past. It's also possible there may be more planned in the future.'

And then Amanda, in a silent gesture, pushed the envelope towards her. 'Have it,' she said bitterly. 'I never want to see them again. Ever.' She tapped the side of her head. 'It's bad enough they're in here.'

Martha nodded and returned to the safe subject of the inquest. 'Have you thought about someone to speak up for Patrick?'

'His teacher.' Melanie's voice was harsher than her sister's. 'Mr Trimble,' she said. 'He was Pat's form teacher. Pat thought the world of him. I'd like *him* to say a few words.'

Martha nodded, understanding. At a guess Mr Trimble might even throw some light on the background to these photographs. She looked forward to meeting him.

At the back of her mind was the solemn promise she had made to the sisters. I will share them with the police and *no one else.*

She would have shared them with Alex (who was police) and no one else. Together they would have decided what to do. Now she had to make that decision alone.

She covered a few more details but when the two women had left she still felt the heat of her own anger until she worked something out. Amanda and her sister had not destroyed the photographs. They had kept them and brought them here today, possibly intending to show them to her. Bridget Shannon might be more protective of her daughter's reputation. Somewhere, if Gina Marconi hadn't destroyed them herself, were there equally shameful pictures? Pictures which would destroy the little Shangri-La she and Julius Zedanski had mapped out for themselves? Or had she burnt them? An action that was probably futile – the person who shared these pictures would have plenty of copies. Backed up and stored ready for social media or any other cruel way of exposing. But why? What was the motive? Money? Blackmail? Patrick Elson wouldn't have had any money to stump up, unlike Gina, so in his case blackmail was unlikely. And he didn't exactly have a reputation to protect. At least not like Gina had. So was the motive simply to cause havoc? Destruction? Simple malice? A feeling of power? It was difficult to fit a twelve-year-old boy into the same frame as Gina. They moved in different circles. She had had power and opportunity, almost celebrity status, whereas Patrick was an anonymous child, an unknown. Was it possible that to preserve her future Gina might have been persuaded to commit a felony, bend the rules a little, distort the facts? Martha recalled the sound of that loud, uncontrolled burst of laughter at the charity evening. There had been something reckless about Ms Marconi. She could have been a risk-taker. But not Patrick. Not that serious, intelligent child. Gina might have perjured herself or kept silent over some inconvenient detail but again, not Patrick. So if there was a connection she must look around them. One thing struck her now. We all have our vulnerabilities. Alex's was his wife. That was his weak spot. His Achilles heel.

Mark Sullivan might already know why and how even though she had not yet discussed with him her idea that there was a link between the two suicides. But he was intelligent enough to have worked it out for himself. Perhaps he too had connected a) with b), unearthed cause and effect.

So now she had to find Gina's weak spot, the place where her defences might have been breached. And in Martha's mind she had the feeling that it was Terence who was more likely to lead her towards an answer than his grandmother, who would be inhibited by overwhelming shame. She suspected the boy would be less inhibited. She also suspected he had more insight into his mother's character than his grandmother. So how could she access him and persuade him to speak out when the law stated he must be accompanied by a responsible adult? And that responsible adult would inhibit him?

Was she right? Were there, out there, similar photographs of Gina to the ones Amanda and Melanie had just produced? Or had Gina destroyed them?

Vain hope.

She would have been smart enough to have covered her tracks and destroy any photographs in her possession, but she would also have known that they could always exist somewhere, out there in the social media ether . . . if someone wanted them to be made public.

The answer bounced back, as clear as a voice in her ear, mocking her. Gina wasn't that smart. She fell right into the hole dug for her. She still died. Martha leaned back in her chair.

This afternoon the office seemed stuffy with secrets. She needed air.

Fortunately her office, based in Bayston Hill, a large village three miles to the south of Shrewsbury, was a Victorian house with a generous private garden. Sometimes when she saw clients, if the day was pleasant, she suggested they speak in this garden, and though the weather today was, frankly, cold and miserable, she still needed to be out there for clarity of mind and not for pleasure. She needed to fill her lungs with pure cold, clear air because she needed to think. She frequently had this moral dilemma arguing at the back of her mind. How much sordid detail did the dead and their families want exposed? As little as possible. But a coroner's court is meant to provide answers. Gina and Patrick had both died because of some reason, some event in their lives and a threat. But how could she, as coroner, who boasted of her voice being the voice of the dead, go against their final wishes? That this event should remain hidden? When she had first left medicine and moved to the coroner's office, in the years before he had died, she had discussed this problem with Martin. And they had recognized there is not one easy answer for all. Each case warrants individual consideration.

She walked, noting with pleasure that her brain was clearing in the damp, pine-scented air that whistled around the garden. The bulbs which had struggled now pushed their way through chilly, wet earth, ready to bloom and welcome in the spring – when it returned.

After a few turns along the paths she had made her decision, drawn up the battle lines and returned to her office, her head clearer now, her thoughts in order. Someone had been bullying Patrick. Someone had taken pictures and destroyed the poor boy. And she believed that someone had found out a shameful secret about Gina Marconi. While it was easy to see why Patrick had reacted in such an extreme way to his humiliation, Gina Marconi was a much more complex and intelligent character. She would have been quite an adversary. If she could have found a way to overcome this without sacrificing her life she would have done so. But she hadn't. With all her intellect and cleverness, her talent as a criminal lawyer, this had been something which she must have known would destroy all that she held dear – her fiancé, her mother, her son. Her career even. And so, without explanation, she had decided to kill herself.

How this malicious person must have revelled in her death. And everything threw up questions.

Who was it? And had his motive been blackmail or simple spite? There would have been no point blackmailing Patrick. He would hardly have had access to funds. So in his case at least, the answer was simple spite.

And if the same person had instigated both suicides, what was the connection between them? Or had the reasons behind them been different? A paedophile for one and a connection with the criminal underworld for the other? Had one been a trial run? If so, she would have expected Patrick to be the first victim and Gina the second. But it had been the other way round. So who was the intended victim?

And lastly, why was she trying to drag Erica Randall into this when the facts pulled her away? The answer was as obvious as the freckles on her nose. Because of Alex, whom she wanted to see off the hook. If her theory was right she could explain both Erica's sad life and her death.

And following the success of two of their plans who, she wondered, was the next intended target?

TWENTY-SEVEN

Friday, 7 April, 1 p.m.

She had waited long enough. Mark Sullivan would have completed his post-mortem on Erica Randall by now and written up his notes. Her fingers hovered over the keypad. She had no business ringing but she had to know. She simply couldn't resist the urge.

It took a while to be connected and she felt increasingly anxious, waiting and worrying what was going on. Then Sullivan's hearty voice came on the line. 'Martha.' He sounded bright – a good sign? She was clutching at any omen.

'I just wondered about DI Randall's—' She got no further before Sullivan dived in.

'Yes – of course. I would have rung you later today but I've only just finished writing it up. Rather a surprise. Bit of a puzzle really.'

Her heart sank. Oh, no. Not a puzzle. She wanted answers, not questions. Certainty, not uncertainty. She wanted Alex off the hook, his wife pronounced the victim of a tragic accident. Plenty of sympathy and he would be a man free of his damaged domestic situation.

'How so?' She wished she could have kept that tension out of her voice.

'We-ell. Not to put too fine a point on it, there's no doubt Erica Randall, poor thing, died from a broken neck consistent with a fall downstairs. It's what came before that's interesting.'

'You mean other *injuries*?'

His tone grew icy. 'Other injuries? Well, more . . . other pathology.'

She was apprehensive but Sullivan hadn't finished. He steamed on. 'The interesting thing was the brain pathology.'

'You mean a fracture or a bleed from before the fall?' She was struggling now as well as worrying. Did he mean an assault? And if he'd found defensive wounds or a blow to the head why was he sounding so bloody jaunty? She'd thought Mark Sullivan and Alex Randall were . . . if not close friends then at least friendly colleagues.

And then as surely as though he was inside the room she sensed Sullivan was backing off. Retreating behind the big convenient screen of confidentiality.

'Look,' he said awkwardly, 'there's still a lot I need to find out. I need confirmation of my theory. I'm not absolutely sure. I'm just hazarding a guess considering the history. I need to speak to Alex and get a clearer picture of his wife's behaviour. And . . . umm.' Now he was sounding more than just awkward. He was having trouble getting the words out. 'I should be discussing this with Mr Steadman as he's the coroner in charge. After all . . .' His voice was almost accusatory. 'It was *your* decision to hand this case over to a colleague rather than handle it yourself, Martha.' It was as though he felt she had abandoned her friend when the truth was so much the opposite. She had needed to distance herself partly so she could be objective but also because it would have compromised Alex Randall to have had his friend, the coroner, conduct the inquest. If it had come out later that they were close, her verdict would *forever* have been open to suspicion. Even so, speaking to Mark Sullivan, she felt cold and uncomfortable, on the defensive and struggling to regain her position. 'OK then, Mark,' she said briskly, 'shall we move on to Gina Marconi?'

She could immediately tell that he was more comfortable in this safe zone. 'Did you know her?' she asked.

'I did,' he said. 'It was a bit tough really. I'd sort of half met her – you know, on the various circuits. She played violin in the symphony orchestra. Not brilliant but . . .'

'Are you happy for me to close the inquest? I take it there's no doubt as to cause of death?'

'Yes.' He puffed. 'Take your pick. I put down multiple injuries. Broken pelvis, broken neck . . .'

Martha winced.

He went on: 'Clavicle, arms, ribs and a nasty tear of the subclavian artery. Shock. Haemorrhage.'

'And there's no indication as to why?'

'No.'

'So have you anything else to add?'

Mark Sullivan gave a dry chuckle. 'You know my remit, Martha. Not to reason why, simply do or die, report my findings. Stick to the facts. If I started to spin stories around my victims' lives and deaths – well, there'd be no end to it. And I wouldn't be able to do my job.'

They chatted a little while longer, but it felt false. Her old colleague, Mark Sullivan, pathologist, was on his guard, keeping something back from her. And although she thought it possible that they both suspected the same scenario, her current concern was that for about the first time since they had started working together they weren't sharing it.

She put the phone down with a feeling of regret and loss, mourning for something gone, but hopefully not forever.

Alone in her office, she had far too much time to reflect. If only Alex was around. She could have shared these vile pictures with him, tossed ideas his way, listened as he considered every possibility as he and she had done so many times before. She was surprised at how much she missed him both as a colleague and as a friend. He would have known what to do, started a police investigation, found this monster and warned him or her off, probably with a criminal charge – but what? There was no evidence of extortion, only of manipulation. Sharing of indecent images? Yes, possibly.

Assault of a minor? Yes.

Alex would have had access to all the evidence the police would have uncovered. And he would have shared it. He would have been her back door. More than once she knew he'd stepped over the mark when they had liaised over a case. Looked the other way when she had exceeded her remit. But, although she could easily obtain his home phone number, where she guessed he would be right now, and although she longed to speak to him, even if only to hear his voice, she didn't pick up the phone. She told herself she could pretend she'd rung to offer her condolences but she knew they would sound hollow. And he would have realized they were insincere. She dared not pick up the phone. Communications between them had to stay cut.

Until all this was all over. If it ever would be.

And now she had a new worry. What was Mark Sullivan's theory? Were they thinking along the same lines or not? Was he worrying about the part Alex had played in his wife's death? What other pathology of the brain? Did he mean trauma? A previous injury? The most likely finding following a fall downstairs was surely a depressed fracture of the cranium or a zygomatic arch fracture, the bone at the socket of the eyes which was as thin as tissue paper. Easily broken in a fall or after a blow to the side of the face. She pictured Alex's long, bony fingers and knew she had only seen them balled into a fist once. And that had been when he was sharing his feelings about his wife.

I hate her.

The history of a broken neck to her had been suggestive of a traumatic spondylolisthesis of the axis – the classic hangman's injury. The broken neck of grisly stories. But this wouldn't be an unexpected finding. And it wouldn't prove anything. So what *was* Mark Sullivan's idea?

And as her mind drifted, tossed on a stormy sea of doubt, her thoughts inevitably returned to DI Alex Randall.

* * *

Who at that very moment was sitting at home without a clue what to do. The house seemed quiet, empty and very small. He didn't know where he was in his life or where he would go next. What he would do. Everything seemed like a faraway never-never land, everywhere unreachable. He'd lost control of his own life through Erica's lack of control over hers. He sank back into the sofa, leaned his head forward and rubbed his forehead as though that would remove his worries and put his thoughts back in order.

The thought that seemed to saturate his mind was that Erica was dead. And he didn't know how he felt about that.

There would be no more embarrassment, no more anxiety, no more emergency situations brought about by his wife's unstable mental condition. The odd thing was that at the moment it seemed like a loss. A hole in his life, a hollow in his core. He had never dared to hope that one day he might be free of her. At the same time he acknowledged the undeniable fact that pushed into him, unwelcome but inevitable as a rat in a sewer. He wasn't free. He might never be free. This might hang around his neck as cursed as the albatross around the poor old sailor. This wasn't over yet. He felt very alone, abandoned and isolated, as though a curtain had fallen between him and everyone else in the living world: friends, colleagues, Martha. He was alone in limbo, somewhere between the living and the dead, alone with Erica. Only he and she populated this dreadful place and this empty house.

There was no one he could ring. Everyone would be compromised by a connection. He was a leper. A pariah. Touch me and you are contaminated. His friends were all in the Force. And the one person he could and would have discussed this awful situation with was way out of bounds. He had to consider his options now, guess at what would happen next. The Force was honour-bound to treat this as a suspicious death until they had all their answers. The investigation would be thorough. And he would be suspended.

But there was one person to whom he owed a duty call: Erica's mother. He picked up the landline.

He'd always liked his mother-in-law and she had been supportive throughout Erica's long years of illness. He'd already told her there had been a fatal accident. With typical thoughtfulness she'd offered to come and stay, an offer Alex had declined. Erica's mother hadn't been upset, simply quiet, then expressing her sorrow, which had morphed into an apology though why he didn't know – her daughter's mental condition was hardly her fault. Now he just filled her in on the day's events, said that hopefully the body would be released for burial soon and a date set for the coroner's inquest. He was fully aware that Martha Gunn had abandoned him, relinquishing responsibility and keeping at a safe distance. Talith had related this fact with as much awkwardness as if he had been responsible for her decision. But Alex understood only too well what was behind it. He had watched her deal with tragedy and complicated situations. He had seen her comfort relatives and practically accuse others of neglect. He had seen her campaign for prisoners' rights, speak out against bullying, stick up for those whose mouths were forever sealed.

But this case would be too near her heart. Too personal. Too close to call. *He* would not be on her list of relatives to be comforted; neither would she be speaking as Erica's mouthpiece. He wondered how she really felt about Erica's death.

That was when his mobile trilled and the caller ID displayed Mark Sullivan's number. Aware the next few minutes could be life-changing, he answered. What on earth, he wondered, was the pathologist about to say?

He made his apologies to Erica's mother and spoke to Sullivan before he rang off or, even worse, left a cryptic and ambiguous message which would worry him until he learned the truth.

Ten minutes later he was staring at the wall. Alex Randall was not a man given to swearing but in the circumstances no other word would do.

'Oh, fuck.'

TWENTY-EIGHT

Friday, 7 April. 6 p.m.

artha was glad to get home and leave it all behind her, even if Sukey was there with Pomeroy taking up most of the kitchen space. They appeared to be on a prolonged

visit. She hadn't heard yet when they planned to leave and return
to Bristol. But Sukey was 'between jobs' and that, she supposed,
was what life was like as a student/actress. She only hoped that
her daughter, beautiful and talented though she undoubtedly was,
had a career Plan B, because in her opinion acting was a profession that needed a decent back-up plan. Pomeroy, her boyfriend,
was far too arrogant to bother with anything so mundane as a
back-up plan, even though he didn't exactly have work lined up
either. He was, as far as Martha could tell, content to do very little
except criticize her daughter. What she couldn't work out was why
the hell Sukey put up with it. She eyed him across the kitchen as
he poured himself a glass of wine. She supposed he was handsome
in a dissolute, lazy, casual sort of way. He had floppy brown hair,
very smooth skin, quite nice brown eyes and good teeth. He was
average height and build but, in Martha's opinion, he was nothing
special. He wasn't unintelligent, but an education at one of the
top public schools combined with overindulgent parents and a
plain and intellectually compromised sister all added up to a spoilt
brat who overrated his place in the world, in Martha's opinion.
Whereas Sukey had more or less grown up in a single-parent
family where her mother worked hard to keep them, and considered
herself lucky to get any acting work, Pomeroy simply lapped them
up as his due – when he got any parts at all. He was, Martha
surmised, not that popular even in the indulgent world of the
thespians. His arrogance, she felt, might well cost him his career.

She'd heard his voice as she'd let herself in through the front
door. Hectoring. 'Well, I wouldn't take it. I mean, it's beneath
you.' The laconic, lazy tone of his voice had sent needles up
Martha's spine. She'd longed to intervene.

Sukey's voice back had sounded timid, cowed – which made
Martha's blood boil. She hadn't brought her daughter up to accept
this lowered state. 'I don't know, Pomeroy – at least it's a job.
It'll pay the rent, you know.'

When she'd entered the kitchen they'd already opened a bottle
of – quick glance – expensive wine. Sukey was looking beseech-
ingly across while Pomeroy looked – well, he looked perturbed.
She looked again, checked she'd read him right.

That was interesting. Maybe her daughter was, at last, sticking
up for herself?

'Hi, Mum.'

Martha scrutinized her daughter's face. It looked thinner these days – a bit like what her mother with her Irish talent for finding the right word would have called 'peaky'.

While Pomeroy looked . . . smug. Instinctively Martha knew her mother would dislike Pomeroy on sight. No doubt about it. Sparks would fly whenever, if ever, they met.

She eyed the half-empty bottle of wine. Sukey eyed it too with a hint of guilt. It was Chasse du Pape, twenty-five pounds a bottle. Without a word Sukey crossed the kitchen, fetched a glass from the cupboard and poured Martha a huge slug, which she handed to her with a look of mute apology from big blue eyes. Martha took it as one anyway. 'Thank you, darling.'

'How was your day, Mum?'

At least she was making an effort.

'I'll be honest, Sukes,' she said, sinking into a chair, 'not great.'

The conversation was halted by a huge noise coming from the front door. Voices, doors slamming, footsteps. A people-quake. The next moment Sam was filling the kitchen with his presence and that of four of his mates. Their sheer ebullience more than filled any awkward silences. All their talk was of offsides and passes, chances missed and a certain amount of teasing about stamina, speed, goalposts hit. Boy talk. Football talk. Apart from a 'Hi, sis' to Sukey, the pair at the table were virtually ignored.

As was Martha, until she said the magic words. 'Anyone hungry?'

Silly question.

There is nothing like one's family to bring you down to earth, Martha thought as she opened the fridge to cheese, tomatoes and olives, defrosted some French bread, found some leftover apple pie and cream.

It was all soon gone.

The evening was saved. Whatever Pomeroy and Sukey had been talking about when she had arrived home was shelved. By the time Sam and his team members had dispersed it was ten o'clock and she was not ready for any sort of confrontation with Pomeroy, who had a habit of scoring points and almost visibly chalking up any 'victories' whether it be about general knowledge or travel or anything else that he considered himself an authority on, which basically covered everything.

And, in Martha's opinion, covered nothing.

Strange that a life can be so neatly divided in half – the traumas and tragedies of her work, and her harum-scarum home life. Unlike Gina, Patrick and Alex, for whom the unhappiness of home and work or school had somehow seeped into their personal life and infected their entire existence.

She wouldn't have it any other way but, it appeared, they had had no choice.

TWENTY-NINE

Monday, 10 April, 11 a.m.

Martha had kept the sad photographs of Patrick Elson in a drawer while she puzzled over what to do next.

From Alex she'd heard absolutely nothing. That was to be expected. But neither did she hear from David Steadman or Mark Sullivan. She was well and truly out of the loop. Fumbling and blind. So she was left to wonder.

She transported herself back to that brief, cryptic conversation and tried to extract something tangible.

'*The interesting thing was the brain pathology.*'

'*You mean a fracture or a bleed from the fall?*' That had been when she had sensed Sullivan backing off.

'*There's still a lot I need to find out. I'm not absolutely sure. I'm just hazarding a guess.*' But pathology is not guesswork. It is scientific and structured. If you don't know something the saying is you don't *guess* but confess.

'*I need to interview Alex again and get a clearer picture of his wife's behaviour.*'

What for? What on earth did Sullivan think he could learn about Erica's death from her behaviour?

And then there had been the final blow. The smack in the face. '*I should be discussing this with Mr Steadman as he's the coroner in charge. After all . . . it was your decision to hand Alex's case over to a colleague rather than handle it yourself, Martha.*'

What had he found? What did he suspect? Were his suspicions mirroring her own? She drummed her fingers on the desk. And that did nothing at all except irritate her.

Use your brain, love. Her father's words, puffing on a pipe he shouldn't even have been smoking. *Use your brain.*

And so she did. She ran through the possibilities, tried and tested her theory by revising the facts.

Erica Randall had been unpredictable since the birth of her damaged baby. Medicine dislikes coincidence. It likes to link adverse events. The shock and tragedy of giving birth to Christopher Randall, the child who had lived for just a few hours, had been the explanation for her mental state. But was it possible that her mental problems had another cause?

What if cause and effect had been reversed? She logged into her medical data account and checked a few facts. An hour later she longed to pick up the phone and ask Mark Sullivan what tests he had ordered.

She plonked herself back down in her chair. He wasn't going to share it with her, which gave her only one option – speak to David Steadman, crawl on her knees and ask him. And that, she reflected, would be a big mistake at the moment. Steadman would know. He was a clever man. Intuitive. He probably already knew that her passing the case to him had been more than politeness and formality. If she continued to pursue the truth he would know that she was emotionally involved right up to her armpits.

Perhaps, she thought with typical optimism, Steadman had already sensed her involvement and would soon get back in touch. And then she could put her theory to the test. Already she was feeling hopeful. Redemption, she thought, followed by justice.

The rest of the day passed in unsatisfactory fashion, an anti-climax after the optimism of the morning. She had still not worked out how to speak to Terence Marconi.

And when she arrived home Pomeroy and Sukey were still there – and another bottle of red wine was opened. Rioja Superior this time.

As she let herself in through the front door to hear his nasal tones she wanted to know how long they were planning to stay.

In other words, when were they going? Martha felt awful, but it wasn't her daughter that she wanted to wave goodbye to. It was the bloody boyfriend. Besides, they had a small but nice rented flat between them in Bristol (paid for partly by her). Surely they would prefer to be there? Private? Without Mother hanging around?

It didn't seem so, and Martha noticed that her daughter was on edge whenever the three of them were in the same room. Was it the snide remarks her boyfriend made, or her mother's tightening of the lips and thinly disguised intolerance for Pom's strongly held views which ranged from 'Trans people' (*Who the hell do they think they're fooling?*) to university degrees (*You just rack up debt. Bloody waste of time if you ask me.*). No one was asking, but that fact seemed to constantly escape him. But when he trod on her job (*Can't see the point of it, quite honestly, Martha. I mean the dead are dead, aren't they?*), he'd crossed the line. It was only the look of panic in Sukey's wide blue eyes that stopped Martha from climbing on to her soap box to defend her role.

Instead she fizzed like a bottle of cheap lemonade that has been shaken and then the top twisted on tighter to stop any gas from escaping. She could almost feel the pressure build up towards an inevitable explosion. She did the only thing possible. She rang her mother, even though she already knew what she would say.

'Don't go shootin' your mouth off now, Martha. If you say how much you don't like him or point out his shortcomings she'll be getting engaged or havin' a baby just because . . .'

'To spite me?'

'No, because she's a girl and wants to prove she's a woman. Tssh, it'll all melt away.'

'Oh, Mum.'

She hadn't told her mother about Erica Randall. For that matter, her mother didn't really know about Alex whom, if she referred to him at all, she tended to call *that detective fellow*.

Oh, Mum. But this time it was a silent plea.

THIRTY

Martha had woken early. No one else was stirring so she did her favourite thing – snuck downstairs, made herself two cups of strong coffee and went back to bed for fifteen minutes to plan out her day. Her mother had instilled in her the philosophy of not fretting about situations she had no control over.

Focus, she always said, *on the things you can influence. Don't waste your energy, Martha. If it can't be done then it can't. Just accept it, preferably gracefully.*

Her own version of the Serenity Prayer. But it is hard to be serene when the words ringing in your ears are *I hate her. I hate her. I wish she was dead.*

Oh, hell, she wished he hadn't said it. Because now it lay, thick and oily, polluting her stomach. She finished the first coffee of the day.

When he'd spoken those words she had seen the passion that lay behind this quiet, self-contained man, glimpsed the life he had led, the sheer damage Erica had caused. She picked up her second cup of coffee and drank slowly, spinning out the moment before she had to face the day.

Another of her mother's philosophies sprang to mind, apt and appropriate: *If you're dressed right it will help your day along.* Her mother was immensely practical and so Martha took this piece of advice too. First of all, what she should wear.

A coroner's work has a negative impact on one's wardrobe. Not for her scarlet suits or bright leather skirts, no jeans or revealing blouses. Her 'uniform' was necessarily sober: grey suit with grey high-heeled court shoes, but as a concession to an interview with Patrick Elson's teacher, Freddie Trimble, she would wear a red shirt underneath. Already she liked the sound of him. He sounded . . . well, like one of the jollier characters from Dickens. Someone just like Scrooge's nephew, Fred. It was only when watching

Dickensian, yah-booing at Compeyson for jilting Amelia Havisham and checking up on the trivia, that she'd realized Fred's last name was never given. What last name, she wondered, would Dickens have given him? He certainly was capable of some very imaginative surnames. Magwitch, Compeyson, Pickwick, Squeers, her favourite, Trotwood, and so on. So having given Fred 'Scrooge' the surname Trimble, she wondered what Patrick Elson's teacher would be like. Would he live up to the image of Scrooge's jolly, Christmas-loving, benevolent and ultimately forgiving nephew?

She continued planning her day. Later in the morning she would make a hairdresser's appointment for next week, with the inevitable scolding about not taking enough care of her hair from Vernon Grubb. Even, perhaps, book a facial, nails, eyebrows, for later on in the week. It was definitely time for a pamper. That would help her to face what was to come, because as a sailor senses an approaching storm she could almost smell choppy waters ahead. Dangerous currents and rip tides which would knock her off balance.

But for now she had a list of people to speak to. She ticked them off on her fingers.

After Freddie Trimble, Curtis Thatcher, as Gina Marconi's partner-in-law, was high on the list. As she sat up in bed, hugging her knees, trying to ignore Bobby's scratching at the door, asking to be let out or, even better, taken for a long morning stroll, Martha pondered. This was her best time of day, her brain sharp from a night's sleep and before distractions crowded in and confused the issue, stifling free thought. She revisited her ideas, pondered their flaws and hoped she was right.

And when she recalled those pathetic pictures of the terrified boy and the consequences of the threat, she was galvanized into action.

She would take great pleasure handing them over to the police and seeing how they dealt with them.

But, inevitably, this turned her full circle.

The police? The police in her mind had always been represented by one man. He had been her constant point of contact. Would he ever be again? Or was he more lost to her than when he had been married?

Luckily her mind returned to Gina Marconi. Think, Martha, think. Work this one out. *Use your brain.* One step at a time.

Climb slowly. One rung of the ladder. Revise what you already know. Gina had contact with the criminal world, the lowlife and felons, thieves and killers. She also had protection from that same world. Start looking in *that* world for someone who knew something they could and would use against her. It would have to be something which had the power to discredit her and destroy the life she had so carefully lined up. So maybe Martha should search among her clients?

She hugged her knees. Was she right or was she wrong to connect the two suicides? Was she making a futile search for connections that simply did not exist? Was the answer somewhere else? Somewhere nearer to Gina's private life than her professional one? Was, for instance, Julius Zedanski a controlling hero? Someone who would eventually stifle her? And had Gina woken up to this and taken the only way out she could think of? Martha shook her head. Gina Marconi was an independent woman who had been on her own for a number of years. She was well able to take care of herself, her son and her mother. And if she had believed that Zedanski was the wrong man for her, she wouldn't have been afraid to simply call it off.

But now, struck by another of her brainwaves, she smiled. She could use *her* powers to redeem Gina Marconi.

She wished she could have run her idea past Alex. She pictured his face, thin, sometimes haggard, unhappy in repose, and smiled to herself. Not exactly a textbook hero. But sometimes it is hard to define what makes a man attractive. Sometimes it isn't as simple as 'good looks' or an 'interesting personality'. Sometimes it is something else – some elusive quality, a reticence, a hesitation that draws you in. She smiled to herself as her thoughts tumbled out.

She'd finished both cups of coffee. She was on her own now. No Alex to fall back on. Her mother's voice again: *You're a big girl now, love.* Usually accompanied by a kiss. When does one stop appreciating their mother? she wondered. *Never* was the word that thundered back at her.

Energized by that thought she threw back the covers, laid her clothes out on the bed, spent minutes in the shower and sat in front of her dressing table to apply her make-up – again fairly subdued – a smear of foundation, blusher, a brush of beige eye shadow and mascara. Red hair limited her palette of make-up to

beiges and greens. No violets, blues or pinks. Then she fought
with her hair, finally spraying with a hair spray almost severe
enough to force even her thick, unruly mop into submission. Ready
to face the world.

There was no sound from Sukey and Pomeroy's room (twin
beds – what a hope) but Sam was already under the shower and
joined her for breakfast minutes later having thrown on a pair of
jeans and a T-shirt, his hair, a little too like hers, still wet. At least
she had breakfast – a dish of muesli and an apple. He seemed to
eat almost the entire contents of the fridge. Rashers of bacon,
two eggs, four slices of toast, beans, mushrooms and tomatoes
before he too dug into a bowl of muesli twice the size of hers.
She watched him with love, and a certain amount of admiration.
Where did he put it all?

He sat opposite her, this tall young man with the crooked teeth
being forced into submission by a brace, *her* red hair – except
even more unruly but much shorter – and his grin which would
melt polar ice caps. He leaned in and said conspiratorially, accus-
ingly and perceptively, grinning from ear to ear, 'You don't like
him, do you, Mum?'

She knew better than to lie. She shook her head. 'Is it that obvious?'

'To me, yes.' His voice was gruff but tender. 'Not sure about
Sukes. She seems to have lost her powers of judgement if you
ask me.'

'So you don't like him either?' she accused and her son's grin
broadened.

'Put it like this, Mum. I wouldn't invite him to my birthday party.'

The image of blowing out candles on a birthday cake drew them
both into a loud guffaw which seemed to conjure up a yawning,
eye-rubbing, sleepy Sukey who appeared, like magic, in the
doorway. 'What are you two chuckling about?'

Which made Martha realize that by allying herself to Pom,
Sukey was isolating herself from her family, from the two people
who loved her and would always love her forever and ever. Amen.

Sukey poured herself a mug of tea and sat down, a thin dressing
gown draped around her bony shoulders.

Martha glanced up at the kitchen clock. She must leave in no
longer than eight minutes and . . .

'Will you take Bobby out for his morning stroll?'

'I will.' Sam stood up. 'Soon as I've finished my breakfast.' He was still shovelling the muesli in.

'So what *was* the joke?' Her daughter's voice was plaintive, uncertain. Excluded.

'Oh, I don't know, Sukes,' Martha said, resisting the temptation to ruffle her hair. 'Something and nothing.'

Her daughter tossed a strand out of her face, licked her lips and sipped her tea, eyes wary. Martha took her chance.

'And what were you and . . .' she hesitated, '. . . Pom talking about when I got in last night?'

Sukey stared glumly into her mug. 'Dominic has got me an offer of a job in a TV soap. It won't last long. I think the storyline gets rid of me in about eight episodes, but Pom doesn't think I should take it.'

'Why not?'

'He thinks it'll typecast me so I'll never get the chance of other work.'

'And what is the part?'

'Oh, a sort of wayward delinquent daughter of one of the main stars. I shoot off and go to live with my father.'

'What does Dominic say?' It was the obvious question. 'He's your agent.'

'We-ell.' Sukey frowned and took another gulp of tea. 'In one way he agrees with Pom. He says if it had been a longer contract it *would* have typecast me.'

Martha wanted to say, *And what's wrong with being typecast?* It was a job, surely, in a precarious world. She kept her mouth shut. 'But?' she prompted.

'As it's only going to be a short contract Dominic thought it might get me noticed and on to bigger things.'

'But Pom . . .?' she prompted. That was the way – leave this sentence hanging in the air or just hanging. Swipe away the vision of Pom dangling on the end of a rope. She could guess the end of the sentence.

'Pom says the part's beneath me and will do my reputation no good.' Sukey was speaking slowly as though evaluating the view herself. Sounding dubious. Atypically unsure. Unconfident. Not trusting her own instincts and those of her agent but relying completely on this young man.

Martha felt her dislike of the youth compounding, growing arms and legs and a fiery tongue.

'Well.' She stood up. 'Pom *isn't* your agent,' she said crisply. It was as far as she dared to go, although lots of thoughts were spinning around in her head. All of them bad. She bent and kissed the top of her daughter's head. Sukey had to sort this one out for herself. She banished the dreadful tug at her heart that mingled with the thought: *And what if she never does? What if this relationship is the one that lasts?*

'I need to go, darling,' she said quickly before any negative words spilled out of her. Once said they would not be forgotten. 'Talk to your brother.'

At that the old Sukey re-entered the room, threw back her head and laughed out loud. 'Sam,' she said disparagingly, 'what on earth does he know about it?'

'Not a lot,' her twin brother responded gruffly.

Martha left them to it.

THIRTY-ONE

Friday, 14 April, 9.10 a.m.

As soon as she reached the office she asked Jericho to try and arrange a meeting with Gina's business partner. She needed more information about Gina's clients. Somewhere, in that rat hole of society's dregs, someone knew something. She believed there was another set of photographs and she needed to scotch the snake before it hatched.

As for her theory about Erica Randall, she had to consign it to the back of her mind – for now. If she needed to act she would. But for now she would be content to wait.

Her desk was piled high with case notes; her computer, when she switched it on, displayed thirty-nine unread emails. And she still needed to prepare for Patrick Elson's inquest next Tuesday.

'Oh, sugar,' she said as she faced the mountain of work ahead of her.

Well, Martha, she lectured herself. *You're not paid to sit and do nothing but look pretty.* That provoked a Sam-like guffaw and an instant lightening of her mood.

Sometimes her mother's mantras were a godsend.

She managed right through the morning not to ring either Mark Sullivan or even David Steadman, and there was no word from them either. Just a woolly silence, but it gave her a chance to clear her backlog of work.

At eleven, when Jericho brought in some coffee (no biscuits this time) and told her that Curtis Thatcher would be calling in at eleven thirty and Fred Trimble at four thirty (after school), her resistance finally broke. 'Have you heard anything more about DI Randall's wife?'

'It's gone deathly quiet,' he said, shaking his head with his habitual pessimism. 'I have no idea what is going on. And to be honest, Mrs Gunn, it doesn't look good.'

Deathly quiet didn't look or sound good to her either. She wished he had chosen a less uncomfortable phrase.

Her voice was subdued and she looked away from her assistant as she asked the next question. 'Is he back at work?'

'I believe not, Mrs Gunn.' Jericho's voice was also quiet and she caught the tone of sympathy with unusual gratitude. He continued, 'I understand Detective Sergeant Talith is still dealing with the case.'

She turned around in her chair so he could not see her face at all as she absorbed this last piece of information. So, no more cosy chats with him. She wouldn't be able to test her idea about Patrick or Gina – no using his position to winkle out confidences and facts. No more bouncing ideas off him, no more working together. Possibly ever. It was frustrating and she felt lonely. Already she was missing it. More truthfully, she missed *him*. His quiet presence, his common sense. After all the years of coping on her own there had been something terribly reassuring about having a man around. Correction: that particular man around. In weeks to come she guessed this sense of loss would intensify. And at the back of her mind was the shadow of his wife, creeping along the wall behind him. Jericho left her to her reflections.

Which was her excuse for making a silly mistake and ringing up a man she'd vowed to keep at arm's length. Simon Pendlebury was the very wealthy widower of Evie, an old friend of hers, who had died a few years ago of ovarian cancer. Called 'the silent killer' by the medical profession because its symptoms presented late, which meant the diagnosis was made late and the death rate was subsequently high. After Evie's death she and Simon had remained platonic friends, even weathering a ridiculous affair he'd had with a young gold-digger.

She'd kept him in quarantine because . . . Because he being a widower and she a widow, it would have been only too easy to have fallen into a relationship which would have been wrong for both of them. There was something cold and damaged deep inside Simon which felt as infectious as the flu. Somehow he had made a lot of money in a short time, which had led her for years to wonder: did anyone become that wealthy that quickly on the right side of the law? Added to that, he had an edgy personality. He was unpredictable, his direction taking turns as abrupt, sharp and unexpected as a dodgem car. Evie might have trusted him implicitly but the farther she was away from her friend's memory, the more Martha thought of Evie as someone *too* trusting, almost gullible. Naive and unable to spot the flaws in the people she loved, she was subsequently blind to her husband's true character. And testament to this flaw were Simon's two frankly horrible, selfish and unkind daughters. Hard as she might try, Martha could see none of Evie's sweetness in that pair of harpies, Armenia and Jocasta.

Hence Martha's resolve to keep him at arm's length. In her mind he was untrustworthy and the last thing she wanted to do was send him all the wrong messages by sharing not only dinner dates but also her problems with him – but she was desperate. She needed to talk to someone and that someone could not be DI Alex Randall.

Simon picked up almost immediately, recognizing her number. She very rarely called him. It was always the other way round.

'Well, Martha, this *is* a nice surprise.' He paused, waiting for her to explain why this break with the usual.

She drew in a deep breath and plunged in. 'I don't suppose you could manage lunch?'

'Today?' He sounded only mildly surprised. And she felt a pricked balloon of relief.

'To be honest, Simon, I need to talk.'

His surprise intensified. '*You* need to talk?'

'Please.'

'To me? I'm flattered.' She could feel the warmth of his smile even over the phone line.

'Surprised but flattered. OK.' His slightly smarmy charm oozed out then, like whitening toothpaste out of a tube. 'If *you* need to talk, Martha, however unlike you it is, then *I* need to listen.'

Inwardly Martha groaned. Was there even a note of sincerity behind his words? But Miranda, her best friend and natural confidante, was currently away for six months on an exchange visit to Belize. Something to do with her job in public health, she'd said airily, so she was out of the picture too. And Martha did need to unburden herself. They arranged to meet at a pub overlooking the River Severn, off the beaten track, where it would be quiet.

Knowing she would be meeting him later and at least have the opportunity to talk helped the morning to slip away.

THIRTY-TWO

Friday, 14 April, 11.30 a.m.

Curtis Thatcher was much as she'd remembered from their brief encounter at the inquest. Smart, smooth and slick, slightly prone to stockiness, with Italian good looks, a hooked nose and very dark eyes. He had a sallow complexion and wore an excellently cut dark pinstriped suit which practically disguised his expanded waistline though not quite. And although he was probably only about forty he even had the greying temples to add silver fox gravitas to his charm. He oozed confidence and the odour of some sort of men's aftershave sweet enough to pass as perfume.

He arrived bang on time, which Martha appreciated. She hated being kept waiting, finding it an insult to her time and a subtle message of superiority. Jericho ushered him in, his face deliberately impassive. Thatcher's dark eyes swept around the room before appraising her with sharp and penetrating intelligence, maybe wondering how far he could trust her. To face him from behind her large mahogany desk which stood in the centre of the room would have implied too much formality for this interview. She wanted Thatcher to feel at home, comfortable, relaxed and off his guard. So she settled him opposite her in one of the armchairs in the bay window. The implication was that in this part of the room everything was off the record. It was, actually, just an implication.

Although she had the feeling that to Curtis Thatcher this attempt at informality would make no difference. She had the feeling that every word that came out of his mouth would already have been carefully edited. Initially he was silent, waiting for her to open the interview, ask the questions. For the briefest of minutes she held back, simply studying him, trying to read the emotion he was hiding below the surface. His appraisal of her continued after the niceties and introductions had been observed.

So she picked up on *something* in his gaze, a frown which from his smooth and untroubled forehead she guessed was not habitually there, and when he did speak she had the impression he was selecting his words even more carefully than when he was in court, whether defending or prosecuting.

She began with the easy questions. 'How long were you and Gina partners?'

'Seven years.' He answered this easily enough, his hands – long, slim fingers, polished nails, bony knuckles – resting casually on the chair. No tension there.

Martha waited and he filled her in, almost anticipating her questions before she voiced them.

'I advertised for a partner and she applied. She was planning for Terence to attend Shrewsbury School when he was old enough so she was keen to move here. I think Mrs Shannon lived somewhere near Wrexham but was planning to move nearer so she could be around for Terence. That would make her work commitments possible.' He frowned. 'Anyway, when Gina responded to my advert she already had it all worked out.' His smile was a tribute to her memory. 'She was like that. She had a very tidy, organized mind, worked things out way into the future.' Another smile, not at her directly, but again, in his partner's memory. 'She could see trouble when it was over the horizon and this made her a very good prosecutor and defender. When she responded to my advert I liked her immediately. She was a charismatic woman, wasn't she?'

Martha often had this problem. Coroners only meet the dead and their relatives. 'I never *really* met her,' she said, awkward at this half-truth. She *had* met her – or more literally *seen* her, noticed her, heard her, felt her presence, her extrovert personality at that party at the golf club two years ago – but she had not spoken to her or acknowledged her. Coincidentally she had attended that party with Simon, today's lunch date. Only now was she catching up with her own mind. Had *Simon* known Gina? Had it been instinct that had led her to ask him out for lunch today?

'Actually,' she said to Gina's partner, 'I did – at least – see her.' She conjured up the curvaceous figure, the large, wide mouth emitting a noisy, almost horsey laugh. The long, thick, dark hair being tossed around to dramatic effect. But the recall was overtaken by her current role in this and her mind swiftly made the connection to the extensive injuries Mark Sullivan had listed. However hard she tried to banish the images of the ruptures, fractures, impacted bone, haemorrhage and facial trauma, that wide, laughing mouth mashed into God knew what, they would not go. To try and replace them with the living woman, she added, 'She was a really beautiful woman.'

Curtis nodded. 'Beautiful in soul as well as in character, Mrs Gunn. She was generous, truthful, honest, warm and as incisive in the court room as a newly sharpened rapier.' He was smiling.

Interesting word that. Rapier. Thin and sharp, used for thrusting.

'So . . .?' Martha was driving towards the point of this meeting.

Curtis opened his mouth but nothing came out. He was struggling. Partly through emotion but also, Martha was realizing, through selective editing. He needed to decide what he should say. He was, like a computer, running quickly through numerous possibilities, leafing through a thesaurus, considering words, phrases, rejecting them, altering them, choosing, cutting and pasting until he found the right text. Martha needed to prompt him. 'Tell me about Gina's cases,' she said, keeping her tone light and only mildly interested.

'Fun,' he said. 'We had some really interesting work. Mosha Steventon's case resulted in more work than we could handle.

Sometimes criminals have unrealistic expectations of what a lawyer – even a brilliant lawyer – can do. But Steventon was a real cool customer. And very generous. We got him off on some quite complicated details of the law. Some of the police work was missing. And to be honest the Inland Revenue hadn't been quite as meticulous as one would expect from a government agency. Steventon was so grateful he sent most of his villainous friends our way, convinced we would be able to get them all off.'

'And did you?' Martha asked curiously. This was an aspect of Gina's life she hadn't really considered enough. Maybe it was time to move outside the family circle, move away from Julius Zedanski and ask herself the real question: who could have wanted to *destroy* Gina Marconi? Or more truthfully: what sort of person could have wanted to drive Gina Marconi and possibly Patrick Elson to destroy themselves?

Surely a disappointed criminal.

'We got some of them off.' Curtis grimaced. 'Not all of them. Some of them should have gone behind bars and didn't; others had lighter sentences because of extenuating circumstances we dug out of some dark hole or other. But others, Mrs Gunn, got their just deserts.'

Which gave them a motive – for Gina's destruction at least.

'Were there any cases where Gina should have got a client off but failed?'

'Well,' he said, reluctantly dragging the words out. 'I always felt she could have done a better job of defending Jack Silver.'

'His crime?'

'Handling stolen goods. I mean, he was caught red-handed.'

'With . . .?'

'Some antique jewellery. The result of a violent robbery which resulted in life-changing injuries to the victim and his wife. It was such a nasty crime, made the headlines everywhere with allegations of torture, that Silver was bracketed with the actual perpetrators. I don't think Gina did the best she could to defend him. Maybe she was distracted by her approaching wedding.'

'What's happened to Silver?'

'He's currently awaiting sentence. And of course now Gina won't be around to mount an appeal.'

'Would she have made a better job of it?'

Thatcher shrugged. 'Who knows?' He was thoughtful for a moment before continuing. 'He was fairly livid, as was his family.'

'But he's inside?'

'Oh, yes.'

Martha was thoughtful. Could Silver have got to Gina? From inside? She didn't think so. And Gina would have been wary of a client who held a grudge against her. 'You like your job, Mr Thatcher?'

Curtis Thatcher gave a long, heartfelt sigh and his dark eyes fixed on Martha's face. 'I could be cynical and say it pays the bills,' he said with a small smile. 'And that's true. It does pay well. Or I could tell you the truth, that sometimes I enjoy my work, the challenge of presenting a case at court; at other times I hate it.' And the note of bitterness that had crept into his voice told her this was the truth that had won through the other considerations.

He turned the tables on her. 'And you, Mrs Gunn? Do you enjoy *your* job?'

'Like you,' she said. 'Sometimes.'

Though she could have expanded on that. Her job too was sometimes distasteful – the death of a child; the demise of an alcoholic; the wrecked life of a victim of child rape; a wife murdered by a husband; the sordid tale of a drug addict; the final release of a child with a congenital abnormality who had suffered every day from birth; the suicides. But at other times, like Thatcher, she loved it.

'Could Jack Silver have any bearing on Gina's suicide?'

The question patently startled Thatcher. 'How? There can't be any doubt that she drove her car into the wall deliberately. She wanted to die.'

Martha kept her thoughts to herself and her voice deliberately dispassionate.

'We don't know everything, Mr Thatcher. She didn't leave a note so we're left with confusion and I have to explore every possibility to indicate her state of mind when she left the house. That includes examining the work which brought her into the circle of some fairly unpleasant and dangerous people. If a violent criminal has reason to hate her he might have wanted to wreak havoc on her life.'

Thatcher looked even more startled. She caught the twitch of worry at the corner of his left eye and pressed on. 'Tell me more about her.'

'Gina had a brilliant brain,' he said. 'Almost intuitively she could spot chinks of light in the law and use them to her advantage. But she did have a strong moral sense.' His frown deepened. 'I think Zedanski brought that out in her.'

Ah, so, back to Zedanski.

'Do you like him?'

Thatcher's feet shuffled. He looked awkward. 'I didn't really know him that well.'

Martha was not going to let this one go. She simply waited. Silence makes a good prompt.

Again, Thatcher chose his words carefully. 'He *seems* a really good fellow.'

Seems? She would have to be content with that. Other people – mainly the general public – had a much higher opinion of him.

Who would know him best? The general public believe they know someone just because they see his face almost every night on the television. They like them, they dislike them, because of something superficial: the wrong tie worn, the wrong word inserted, the wrong angle of the camera. The truth is they don't know them at all. Only people close to them know the real man behind the television screen.

'Because of Steventon she brought in a lot of business,' Thatcher volunteered.

'Does that mean you could pick and choose?'

'To some extent, yes.' Again, she was struck with the care he was taking over these words and their significance.

She moved on. 'Tell me,' she said. 'Were there any . . .' Like Thatcher, she too was choosing her words very carefully . . . 'loop-holes Gina might have employed that were . . . questionable?'

Curtis Thatcher wasn't even embarrassed. 'We all do to some extent.'

They both knew what she was asking. Which won – Gina's integrity or her manipulation of the law?

Martha was seeing Gina Marconi in a new light – an unfamiliar light – not with a halo, not as some beautiful, talented paragon but as a woman immoral, a woman not above using the gaps in the law to free criminals and feather her own nest. It was those two words he had used earlier when talking about Steventon.

Very generous.

She reminded him. 'You said that Mosha Steventon was very generous.'

Thatcher's eyes were full on her.

'Did you mean by that that there were backhanders? Bribes?'

Curtis seemed unperturbed by her question. 'Not as far as I know. I mean I don't think so.' He gave a small laugh. 'Our fees are plenty high enough. No, what I meant was that he provided us with clients. In the beginning, when a new partner is taken on you can be a bit short on the briefs sent your way. After she got Mosha off we were never short of work again.'

Time to use that rapier and thrust. 'You must have made some assumptions about her suicide, Mr Thatcher?'

Again Thatcher was unperturbed by the question. His body language didn't change. Hands, feet, legs, eyes, mouth – all remained still. Except he nodded. Just the once. 'I . . .'

Martha waited. She would not prompt or lead. This must come purely from him.

Photographs.

Curtis shifted slightly then his eyes fixed on Martha's face. Puzzled but honest. 'Look,' he said awkwardly, 'Gina was good at not showing her emotion. Her talent was for hiding things.'

Again Martha waited.

And he continued, proceeding very slowly, testing the water as he spoke, measuring out each word. 'In general,' he said, 'she was careful. Very careful. She was mixing with some dangerous people and she knew it. Some of them were psychopathic, sociopathic, malicious and cruel men – and women – who would not hesitate to use anything against her if they thought it might buy them freedom or a lighter sentence. These are people who are born twisting arms, manipulating people, using people merely to get their own way, using them like pawns in a chess match. They'll do anything without regard to loyalty or friendship or what's right and proper. What's right and proper to them is what *they* want. Just that. The only language they speak is violence.' He leaned forward, spoke with urgency. 'You know the saying "honour among thieves"?'

She nodded.

'There's no such thing. They will drop anyone in the shit if they think they can get away with it. They don't have social values of loyalty. They don't have those sorts of emotions.'

Women. Martha almost breathed the word. He'd said men and *women.* He'd dropped that in to his rant deliberately. *The subtlety of women to needle and goad is well known, like the ability and talent to push someone into a corner and wait. And with women Gina's good looks might have counted against her rather than for her.*

Thatcher's eyes were boring into hers as though he was trying to convey something else. Something beyond words, a phrase not to be found in any dictionary.

She tried to pick up on it. 'You mentioned women.'

'The wives and partners of her clients.' She knew again this sentence was deliberate. He was pointing her in a direction.

'Anyone in particular?' She kept her voice casual.

And then he backed off. 'Look,' he said awkwardly, 'I don't want to point the finger. Gina recognized the danger of mixing – no – of getting too close to these people and was guarded, but like many strong people she had an Achilles heel. Peter Lewinski, the guy accused of road rage, seemed to have some sort of hold over her. He visited her once or twice at the office and seemed to bother her, threaten her, upset her. He's a scary guy.' He leaned forward slightly in his chair. 'But this is pointless. *I* know and *you* know, Mrs Gunn, that Gina set out that night to destroy herself.'

Martha kept her thoughts to herself and listened without responding.

Curtis continued. 'She knew she wasn't going to come back. This was obviously *not* an accident.' He settled back in his chair, certain of his facts. 'Only a fool would even consider that option. So that means that she was leaving Julius, whom she adored. She really did. She was devoted to him and he to her. She loved . . . no, that's not enough. She was proud of him and the work he did.'

Again Martha was reminded of Sukey. That adoration. One way in her case. No sign of Pom returning the favour.

'And Zedanski,' she prompted. 'Was *he* proud of the work *she* did?'

Thatcher looked startled by the question and didn't answer straight away. 'You know,' he said, 'I've never really considered that angle. I suppose. I mean, I'm sure so. She would have made him a beautiful, lovely wife.'

Trophy wife? Trophy wives must remain so – perfect – an asset. Perhaps, Martha thought, *she was beginning to thread the black pearls together to make a necklace. Or the beads of a rosary.*

Thatcher seemed to think he needed to contribute more. 'I've seen them together,' he put in. 'They would have been a perfect couple.'

Martha smiled. Curtis sounded almost sentimental. She wondered about his own domestic arrangements. Married? Partner? Single?

He continued. 'Her suicide means she was abandoning Julius as well as Terence and her mother. Gina was a loving person. She would only have done that under the most dreadful threat.' He paused again to let his words sink in. 'A dreadful threat. And that means something . . .' Again he couldn't find the word.

And Martha wasn't going to supply it. She didn't want to hide behind euphemisms or meaningless words. She did not have the time to play games. What she wanted was the truth. Pure and simple. And then she could work with that, mould it like soft Plasticine.

'And you wonder if this Pete Lewinski . . .'

'I only wonder,' Thatcher said firmly. 'Just wonder. It's the only time I'd seen her rattled. Frightened.' His eyes clouded. 'Defeated. We were at a party a few months ago. He was there and he just stared at her. Even I felt the chill. It felt like a threat. Though it was a warm night and the place was overheated, Gina actually shivered. She looked cold.'

'So what's happening with him?'

'The trial's yet to come up. Date's not been set. He's currently on remand but initially she thought she'd win it.'

'On what evidence?'

'The police notes,' Thatcher said reluctantly. 'Bits had been added. She got some expert in forensic dating ballpoint pen entries and found that the notes had been tampered with. They weren't all contemporaneous. She thought the CPS mightn't proceed and the judge would throw it out of court but it didn't happen. Now the odds are stacked against Gina. Lewinski is suspected of knifing a man in a road rage incident on the A5 but the witness "couldn't remember". The police knew their case was weak. The CPS might still throw it out. I think that's why they tampered with the evidence. All that work and he'd get off?'

Martha pointed out the obvious. 'Lewinski surely wouldn't have driven her to die. He needed her.'

'That's what I'd have thought but there was something weird going on.'

Martha looked up, her mind busy digesting these new facts. 'Were you surprised at the effect Lewinski had on her?'

He nodded and then sighed. 'Yes,' he said, 'I was. She's dealt with these people practically all the years she's been in Shrewsbury. I've never seen her like that, Mrs Gunn. Never.' He thought for a minute before adding, 'I didn't really understand it.'

She decided to take a leap in the dark. 'Do you know anything about some photographs?'

'Photographs?' Thatcher shook his head and looked blank.

She took another leap. 'Do you know or have you heard the name Patrick Elson?'

Again the question drew a blank.

'Or Amanda Elson?'

'Sorry.'

'Is there anything else you think might help me understand Gina's death?'

Thatcher kept shaking his head. 'No,' he said. 'Nothing. I've told you everything I think could have a bearing on that night. I wish I could help you. I wish I could understand, but I can't. Sorry.'

She stood up and the interview was at an end. They shook hands and Curtis Thatcher left.

Martha sat for a while trying to thread together the various strands he had spoken of. So what was she left with? Gina Marconi played with fire. And it looked like she'd burned for it.

And now it was time for lunch.

THIRTY-THREE

Simon Pendlebury was already at the pub when she arrived. His maroon Rolls-Royce was parked ostentatiously right at the front of the car park. A *look at me, I'm rich* statement which only served to irritate people. Why did Simon constantly feel he had to rub everyone's nose in it? Inferiority? She felt like kicking it as she passed. Who the heck drives a Roller these days? Maybe she'd suggest he bought himself a Smart car. She stifled a giggle. Now that was one thing even she couldn't quite conjure up, Simon peeping over the wheel of a Smart car. But here it was, his status symbol, shouting to people that *he* was here. Rich people eat here. And yet she didn't kick it. Instead she felt an unexpected pang. There was something almost vulnerable about Simon. He *had* to have the money, the car, the house, the designer suits, the trimmings. Take it away from him and she knew he would feel he was nothing. So all the flashy trappings were, in actual fact, a sign of his vulnerability, of his feeling that he had to be better than everyone else. Because if he wasn't better, richer, more successful than everyone else, he was nothing.

Her heart sank. This was a mistake and she knew it. She shouldn't be here. Of all the men in the world Simon Pendlebury was about the last man on her list of potential confidants. He wouldn't understand. He was too wrapped up in himself. This really was a mistake.

She walked in anyway.

And when he stood up to greet her, kissing both cheeks before gripping her shoulders and giving her a long hard stare, she was still thinking what a stupid move this had been.

But when he sat down, handed her a glass of fizzy water and waited for her to speak first she began to revise her poor opinion of him.

He was about six foot one, slim built, with straight dark hair cut a little too long to be currently fashionable but very neat. He practically always wore a suit. Even when he was 'casually' dressed in a jacket and chinos he looked as though he was still wearing a suit. Maybe it was the fact that he always wore good quality leather shoes so the casual look never extended to his feet and appeared almost as a disguise. Maybe it was his bearing – very erect, straight shoulders. Maybe it was the Rolls sitting outside.

'Hey,' he said, grinning, his bright dark eyes scanning her face. 'Surely things aren't so bad?'

It all spilled out then, chaotically, tumbling out like children at the bottom of a helter-skelter. The death of Erica Randall, her unpredictable state of mind; the cloud of suspicion over Alex Randall, the questioning by his colleagues; the impossibility of a

verdict other than 'Unknown'; the handing over of the case to
David Steadman, resulting in her being out of the loop; the unhappiness of Alex's rocky cake-walk marriage, the query over the
post-mortem, finally confiding something she had never even
admitted to herself: 'I'm really fond of him, Simon. I trust his
integrity. When I'm with him I am . . .' She could hardly pick out
such an anomalous word. 'Relaxed. I feel at home with him.' She
fell silent then, recalling the few moments she and the DI had
snatched time together. Stolen time.

'Whoa,' he said, finally holding his hands up after she had
talked non-stop for at least ten minutes. 'So where are you now?'

She plunged back in again, focusing on the fact that she'd
handed over the case to David Steadman. 'Steadman,' she said.
'Of all people. David Steadman. I don't even like the guy.' She
wagged an index finger. 'And I'm not sure he's that struck on me
either, so there will be minimal communication there. How he will
handle it, Simon, I do not know. And at the end of the line . . .'
She paused. 'Is Alex. But . . .'

And then, for the first time to another human being, she shared
her Great Theory.

Simon listened then leaned back in his seat, smiling at her with
more warmth than she had ever seen in his rather hard face. He
was apparently enjoying having to deal with her conflict. 'And
you came to me,' he said, leaning forward right on cue. 'I'm
flattered.'

Don't read anything into that, she thought warily.

But he was oblivious. 'If you want my opinion, Martha, you
did the right thing handing the case over to a colleague.' His face
was intense. 'It could have been awful – if you'd handled it badly,
if anyone had any idea how much you thought of him. God, Martha,
it could have really compromised you if anyone else knew how
you felt about him.'

'Thanks,' she said bitterly. 'You think I haven't gone over all
this in my mind?'

He simply nodded.

'Trouble is I'm right out of the loop.' Now it was she who was
leaning forward. 'Mark Sullivan appears to have unearthed new
evidence and I can't even get near it because,' she finished bitterly,
'I abandoned his case. I abandoned my friend.'

'Hey, Martha.' Simon looked shocked. 'This is so unlike you. Whatever's come over you? I'm sure that to hand the case over was absolutely the right thing to do.' He frowned. 'I mean, otherwise the findings could have been compromised. And how would that have helped this Alex Randall?' Then he asked, with bright-eyed and unashamed curiosity, 'What do you think Mark Sullivan's unearthed?'

'I don't know.' She knew she was speaking wildly. 'At first I worried about defensive injuries, anything not consistent with the fall, maybe a head injury that doesn't quite fit, evidence of previous assaults.'

Simon looked concerned. 'You think he's capable of all that, a man you're so . . .' He hesitated, his eyes running right over her before plunging back in. 'Fond of?'

'No, not really.' She felt helpless.

'So why are you beating yourself up over this? I don't get it, Martha. You think you could like a wife beater or a wife killer? Trust your instincts.' Then his eyes narrowed. 'Hey,' he said. 'What are you saying? That you don't care what he's done?' He put his hand on her arm, his fingers tight over her wrist. Then he slid it down to cover her hand. 'He's a lucky man,' he said, 'to have attracted so much devotion from you.'

She felt very uncomfortable. Felt her face fold into a frown. 'No,' she protested.

But he was watching her. 'What then?'

She shrugged and his face relaxed. 'Let's get something to eat and then I'm sure I can get you to put things back into perspective. OK?'

It gave her a few minutes' grace. They bent over their menus. She elected for salmon with new potatoes while Simon, true to form, chose a bloody steak. She drank Perrier water and he J2O. Neither wanted their senses impaired now or during the afternoon. And both were driving.

Martha watched him stride back from the bar. Savile Row suit, long legs, dark hair. Evie had always stood up for her husband, protesting that no one really knew him as she did. And now Martha was wondering. Maybe Simon was a nicer person than she had given him credit for. So how, her mind argued, had he produced that pair of selfish shitbag daughters, Armenia and Jocasta? Their genes had come from somewhere – certainly not from their mother. Evie had been a saint.

Simon settled back beside her with a waft of a man's fragrance and she gave a slightly embarrassed laugh. She was rarely aware of him as a man. An attractive man at that. Actually much more attractive than Alex Randall, whose frame was spare, his features angular and craggy. It had been his eyes, warm and perceptive, which had made him, in her eyes at least, irresistible.

They ate quickly, Simon trying to reassure her, and in some way he did. 'Trust your judgement, Martha,' he said finally. 'I don't believe that you could feel anything for this detective fellow if he was an explosive wife beater – you'd have picked up on that somehow – and certainly not if he was a killer, whether calculated or not.'

'But provoked?'

'I still think you'd have sensed something wasn't right. You would have sensed something.' He placed his knife and fork together tidily, looked up and smiled. 'Put it like this, Martha,' he said slowly, 'if this DI Randall is capable of murdering his wife, you're better off out of it. If, on the other hand, he put up with a mentally sick woman for years then he's a bit of a saint. Either way the truth will out. I'm sure of it.' He put his hand over hers again and even that hand, nails manicured, skin soft, was different. Alex's hand was bony with long fingers, knuckles pronounced. Simon grinned. 'So relax, Mrs Gunn.' He drained the last of his fruit juice. 'Anyway, it isn't your problem so let others sort out the mess. Now then. Dessert?'

She declined but accepted a coffee – double strength with at least two shots. As they drank he eyed her over the rim of his cup, hesitated, put the cup down and met her eyes. 'Be honest. What does he mean to you, Martha, this detective? Where are you taking this?'

She didn't answer straight away because she couldn't. She needed to think about her response as she'd never really asked this question of herself. 'I don't know,' she said. 'I really don't. I like him, Simon. Sure. I think he's had a tough time. Things haven't gone his way, but he is – or was – married. And that dropped a gate between us. He's intelligent, intuitive, perceptive, but these are all just qualities. They don't really encompass the man.'

He levelled a very direct gaze at her. 'Do you love him?' He looked slightly confused – and she gave a confusing answer.

'I don't know. I don't think so . . .' She frowned. 'At least, not what I remember of love.'

'You mean Martin.'

She nodded.

And he settled back in his chair, eyes half closed. 'Love changes,' he said. 'The love you feel for someone in your teens and twenties is different from the love you feel later in life.' He gave a lop-sided, slightly regretful smile. 'It's more like embers than a fire. And then . . .'

She couldn't resist raising the subject. 'And Christabel?'

But if she'd thought by bringing up the young woman, labelled as a gold-digger by Simon's two daughters, she'd embarrass him, she'd failed. He simply gave a huff of a laugh. 'Well, that,' he said, 'is a point in question. That was a spark that never quite got the fire going. Or shall we put it this way – it soon went out.'

And she had to leave it at that. 'Suffice it to say that I don't know. Only that there's something about him.' She tried to put it into words. 'I feel . . . comfortable around him, I think that's how I feel – just comfortable. Happy. Relaxed. He's easy to be with.'

'Hmmm.' His eyes flickered. He put his cup back down on the saucer and made a dubious face. 'Not sure about this.'

She laughed out loud then. 'You're not my brother, you know. But if I'm right, Erica is the true victim. A test might prove it.'

He nodded and touched her hand again. 'You should talk to Mark Sullivan,' he said. 'See if he's done this test you're talking about. You kind of owe it to Randall.'

She nodded and gave him a grateful smile.

But his face changed, looked almost bleak. 'So if that's how you feel about him, how do you think of me?'

She laughed, avoided the question, shook her head but then met his eyes with a merry smile. 'Good friend?'

'OK,' he said. 'I'll settle for that.' And he didn't pursue that subject.

'Anything else interesting going on in your world?' The question was casual, a conversation filler.

She told him about the two suicides, the interview she'd had with Gina Marconi's partner that morning and the impending interview with Patrick Elson's teacher later this afternoon.

'You seem to be digging in a bit hard when it seems obvious both are suicides.'

'Yes. But there's a lot more to them than that. There's always a back story, a missed opportunity. Patrick – well, it wasn't just bullying, Simon. The photos. They were horrible. And deliberately set up. I suppose I'm hoping that at some point someone will be able to point the finger at the culprit and stop them in their evil game. Punish them. Who better than a teacher to know a child? I've already interviewed his mother and the unfortunate Mrs Tinsley whose car bonnet Patrick landed on before bouncing along the road. His body – parts of it at least – were found up to six hundred yards away from where he'd fallen. Cars can't stop straight away. His DNA was found on eight separate vehicles.'

'I couldn't do your job,' he said.

She looked straight back at him. 'And I couldn't do yours.'

He laughed loudly then. Open-mouthed, merry and mocking.

She returned to her case. 'The pictures would have been enough to tip the poor boy over the edge.'

'And you're connecting the case to Gina Marconi's?'

She felt defensive. 'I'm just *wondering* if she was the victim of something similar.'

'Gina Marconi? Who drove her car into a wall at about ninety miles an hour?'

She nodded. 'Sixty, actually.' Then, picking up on something in his voice she looked up. 'Did you know her?'

He was unfazed by the question. 'Not well. I had some dealings with her a while ago. She was quite a girl.'

'So I understand.'

'You never met her?'

'Just that once,' she said, 'at the golf club. I went with you, remember?'

'Oh, yeah, that's right. She *was* there, wasn't she? Quite a noisy sort of girl but a clever lawyer.' He thought for a minute. 'Extrovert.'

'Do you know anything *more* about her?'

Simon shook his head. 'Not really.'

'She died of multiple injuries. Fractures, multiple head injuries, a ruptured aorta.'

Simon looked frankly nauseated at these details so Martha changed the subject. 'And what about you? How is *your* business going?'

The look he gave her was almost sentimental before he threw his head back and laughed again out loud, causing a few other diners to glance across, curiously. 'What on earth do you care about my work, Martha? The bits you don't understand go straight over your head and the bits you do understand bore you to tears.'

She was too honest to deny this. But *he'd* listened to her. She owed him this courtesy to at least make the effort. 'Go on then,' she said, teasing him out. 'Bore me.'

And the tale he told was so exotic and foreign about acquirements and land, about buying up entire companies investing in futures and . . .

'Stop,' she said laughing and holding her hand up. 'I don't understand a word of it.'

He drained his coffee cup and wagged his finger at her. 'I knew it,' he said. 'I just knew it. Anyway, the truth is that the whole thing's going really well, thanks. It's funny. I spent ages slaving away for the first million. And now it just seems to happen. Rolls into my lap. Money makes money, Martha.'

'I wouldn't know. I just work for a living and pay my bills.'

'*C'est la vie.*'

'And your love life?' It was as though he really was her big brother.

He laughed, no embarrassment, no awkwardness. 'Once bitten,' he said. 'Since Christabel I've kept myself to myself.' His face softened. 'And how are the twins?'

This provoked another confidence about Pomeroy. 'I really don't like him, Simon. Worse, I think he's bad for Sukey – giving her advice that goes against her agent's. Dominic's been an agent for years. He's had some real successes. Sukey was thrilled when he agreed to take her on. And now Pomeroy seems to be undoing all the good that Dominic's been steadily building up.' She appealed to Simon. 'And you know how difficult it is to get anywhere as an actress these days. Even if you look like Sukey and really can act.'

Simon nodded. 'And Sam?'

This was so much easier. 'He's great. Really great. Happy with his football and happy with his studies. He's planning to play for Stoke City hopefully for a few more years and then believe it or not he wants to be a teacher.'

'Wow.'

It was only polite for her to return the compliment. 'And Armenia and . . .?' She got no further.

Simon rolled his eyes. 'Awful as ever,' he said. 'They were rude to Hannah the other week. I mean, Hannah is about the best housekeeper in the world. She runs that place like clockwork. I almost lost my temper with Jocasta. She just waltzes in and waltzes out again, leaving a trail of misery behind her. She's an absolute pain. Where they get it from, Martha, I don't know. Evie was never like that.'

Martha bit her lip to stop herself from smiling. She'd always disliked the girls but had never heard Simon speak this forcefully against them. But that wasn't all. He hadn't finished.

'After Christabel, poor girl . . . I couldn't possibly submit another woman to that.' His expression was suddenly appraising, his eyes thoughtful. 'At least no woman except you,' he said slowly. 'For some reason the pair of them absolutely adore you.'

She had to stop herself from shuddering. She didn't know where he was going with this confidence. All she did know was that she felt extremely uncomfortable. The truth was she'd rather hug a pair of Rottweilers on anabolic steroids.

But she could hardly share this with Simon so she simply shrugged and stood up. Time to go back to the office. 'I'd better be going,' she said. 'I'm meeting Patrick's teacher later. I think it'll be tricky. But I hope it'll give me some answers.'

'Me too.' He stood up. 'I'd better get back to my empire.' And now he was mocking himself. He kissed her gently on the cheek. It felt like true brotherly affection. She took a few seconds to step back and look hard into his eyes. Simon? That most certain, arrogant person, being self-effacing? Someone who never questioned his judgement even when he got it horribly wrong? He returned her gaze with something like surprise boring back into her soul and then he smiled. The moment was gone. 'Dear Martha,' he murmured and escorted her to her car where his mood did an about-turn. He grinned mischievously, touched her shoulder. 'Hey,' he said. 'As my mum used to say, "Worse things happen at sea".'

Now that *was* a surprise. Simon had come from humble beginnings, his father abandoning the family when he was small. His mother had been a cleaner. Simon rarely mentioned his roots. She wasn't even certain whether his mother was still alive. She had certainly never met her.

'Worse things happen at sea,' she mused. 'My mum used to say that too,' she said. 'Right up until Martin got cancer. I don't think she's ever said it since.'

Simon bowed his head. 'Ah,' he said, turned his back on her and headed back into the pub, presumably to pay the bill.

Martha drove back to her office. She had given up musing over Simon Pendlebury a long time ago. It was a path that led nowhere. Like a maze without a centre or a way out.

On her return Jericho told her that DS Paul Talith had asked to speak to her so, with trepidation, she picked up the phone and connected.

THIRTY-FOUR

DS Talith was awkward, fumbling with his words. She sensed his embarrassment even over the phone line. 'I know this isn't your case, Mrs Gunn.' He was hesitant. 'I'm hoping DI Randall won't be on gardening leave for too long. Just until we've sorted all this out to everyone's satisfaction,' he added quickly. 'I expect he'll have a lot to do anyway, organizing the funeral and such.'

Her ears pricked up. A funeral? That must mean that David Steadman would soon release the body for burial. Or cremation. So he had made up his mind. She needed to speak to him.

She couldn't resist prompting the DS. 'Doctor Sullivan intimated he had unearthed something at Mrs Randall's post-mortem?'

Talith's response was typically stolid. 'We haven't heard back from him. Not yet. At least not the full report. We're still waiting but we're not really investigating DI Randall. There's no hint he's done anything wrong.' And now she felt a traitor. Talith sounded a hundred per cent certain. There was no doubt in *his* mind, only in hers.

Which was almost a relief, but she was still picking up some doubt.

She couldn't resist pumping him. 'It looks like an accident?'

'Well, no. Not as I understand it. Not exactly anyway. I don't think that's what Doctor Sullivan was saying.'

So what then?

'So . . .?' She waited for him to fill in the detail.

But he didn't. 'I can't really say,' Talith continued even more awkwardly. She sensed he was being selective, deciding what she would want to know and what to hold back – for now. And he was confused, uncertain what to say – and what to leave out.

With the result that his next words came out in a rush. 'I'll let you know when we get the full report if you'd like.'

'Well, thanks for that,' she said drily. *At least*, she added silently, *Alex is free. Back home, not incarcerated.*

But Talith had another reason for ringing. He pinned her down to her proper role. 'And the two suicides, Mrs Gunn? Are you any nearer completing your investigation?'

'I'm still gathering evidence,' she said curtly, and made the decision to keep mum for the moment – or at least until she had spoken to a few more people, one of them Sullivan. But she was getting there. She knew it, inching nearer, and with every move she coloured in a little more of the picture. 'I think I'm beginning to understand a little more about Patrick Elson. He was victimized.' For now she left out the photographs, the fact that the boy's mother had hidden them from the police only to reveal them to her. 'I have yet to know by whom, Sergeant Talith. But the answer to Gina Marconi's death is, I sense, a little more involved.'

'Oh,' he said, and seemed to wait for the silence to be filled. It wasn't.

It was she who brought the awkward telephone conversation to an end, keeping it formal. 'Thank you, Sergeant Talith. I appreciate your ringing.' She decided to take one small step forward. Step out into the open. 'And thank you for letting me know about DI Randall. I consider him both a colleague and a friend.'

There was something like relief in Talith's response. She heard the release of the breath he'd been holding. 'Yes, of course, Mrs Gunn.' Followed by, 'I'll keep you informed.'

THIRTY-FIVE

Martha sat quietly. She had Alex's home phone number as well as his mobile and her fingers itched to press the keys. She even picked up her handset at one point and studied it for a while. She had *never* used his landline, fearing that it would be his unbalanced, unstable wife who would pick up. She had also avoided calling his mobile when she thought he might be at home. She put her own mobile back in her bag with an empty feeling. She was swamped with unexpected sympathy for Erica Randall.

Friday, 14 April, 2.30 p.m.

She prepared to face the afternoon, cleared her desk ready for the teacher's arrival and read through her notes trying to search for clues in Patrick Elson's case as to who had been victimizing him. Almost certainly someone from school. Hopefully the teacher would have names. Neither Patrick's mother nor his aunt had come up with anyone.

Freddie Trimble arrived at four thirty, looking flustered and a touch knackered, a rumpled figure in his early forties, wearing a corduroy jacket and grey trousers, scruffy, scuffed shoes, bags under his eyes, messy brown hair and a harassed expression. Very different from her lunch date, she reflected as she greeted him. Neither was he exactly the Dickensian character she had been imagining – much more contemporary. His expression was far too gentle and tired to ever wield a schoolmaster's cane. He managed half a grin. 'It's been a hell of a day,' he said frankly. 'Bloody twelve-year-olds, think they know everything. Such smart-arses.' Then his grin broadened. 'Sorry,' he said, 'don't mind me but teaching geography to year eight – they think they understand the world because they've been skiing in France and flopped on the beach in the Philippines, all inclusive. They think it's all them and us, Muslims and the rest. See everything through holiday eyes.

Swaggering around with dollars and euros in their pockets. It's hard, you know, Mrs Gunn, getting them to *recognize* the world, its cultures and religions or lack of them, let alone respect it and put it all into perspective. Particularly when their parents read the *Daily Mail*.' He grinned to rob the words of any real antipathy but there was an underlying frustration.

She was amused at his semi-rant but it felt authentic and heartfelt. So often when faced with a coroner people acted abnormally. Put on an act of fake sympathy, empathy or understanding. This, she felt, was the true Freddie Trimble – no holds barred. And she liked him. To the right children he would be a good teacher. But sometimes the measure of a really good teacher is to reach those children who were not initially the 'right' kind, the children who disengaged themselves from teachers, authority, education. Maybe with these children his knowledge, likeability and charm would transform them.

The teacher's grey eyes twinkled as though he had read her judgement. 'It must seem awful my having a moan when I'm here to talk about poor Patrick.' His face clouded and he looked straight at Martha. 'He was a nice kid. Bright too. Very bright.' He was frowning. 'I've had nightmares about it, you know. Seeing him fall, his friends peering over the bridge, watching him jump, seeing him land. *Hearing* him land.'

'Which friends?' she asked quickly. 'The witnesses claimed that he was alone when he jumped. No one was there to peer over the bridge.'

Trimble looked confused. 'You know dreams,' he said noncommittally. 'They fill in bits.'

Martha leaned in. It was exactly these 'bits' that she wanted. Not what had *actually* happened. She knew that only too well from the numerous witness statements. She wanted to know what Trimble, with his classroom knowledge, could colour in.

She repeated her question. 'Which friends?'

Trimble met her eyes. 'What exactly are you . . .?' The words faded. His eyes had a shine in them and he half closed them as though to see the dream again. 'Paul Jamieson, Saul Matthews. Nice kids,' he said stiffly. 'His mates. And a couple who definitely weren't his friends, Warren and Sean.'

Martha picked up on it immediately. 'Warren and Sean?'

'Pair of junior thugs.'

Martha mentally tucked them away. She would return to the junior thugs later. For now she wanted to explore other dimensions. 'But they weren't *really* there, were they?' Martha prompted gently. 'The boys were all reported as being at school that day. Except Patrick.'

'Yeah. I know.' Trimble looked embarrassed. 'Just a dream, Mrs Gunn. You know?' There was something boyish, hopeful in his face, to which she responded with an encouraging smile.

He continued. 'We've had counsellors in the school but I can't say they've achieved much. His classmates have been quite affected.' His face twisted.

'Ah,' Martha responded, picking up on it. 'His classmates. He was a popular lad?'

Freddie Trimble frowned. 'I wouldn't say popular,' he said tentatively. 'He had his mates, a tight little circle, but he wasn't one of those lads whom I'd describe as generally popular. He was too quiet for that. Contained.' He lifted his eyebrows. 'You know?'

She did.

'And too intelligent,' he added.

'Tell me more about him, Mr Trimble,' she prompted. What she really wanted to say was this: *Make me see him through your eyes.*

Freddie Trimble leaned back in his chair, patently more relaxed now. Martha offered him tea or coffee and he accepted decaffein- ated tea. When Jericho had obliged, he took a sip, half closed his eyes and breathed in through his nose before fixing her with a very direct stare. 'I don't know how much you know about school life these days,' he said.

'My twins are almost twenty,' she filled in. 'Year eight was a long time ago for them – and for me. Start from scratch, Mr Trimble.'

He took a larger slurp of tea and set his cup down on the small table between them. 'Kids these days,' he said. 'Well, kids have always been cruel to anyone who doesn't quite fit in.' He was thoughtful for a moment. 'In that way I don't suppose things are any different from what they've always been.' She nodded and he continued. 'It's just their tools that are different.'

'Ah.'

He met her eyes. 'Facebook, the internet, mobile phones,

WhatsApp, Instagram, YouTube, Snapchat.' He smiled. 'In days gone by it might have been a sling, throwing stones, openly mocking someone. These days it's so much more subtle and far reaching. More difficult to prove – less physical, more mental. If you're an outsider it can be cruel and public. Patrick was quiet and self-contained, sensitive and intelligent. There's a couple of kids in the school who probably belong in a young offenders' centre.'

Ah, she thought, *I knew we would return to them.* Warren and Sean.

He gave a rueful snort. 'But if they ended up there, their very vocal parents would accuse people of discrimination, of prejudice, of picking on them. That's the way things are these days.' He paused, still thoughtful. Martha guessed he was wondering how much to tell her. How much she needed to know. Whether he could trust her.

He made his decision, dived back in. 'He was small for his age. I mean, at year eight some of the kids – well, they're big and quite meaty if you know what I mean. Pat – he was skinny. He could run fast.'

Not fast enough.

'He loved space and the planets and adored Professor Brian Cox. He'd bring his name or something about space into the conversation whenever he could. Cox and Tim Peake were his heroes. He was going to be an astro-physicist or a spaceman. But that meant . . .' His speech slowed to a dawdle.

'Ridicule?'

'Other kids – I mean, some other kids; not all, to be fair – they took the piss out of him, called him a geek. It was the class bullies, Warren and Sean. They're brothers – only ten months between them. They're in the same school year. It makes them close. A bit united and very aggressive. It doesn't help that their dad's in prison. It makes them even more defensive. Labelled as trouble.'

Martha sat up. 'Their surname?'

'Silver,' the teacher said, unaware that he had just dropped a brick. Martha breathed out slowly, as though in a yoga class. So there was the connection. Just a thin thread at the moment. Trouble was if Silver was in prison, on remand, *he* couldn't have got at Gina. But . . . She forced herself back to the teacher's words.

'About three weeks ago they chucked his shoes over a telegraph wire.' He looked almost apologetic. 'It's nothing really. That sort of thing happens all the time. You'll never stamp it out but Patrick's were Nike. They were expensive and probably cost his mum money she could ill afford. Amanda's a nice woman. I really respect her. She'd done a good job bringing him up alone. Patrick was well behaved and polite but she couldn't be everything to him. It doesn't work like that.'

She inched closer. 'After the shoe-throwing incident?'

'He became very quiet. He'd never been pushy or noisy but he became almost withdrawn. Something happened round about then. Not the shoes. That was just the start of things. Something else. He became quieter, stopped talking about his ambition. Damn.' He punched his left palm with his right fist. 'I should have picked up on it.'

'His mother didn't,' Martha put in gently.

Trimble seemed not to have heard her. 'He was almost ashamed.' Freddie was frowning now. He drank his tea abstractedly, looking into the distance. 'Pat buried things very deep, you know. If he could have got to the right university to study the right subjects with the right friends to back him up and encourage him, he would have shone. He had a head full of knowledge and the sense to sift through it. He might well have realized his ambition, been an astro-physicist or a cosmologist or something. But . . .'

'That last day,' she prompted.

'Well, he didn't come to school.' It was the first sign of anger. Of irritation – with her. Trimble could be sparky, she realized.

'Was that the only day he didn't attend school?'

The teacher shook his head. 'No. He was away for two days in the previous week. I checked. I think his mum sent a note in saying he had a cold or something.'

Amanda Elson hadn't mentioned this.

'Tell me something. When you heard . . .'

The dark eyes flew up to her face. 'I wasn't surprised,' he said. 'It's as though I knew something was brewing. But not that. Not that, or I would have stopped it.'

'You think you could have stopped it?'

'I'd tried to speak to him on the previous Thursday but he didn't want to know, not really. But . . .' His eyes met hers fearlessly.

'I could never have anticipated anything like that. Not suicide. If I had I would have done absolutely anything to have stopped it.' He paused. 'With most suicides, surely it's just a phase you have to get through and come out the other side.'

She nodded. That was one way of looking at it.

'He was a nice boy. It shouldn't have happened.' He looked at her, pain clouding his eyes. 'You know the worst thing about a suicide?'

She already knew what he was going to say. Because she'd heard it all before – the guilt, the feeling that you could, should, have prevented it.

He didn't fail her. 'We let him down,' he said. '*I* let him down, but I could never have imagined . . .'

'No,' she said. 'You couldn't. Patrick couldn't live with himself.' She was tempted to complete the question. *Because* . . .

Partly to divert him away from the river of sadness, she pursued another aspect.

'Tell me,' she said, 'more about the two boys, Warren and Sean.'

Trimble looked alarmed. 'We can't do anything unless we've got proof. The parents would be down on us like a ton of bricks. Their mum has been down the school a couple of times with complaints that her sons weren't being treated fairly, that they've been given grades that were too low or excluded from a trip just because of who they are, who their dad is.'

'Their mother's a tough nut?'

His face looked almost humorous. 'You wouldn't want to take her on, Mrs Gunn. She's a lady with an interesting collection of tattoos and language that would make most men blush. The boys are big for their age.'

Martha simply nodded. She knew now in which direction she was headed. But Gina Marconi hadn't committed suicide because a couple of schoolboys had intimidated her. It would have taken much more than that. She hadn't found the bottom of the muckheap just yet. How this all connected, she didn't know. But she had a feeling that these cases, murky and stinking like rotting fish, had another lesson for her. She might not have DI Alex Randall to walk her through but that didn't mean she couldn't run her own investigation. She was on her own now.

So be it.

THIRTY-SIX

After Freddie Trimble had left her office, Martha sat for a while taking stock, trying to work it all out. Because now that she'd found a link between Gina and Patrick, what was her next step?

She rang Amanda Elson's mobile phone and asked her about the note she had sent to cover her son's absence from school the week before he'd died. And as expected, Amanda knew nothing about it.

'I don't understand,' she said. 'He wasn't ill. He was at school . . .' Her voice trailed away. She was wondering how well she'd actually known her own son.

Before she could put two and two together Martha thanked her and ended the conversation. At the moment she couldn't help her. She started putting known facts in order.

Patrick Elson's schoolmates' dad was to stay in prison. And Gina Marconi had put him there – or at least hadn't managed (or wanted) to keep him out. But it hadn't been a man in prison who had taken those horrible pictures.

And Gina? The pictures she would have been sent of herself? Electronically? Yes, an electronic version existed but Martha believed she would have been confronted with an actual photograph. Somehow it is more shocking. The threat of spreading them around would have accompanied the full Disney Technicolor. So if they existed, had Gina destroyed them? Or was someone hiding them? The police had found nothing like that. So who was hiding them? Terence? Her mother? Julius? And more importantly, who had sent them? She could take her pick. Gina had mixed with a dangerous crowd, but Mosha Steventon would have protected her. He was her guardian. So who was intimidating her under Steventon's radar? Who else was lurking there, in the shadows?

For her money the thread was Pete Lewinski, who had not only gone to Gina's office and threatened her, but the threats seemed to have struck home. Trouble was Lewinski needed Gina. But

Martha felt that Lewinski had something over Gina just as Gina
had something over Lewinski.

She reminded herself that Alex had had contact with the criminal
world. She wondered if he knew Lewinski. But it was a mistake
to return to him. She put her head in her hands. How tantalizing.
DI Randall was now single but, ironically, even more untouchable
than before. Thank you very much, fate, she thought bitterly. You've
just made certain nothing can *ever* grow between us – not even
honest affection. He is farther away from you now than he's ever
been. So, Martha Gunn, analyse your feelings and be truthful. Sort
yourself out. She scooped in a deep breath. If her theory about
Erica was right, she knew it fitted like a glove. She'd done the
research. She was just missing one small blood test to confirm her
horrible suspicion. If she was right, Alex Randall would feel guiltier
than ever. Bugger. She felt tempted to kick the base of her desk
but today she was wearing some rather smart, very expensive,
black Italian leather high-heeled shoes that she'd paid an eye-
watering price for. She was not going to ruin them in frustration
over Erica Randall's death – as doomed a death as her life had
been for the previous six years.

Time to find out the truth and share her theory. She picked up the
phone and connected with Mark Sullivan. He had done the three post-
mortems. If there was any proof, he would be the one to have it.

THIRTY-SEVEN

Monday, 17 April, 10 a.m.

In Church Stretton, DI Alex Randall was at home, searching
the computer for any reference to his current suspension, when
the phone call came. He answered it with a touch of apprehension. Apart from his mother-in-law he'd had no good news over
the line and any minute now he expected a call from the press.
'Detective Inspector Randall?' His wariness compounded when
the voice was male and unfamiliar. 'David Steadman here.' Alex
was struggling to remember who he was until he introduced

himself. 'Coroner for South Shropshire. I'm not sure whether you're aware but I shall be dealing with the unexplained death of your wife. Mrs Gunn has asked me to take over.'

Alex felt even more cheated. Martha was his friend. Surely she could have . . .?

And then he put his head in order. Of course Martha couldn't have managed the case objectively. They had been too close.

He listened carefully to what David Steadman was saying. 'I think you should come into my office in Ludlow so we can discuss the findings of the post-mortem – so far. Obviously we're waiting for more results but I expect you want to proceed with the funeral, DI Randall.' A statement not a question. 'I hope to release your wife's body before too long.'

Randall searched for some clue, some hint. What was going on? What was he saying – nothing? Steadman was giving *nothing* away.

So Alex mirrored his neutral tone. 'Certainly, Mr Steadman,' he said, his voice icily calm and controlled. 'When would you like me to come? I can manage any time – I'm on *gardening leave* at the moment.'

Steadman pushed the sarcasm aside and wasn't above inserting just a tinge of it himself. 'Well, how about tomorrow morning then as you're busy? Nine o'clock. Does that suit you, Inspector?'

'Just fine.' Randall put the phone down with more than a touch of irritation. *Don't give me a clue as to what's going on, will you, Steadman?* He eyed the phone balefully as though it could tell him what credence they were putting on Mark Sullivan's post-mortem findings. Still, at least he wasn't being forced to wait too long.

Just until tomorrow morning.

Long enough.

In her office, Martha was on the internet, googling some names, among them Peter Lewinski. Quite a record. Quite a man. The face that glared out of her screen was thin, hard and uncompromising. The question was, did he have the subtlety to drive a bright woman like Gina Marconi to her death? Martha wasn't convinced. But there was something there. She looked again and wondered what had gone on between Gina and Lewinski, though when did a photograph indicate a true picture of character? She had seen mug shots of saints and sinners. They all looked evil glaring into a camera lens.

Next she googled Jack Silver and again faced a person with staring glaring eyes and a Desperate Dan chin but this man looked a little more interesting. There was a sharpness there, some alertness, like a meerkat on guard, ears pricked up, listening for some sound. There was also a ruddiness, an earthiness and a certain cockiness in his face. She stared at him. Question was, how could she find anything out? Her fingers hovered over the keyboard as though it was a Ouija board waiting for instruction. Something was there right underneath her fingers.

Patrick and the two Silver boys attended the same school and were in the same class. And the boys had picked on Patrick Elson. Forget Gina for now. She wasn't a twelve-year-old boy. Focus on Patrick. But she was finding it hard to detach one from the other. Gina would have had better judgement. She would have had the sense to fend off any encounter or recognize any deal which could impact on her life or career. *Unless* . . . Martha found herself drifting into another world. Unless her judgement had been impaired. Was that the issue?

She tried to think. And returned to her earlier conversation with Mark Sullivan.

'*The post-mortem findings on Patrick?*'

Put that with the photograph and she had it.

'*Semen?*'

'*No.*' He'd sighed. '*They all know to wear a condom these days.*'

A blind alley. She wasn't there yet.

Back to Gina. What if she had warned him that she might not win the case? What if Lewinski did not want Gina to represent him at trial? Had he been anyone else he would have simply changed lawyers. But Lewinski did not act predictably. So how would he respond? Exactly as he had. He would burst into her office and threaten her. But what if she had ignored his threats? Then he would have fought back. How? A lawyer whose judgement is impaired by, say drugs or alcohol, might be held up to ridicule. And more. She could lose her licence to practise. Professional bodies check up on their members and the law has a strict code of ethics. Any slur on Gina might have rubbed off on Julius Zedanski. Would their relationship have survived? *Nothing sticks like dirt.* Another saying of her mother's. Martha smiled to herself. Did her mother have a mantra for every occasion to support any view?

Probably.

In this case the dirt was scandal. That would be how Lewinski would have punished the lawyer who was going to fail him at trial.

She worked steadily through the day, feeling hopeful that eventually all would be explained, that her ideas would be proven and, more importantly, that she could use her powers to mitigate the damage and achieve something through the inquests she would be conducting. And as for Steadman, if she was right, her theory confirmed by tests, there would also be an explanation for Erica Randall's life and death. It was only as she was packing up to go home that she realized. Even if she was right it didn't necessarily let Alex off the hook.

6.45 p.m.

It was late. Martha's mental meanderings had made her lose track of time. And now she should go home. But her normal enthusiasm for returning to her home, the White House, was marred by *him* being there. Sneering and criticizing. And the worst thing? The thing she hated most? The thing she could not forgive him for? It was the effect he had on Sukey, her own beautiful, talented, darling daughter. She would be glad when they returned to Bristol and resumed their studies. But that meant exiling her beloved Sukey.

'Oh, shit,' she thought and left her office.

It was dusk, the town's lights twinkling in the distance. What a day it had been, even more interesting than usual. And now it was time to face the drama of home. But out here, three miles away from the town, her office hidden behind a private driveway overgrown with rhododendrons, it took her a while to realize something was different.

Jericho had left half an hour ago, leaving her to lock up. She was alone and suddenly felt vulnerable without knowing why. Then she turned and saw. Scratched on her car was some advice. *Don't turn over stones.*

Martha wasn't someone who scared easily; neither was she a woman who had an obsessive love for or pride in her car, but hell's bells she'd only had it a year, kept it reasonably clean and quite liked it. She'd paid a good price for the Merc as it had been showroom almost-new. And some cheeky bastard was using it to threaten her? Just as they had Gina and Patrick? Did they sense she was inching too close? Or were they simply targeting her as they had them?

Don't turn over stones.

She sensed that as she had worked out Lewinski had warned Gina, he was now turning his attentions to her. Well, they didn't know her, did they? She was not someone to be threatened. It was more likely to goad her into action. And she believed there was nothing they could use against her because she was forewarned. She wasn't going to take this advice/threat seriously. It was a red rag to a bull. Simply a challenge. And then she realized she was acting in exactly the same way that Gina had. Look where she had ended up. It was a chilling thought.

As she fished her mobile phone from her bag and held it to her ear she was working things out. She had CCTV cameras along the drive. She knew from bitter experience that bereaved relatives could act in unpredictable ways after an unsatisfactory interview with a coroner or else dissatisfaction with the verdict at the inquest. Sometimes they argued or grew angry. Sometimes they wanted a verdict other than the one she was prepared to give – particularly in the case of a suicide. She'd been stalked before in just such a case and this had resulted in the installation of the cameras. The family had suffered financially from her verdict and had not accepted her reasoning: *a bloody note, for goodness' sake, stating intention. How arguable was that?* At least *initially* they had not accepted her verdict. Later she had convinced them but at the time it had been unnerving enough for her to feel threatened. Hence the CCTV cameras watching the approach to her office beamed to a couple of monitors which Jericho watched like a hawk.

She ran through her recent contacts, rejected anyone from Gina's family, struggled to imagine Amanda Elson or her sister doing such a spiteful act. Had Freddie Trimble been angry when he'd left her office? She quickly rejected this idea too. No. This was someone else who had waited for Jericho to leave and then acted. Jericho would not have walked past this. His nosiness had a payoff. He was the most observant man she knew. He would have noticed someone loitering in the drive or a strange car parked where it should not. She eyed the cameras and hoped they were in the right place. Eyes still on the car and the bushes watching for any movement, she called the station, this time getting through to a sympathetic PC Delia Shaw.

This smacked of Lewinski and his associates. Shock set in and Martha began to shake. Admitting she was frightened was foreign to her but she knew where this message came from.

Gina Marconi had believed she too was a strong and independent woman, immune even to her links with the underworld, protected by Mosha. But in the end *no one* had been able to protect her. And now Alex had been suspended, Martha had no one either. If Alex hadn't been suspended he would have been here by now. And he wouldn't have left her side until she was safely home. And then *he* would have initiated investigations. A result of Erica Randall's death had been to remove Alex from her side. So she waited. And they finally arrived.

PC Delia Shaw was accompanied by a young special constable called Rosie who shadowed her superior's footsteps like an obedient, reliable and faithful puppy.

Delia shook her hand. 'You OK, Coroner?'

'I'm fine. Unlike . . .' All eyes turned to the car.

'We've got the photographer coming,' Delia said quickly. 'We're a bit stretched for someone to go through the CCTV now so we'll take the tapes away with us. Any idea what time it happened?'

'Jericho left at about six fifteen,' Martha said. 'He's hawk-eyed and I don't think he'd have missed this so I'm assuming that this was done between six fifteen and six forty-five when I found it.'

'Narrows the field a bit,' Rosie put in.

Everyone turned to her and she flushed.

Delia Shaw resumed charge. 'OK, leave it with us. We'll lock the gates up tonight and stick some *Do Not Cross* tape up then we'll take a proper look in the morning.' She scanned the floor around the car in the fading light. 'Nothing too obvious.' She tried to give Martha a reassuring smile but Martha was thoughtful.

'I'd like to know what you turn up,' she said, 'just in case it's someone I've had dealings with in the past and I need to be more watchful.'

Both police officers nodded. 'Yeah. Of course.'

Then it was Delia who turned to the practical. 'Would you like me to run you home?'

THIRTY-EIGHT

Tuesday, 18 April, 9 a.m.

Alex was at the coroner's office dead on nine o'clock.

David Steadman met him on the staircase and held out his hand. 'Inspector Randall,' he said genially. 'Good of you to call.' He ushered him into an interview room. 'Sit,' he invited.

Alex was contrasting David Steadman with Martha. In spite of the obvious differences – age, sex, appearance – his manner was oddly similar, warmly formal, perfectly polite, demeanour genial. His face was less animated but perhaps she kept that particular face just for him. Did they instil these traits in coroner school?

His study of Steadman continued. His physical presence was quite different. He was red-faced and overweight, puffing slightly on the stairs as they'd ascended. He had Martha's direct gaze but his eyes were faded blue instead of that brilliant, almost iridescent green. He had hardly any hair and what he had was white and wispy. In spite of the seriousness of the impending interview – half an hour which could change his life – Alex Randall couldn't quite suppress a smile when he recalled Martha's thick unruly red hair which she should have dyed sober-black and had cut short if Coroner had been her life's ambition.

He made himself comfortable and forced himself to focus on David Steadman's statement.

'We've got most of the results of Doctor Sullivan's post-mortem,' he said crisply, leafing through papers as he spoke, glancing from time to time towards the computer screen. 'We also have some initial results back, DI Randall. I thought it only fair to prepare you.'

'Thank you.' Alex was wondering what was coming next.

Half an hour later Alex Randall practically staggered out of Steadman's office. This was Erica having her revenge. This he had not been expecting. This changed everything. He felt terrible.

Martha received a call at ten o'clock. She had arranged a hire car to be delivered to her home and fended off questions from Sukey and Sam and even Pomeroy who appeared sympathetic to her tale of a 'breakdown'.

'Crikey,' he'd said. 'Poor you. Practically brand-new Merc and it cranks out on you.' Was she imagining a hint of malice? She eyed him suspiciously, but this time read only sincerity. Had she been wrong about him? Was he possibly just one of those people who had an unfortunate manner? Said things out of awkwardness rather than true malice? Well, she had enough to deal with now without undoing her character assassination of Sukey's current boyfriend.

The Toyota they provided wasn't quite the Mercedes but it would do for now. However, a little like having your home violated by a burglar, she knew she wouldn't feel quite the same affection for the car when she had it back, doubtless as good as new. She would still run her fingers along the paintwork and, however skilled a job they managed, would still feel all the letters of Lewsinki's message. She would be swapping it in the near future.

On the other end of the phone was PC Sean Dart, the one Alex had described to her as a 'dark horse'. Somewhere in his past a dark secret lurked but this morning that was far from her mind. He was simply passing on information that he'd gleaned from the CCTV set up along the drive. 'Two guys,' he said. 'One's small – could be a kid even. We've picked them up on the CCTV and we might – we just might have part of a number plate.'

'Careless.'

'We-ell, I don't suppose they'd be expecting a camera to be stuck up there in the trees, Mrs Gunn.' His tone was stolid but there was a note of humour in it. She smiled too.

'True. So who are my villains?'

'Well, we haven't actually got them at the moment.' A pause. 'We've got the forensic boys to take a look around both the car and your rather secluded drive but they haven't found anything obvious so far. I take it you want the car removed to a garage for a facelift?'

Sean Dark Horse did not appear to be taking this seriously enough. But what could she say except, 'That would be good. Thank you.'

She worked through the day but was distracted. She was trying to piece together the facts as she knew them and needed to do something. She finally decided she would begin by eyeballing the Silver boys who had been bullying Patrick. As this was something she knew for definite it seemed a good place to start. The best thing to do, she decided, would be to hang around the school when they came out. She would recognize them. What she didn't want was for *them* to recognize *her*. Trouble was her red hair was a beacon so she found herself a dark green beanie and stuck it over her head, then donned a pair of tinted glasses to hide her eyes. Luckily the rain was sheeting down so over this she belted up a shiny black mac and turned the collar up. Flat shoes to disguise her height and she was ready for battle.

That stopped her up short. What on earth was she saying? Ready for battle? Do battle with a couple of twelve-year-olds? A bit dramatic, Martha. And yet what could be more dramatic than the two suicides, the boy's dive on to a busy dual carriageway and Gina's determined impact with the wall?

She hoped the year eight brothers would be easy to spot. She had a vague description from Freddie Trimble and she guessed they would walk home together. If the worst came to the worst she could always ask some of the other children to confirm their identity. She took up her place on the pavement with a crowd of jostling mothers, fathers, grandparents, childminders, some of whom already had their hands full with smaller infants. A couple of them were pregnant. Most of them wore jeans. No one took any notice of her. The sun came out from behind a cloud. The rain stopped abruptly and shadows danced in front of her on the still-wet pavement. She looked up at the sky at the source of one of the dancing shadows. And there they were, the shoes still pirouetting over the telegraph wire. Left there long after he died. What happened to these shoes in the end? she wondered. Dumped by Openreach workers? Taken home for *their* kids? Thrown away? Who knew.

As the stream of children trickled through the gates Martha hit a stroke of luck. A plump little girl with plaits called out. 'Hey you, Warreny.' Two boys turned around simultaneously and Martha caught her first sight of Patrick Elson's tormentors. Two stocky lads with buzz haircuts, a tough air about them, swigging Coke from plastic bottles. Bingo. And yes, they looked as though they were walking home. And so she followed them. Simple.

But as she walked behind them she knew there was more to this. *They* were not the ones who had assaulted Patrick Elson. It was somebody else. An adult. Not their dad. He was out of the picture. Somebody else was involved.

She revisited the conversation she'd had with Mark Sullivan two hours after her original call. He'd agreed with her first point but when she had followed this up with a question about Gina's suicide he had sounded surprised. 'Don't quite see where this is heading, Martha. Yes, she'd had recent intercourse. But she *was* engaged.'

'When you say recent?'

'Within the last few days.'

But Julius Zedanski had been in Syria for the last *month*. Little cracks were appearing in Gina's perfect life.

She trailed the boys, noting their manner. They were true clones of their father, potentially criminal material. What was it Trimble had called them? Junior thugs.

They pushed and jostled their way through the smaller children, the two boys easy to pick out, taller and bulkier than the others, both big for their age. The two Silver boys must have been fed on hormones and junk food. Martha could well imagine their feeling of power. They were the sort of boys who would have pulled the legs off frogs, enjoyed inflicting pain, frightening the younger children who stepped aside pretty smartly to let them through, one or two spilling dangerously on to the road. Even the mothers who were picking up the younger children gave them a wide berth, avoided their eyes and steered their children's scooters tight into the side. Martha walked steadily behind them, keeping her distance and her head down. She did not want to be recognized. But she needn't have worried. The boys were far too busy with their own agenda to notice someone following behind them. In her beanie and mac she was invisible. Besides, the pavement was crowded with children, parents, pushchairs, scooters, a couple of bikes, one or two pensioners on their mobility scooters. The one called Warren deliberately stood in front of one, causing the elderly gentleman to brake sharply and curse loudly. But he too backed off when he met the boy's eyes. Warren gave a mocking giggle, sticking his middle finger up. And the gentleman hurried away as fast as his scooter would let him from the two thugs. These were the sort of boys and men they would become, Martha mused, as she too moved along the pavement, head down. People would shy away from them all their lives. And those who didn't would come to regret it.

Their home was a fifteen-minute walk away but in that time their tormenting was relentless. They pushed a girl out into the road, almost in front of a car, threw a small boy's school bag into a skip full of broken glass and old wood, drew a key along a car, one committing the act, his brother keeping watch for tale bearers. They grabbed another boy by the scruff of his neck so he handed over the chocolate bar he was halfway through eating. All the time they were watching for someone to pick on, preferably someone small. Finally both boys let themselves into a house, quite a smart house, modern, detached, probably three or four bedrooms, no car in the drive. The window to the right of the front door had rather feminine draped net curtains – unusual for these days. And on the window sill stood a Doulton model of a girl in a red windswept crinoline. Juliet. It pricked a memory.

Gotcha.

Martha's breath quickened. *I have you now*, she thought. *I have you. Or at least I nearly do.*

The memory of Patrick Elson's face, terrified, humiliated, made her clench her fists. But how on earth could she ensure these boys were punished? Bullying is hardly an imprisonable offence. An adult male was involved here somewhere. She recalled the man who stood by, waiting. These two lads were not capable of rape . . . not yet. Again she recalled Mark Sullivan's words: *'They all know to wear a condom these days.'* She knew it would be difficult if not impossible to prove. So she could do nothing and these boys would continue in their ugly ways. And in the future, as they matured, there may well be more vulnerable victims. More boys determined to destroy themselves because of these two villains. It was a terrible thought.

A second memory augmented that thought, the list of traumatic injuries Mark Sullivan had picked up on during the post-mortem along with the jaunty comment that had failed to hide his revulsion.

Take your pick, Martha.

And then a third image superimposed itself on the first two: Amanda Elson practically propped up by her sister. Martha stood still, appalled by the image. *How, as coroner,* she asked herself, *can I prevent this in the future?*

And the politically incorrect answer? *By removing them from a harmful environment.*

Minus the beanie, glasses and mac she returned to her office. Jericho, sitting at the front desk, gave her a swift, searching glance as she entered but he said nothing. The office – and her pile of work – was waiting for her. As unwelcome work always does, sits and stares at you, pricking your conscience. She sat at her desk and leafed through the photographs yet again. She needed that anger to propel herself through the stormy waters that lay ahead.

And there it was, her proof, the pictures that she could use. Taken from the outside through the window. Lace curtains, swept back from the middle, the same lady in a red crinoline standing on the sill like an actress centre stage, back towards her, flouncing her skirts into the room. Doulton pretty lady figure, Juliet. So what had Juliet's china eyes witnessed? She could picture the scene. Mother not at home, they had lured Patrick to their house while a photographer stood outside and recorded. Someone had forced Elson to bend over. Why? She joined her question to the others. Why him? Jealousy because he was smarter than they? Had Patrick been a natural victim as his teacher had assessed? Why go this far with this particular child? Just because he was a geek – clever?

Her hand moved across to the other file. Like a missing piece in a puzzle she was manoeuvring this case over Gina's, fitting it together. The natural instinct was to link the boys, Patrick Elson and Terence. But Terence Marconi was at a different school from Patrick so not exposed to this pair of embryonic psychopaths. And besides, he was four years younger. With the information Mark Sullivan had given her, the link was sexual. She shook her head.

It was not enough. She needed more. Her frown turned into a
scowl. She was still missing something. Was she skipping along
this theory of hers, bridging the gaps, jumping to all the wrong
conclusions? Forcing facts to slip into her theory? She jumped
anyway. She had found the link between Silver's two sons and
Gina Marconi, who had defended their father. And now it was up
to her to find the still missing gaps, find the proof and present
it to the police. Minus DI Randall.

Patrick's suicide had been the result of bullying and almost
certainly rape. But she was still missing Gina's back story.

It couldn't be a couple of lads tormenting her, but something
and someone more equal to her in both age and intellect. Someone
who had caught her out. Someone who was intelligent and presumably charismatic enough to lead her into a trap and she, with all
her lawyer's clever instincts, had not seen it for what it was. It
had also been under Mosha Steventon's radar. That pulled her up
short. In the main the clients Gina dealt with were thugs. She
would have seen right through them, fended off any attempt to
manipulate or blackmail her or manoeuvre her into a position of
vulnerability. She was just too smart. She would have seen that
coming like a steam train four miles down the track. So why hadn't
she taken heed? Had she had sex with someone when there was
so much to lose? Everything destroyed. Was Gina, perhaps, not
as smart as everyone thought, but a fool, to let this lust get the
better of her? And they had won in the end. The villains had beaten
both Mosha and the clever lawyer. Question was who were they
– or rather who was he? And how had he pulled this one off? How
had he backed her against a wall – literally – where the only way
out she could see was suicide, with no explanation, an act hurtful
and cruel to her family?

She didn't know enough yet but at some point she should
confront Gina's family with her beliefs. Not now. When she had
proof and saw the full picture she could explain. Agitated, she
picked up the phone. She had to speak to Gina's mother again
and, if possible, Terence. Terence, the quiet little boy with the
all-seeing, wary, watchful eyes. There was something destroyed
in those eyes.

Mentally she zoomed back out to the wider picture. Curtis
Thatcher would have been anxious to protect his reputation,

preserve the integrity of the partnership and distance himself from anything that might damage the firm. And Zedanski? These days the BBC was a notoriously conventional employer with a strict moral code. Correspondents with a tainted reputation would soon be dispatched. So perhaps Zedanski's high profile had been another nail in Gina's coffin. Martha flicked back to the last broadcast she had seen him make. His almost messianic reporting of the world's troubles. Had *she* died because of who *he* was? Fame and fortune are equally fickle entities. Both her law firm and Zedanski could have easily been tumbled from their perches. Did that put them in the picture? How far would *they* have gone to protect their images? And, realizing this hard fact, was that why Gina had decided to end it all? But there were differences. While Curtis Thatcher had been there, every day, sharing offices, Zedanski had been away covering the refugee crisis from Damascus. When, she wondered, had they last actually been face-to-face?

One way to find out.

She hooked up with Zedanski on his mobile phone. He responded quickly, perhaps recognizing the 01743 telephone number. 'Mrs Gunn,' he said, his voice wary and guarded. 'Thank you for calling.' It was mere politeness. His tone was flat.

'Are you still in Shrewsbury?'

'Yeah. I have to wind up things here, organize completion of the building work on the rest of the house and then put it up for sale. Bridget is kindly putting me up.' He tried to laugh. It was a miserable failure. 'Or rather putting up with me. I can't bear to be inside that place. We're managing.' It was his response to a question she had not asked.

'When did you last actually see her?'

'Not for two months. There's so much going on out there I couldn't really take a break.'

That would take them back to the end of January.

He seemed to think he needed to add something. 'We spoke daily about stuff – the wedding, the house.' He was sounding defensive. 'It's the same, really.'

But, as Martha knew, speaking on the phone is *not* the same as seeing someone face-to-face, sharing innermost thoughts or making love, sleeping beside them through the dead hours of the nights, putting your hand out, knowing he is there. She blinked away that particular distant memory. More than fifteen years old.

Telephone conversations can never be a substitute for that. They are not intimate or perceptive. One can keep up a pretty good farce over the phone. Seeing is different. 'You Skyped?'

'She wasn't keen on it, thought it made her look odd.' A slightly more genuine attempt at mirth. 'Said I'd dump her if she looked as distorted as that in real life.'

Distorted. The word bored into Martha's mind – and stayed there. Latent for now.

'Hmm. Did you think she was lonely? Did you pick up on anything?'

There was a long silence in response and then Zedanski said softly, 'I thought it was the wedding. I thought . . .' Whatever he had been about to say he substituted for: 'There *was* a distance.' Another pause during which she could hear him breathing. 'The distance seemed to be widening.' There was a pause and then he added, 'Are you any nearer . . .?' The question faded into nothing.

She said that she wasn't, but that she had an idea she would like to discuss with him before the inquest. Then she said goodbye and thought. She *would* get to the bottom of this. She *would* take this bull by the horns. Now. Because now she could approach this from another direction. Before she could change her mind, she picked up the phone again and asked to speak with DS Talith.

'I take it you're still the SIO in the two suicides, Patrick Elson and Gina Marconi?'

'I am, ma'am.'

So Alex was still off.

'I think I have some evidence that Patrick was being intimidated, threatened. Possibly raped.'

'Ma'am?'

'The family are in possession of some photographs – rather unsavoury. The boy was being victimized.' She held back on the rape. She had no proof. Even Sullivan had said there was a chance the boy had suffered from constipation. 'I shall be bringing this out at the inquest. I'm quite happy to deal with it myself for the moment but you should have copies of these pictures and I'm hoping that you'll be able to act on them.'

Talith was silent for a moment, then said, 'I take it the perpetrators were also youngsters?'

'The bullying – yes. The other I don't think so.'

'The other?'

'You know Jack Silver?'

'Who doesn't?'

'He appears to have two sons who are following in their father's footsteps.'

'Doesn't surprise me.'

'Nor me. But without proof and perhaps a lead to an older man you're going to have a struggle to do anything about this.'

'Yeah. Not for the first time.' Talith was growing cynical.

'Have you unearthed anything more about Gina Marconi's private life?'

'We-ell. She mixed with some unpleasant characters.'

So he was trudging along the same road. 'Through her work, surely?'

'Mm.'

'Anyone in particular?'

'We've got our eye on a Mr Lewinski and his accountant, a slick old fellow named Donaldson.'

'Lewinski I know about – racial hatred, money laundering. But Donaldson?'

'Financial advisor,' Talith said, grumpy at the implication of wealth. 'We've had our eye on him for ages – as have HMRC, but nothing provable yet. We can't get a case together that the CPS will have anything to do with. There's another guy called Lenny Khan who's of interest to MI6, maybe connected with terrorism, maybe not. She got him off anyway so he's free. But again we've nothing concrete. She mixed in such a witches' brew of odd company.'

'This Mr Donaldson,' she said curiously, the name new to her. 'Tell me about him.'

'He's a financial advisor, business in town, offices in Milk Street, hangs around with a guy called Victor Stanley.'

This was another new name to her. 'Stanley?'

'A sort of a . . .' Talith hunted down the word. 'A gigolo.'

Martha stored the description away, aware that she would bring it out at some time. But how would she get to him? 'Tell me more about Donaldson.'

'Bent as a ten-bob bit.'

Martha smothered a smile. When would DS Talith have even seen a ten-bob bit?

'Most of his clients appear to be . . . questionable. His returns seem to bear no resemblance to the current interest rates. He's just . . . dodgy, Mrs Gunn.' Talith sounded more pleased with his description.

'I see. Nothing concrete, just that?'

'Her Majesty's Revenue and Customs have had their eye on him for years but he's a clever customer. Leaves a trail more difficult to follow than a fox. Runs to ground every now and then, hides money in all sorts of offshores. We haven't turned up anything and so far neither have they. Gina defended him successfully eighteen months ago on a minor charge. There was a question of some money he'd handled for a client and it was proved the money was the proceeds of an art theft.'

'Tell me more.'

Talith backed off. 'I'm hardly an expert, Mrs Gunn. It was handled by the Fine Art Department in Birmingham. Some art that was stolen appeared to turn up in one of the city's salerooms but when the team swooped it turned out they were fakes.'

Martha frowned. 'So . . .?'

'The opinion was that there had been a swap sometime between the saleroom assessing the work at a private home and them turning up at the saleroom in time for the Fine Art Department to reclaim them.'

Martha's frown deepened. She still couldn't see the connection.

Talith continued. 'Trouble was they weren't old like Old Masters, they were all pieces of modern art so a lot of the usual checks – carbon dating and paint analysis – just weren't any use. The whole thing was dropped because there was no proof. The real ones were stolen, the fakes turned up. What happened to the real ones is anybody's guess. A bit habeas corpus, if you know what I mean. No body, no conviction.'

'I see.' She was about to replace the handset when Talith cleared his throat ostentatiously. 'Word is DI Randall may well be back at work in a week or two. His wife's funeral is next Thursday at the crematorium. Private ceremony.'

So Alex was free.

'Thank you.' She disconnected.

Alex back at work? What did that mean? Erica to be cremated. Next Thursday. Cremation destroys every single possible forensic detail. That is why two doctors have to sign the forms. Because once a body has been cremated evidence is gone forever. It can never be resurrected.

David Steadman had, so far, and in spite of his promises, passed on nothing; neither had Mark Sullivan. She was still in the dark waiting for confirmation of her theory. These decisions had all been made without her – for Alex to return to his role as DI, for Erica's body to be released for cremation, for the funeral to be held.

Why had none of them kept her up to date when the enquiry must have reached a conclusion?

THIRTY-NINE

t was all very well distracting herself with the two suicides but Martha's mind never drifted far from Alex. With an effort, almost a creaking of the wheel, she turned back to her own two cases.

One name seemed to present itself for consideration: Ivor Donaldson, financial advisor.

Well she thought, smiling. She could do with a little financial advice herself.

She could almost hear Alex Randall's voice warning her. *'Leave it, Martha, these are dangerous people. You don't want to get involved here. Not safe.'* It would have been accompanied by that knowing look that understood she would be involved even though his advice was sound. *'Leave it to us.'*

She could feel the pressure of his hand on her arm, staying her. And she shook it off. 'You're not here, Alex, are you?'

She didn't realize she'd spoken out loud until Jericho was standing in front of her, his expression curious. 'Did you want something, Mrs Gunn?'

'No. No. I may have to go into town for an hour or so.'

He nodded and she looked up the telephone number and dialled it, spoke briefly.

She was interested in hiring his services to invest some
money? A legacy? Of course he was happy to oblige. He had an
appointment free for two o'clock.

She was going to put her head right into the lion's mouth.

Ivor Donaldson looked like what he possibly was – a thug with
a smooth coating, sharp eyes, a warily expectant look. He had
coarse skin which went perfectly with a coarse manner, a way of
sizing a woman up as though he was giving her marks out of ten
for her performance in bed. She appraised him right back, coolly,
and decided he was probably selfish in bed, someone who satisfied
only his own needs. Such men made rotten lovers and would always
drive a woman towards another man, someone who 'understood'
them. Victor Stanley perhaps? She certainly found the financial
adviser singularly unattractive. That much she decided within
seconds of meeting him. She had parked at the bottom of Wyle
Cop and walked up the steep hill bordered by pretty black and
white individual shops including the antique shop and her own
personal favourite, the Period House Shop. As she had walked
she had pondered the reasons behind Gina Marconi's suicide, the
humiliating loss of face which would destroy the opinion of
the only people who meant anything to her.

And that, after all, is what defines our life – the esteem of those
whose opinion we hold dear. It was the best she could come up
with. Perhaps the truth was something even deeper.

But how could she steer the conversation round to Gina while
Donaldson was rabbiting on, asking her, greedy eyes fixed on hers,
exactly *how much* money she wanted to invest, did she want it
safe or was she prepared to *take a risk*? His eyes continued to
bore into hers as she said, quite sweetly, that she was perfectly
happy to take a risk.

'And how much money are you thinking of investing?'

'Oh,' she said casually, 'round about fifty K – initially.'

The amount and comment seemed to please him. She saw a
little light flicker in his eyes, a light that shone with happiness
and optimism and pure unadulterated, undisguised greed. 'Good,'
he said, and just about managed to avoid rubbing his hands together.

'We could talk about this over dinner.' It was the nearest he
would get to charm but although something in Martha revolted
against it, she said yes, she would love to have dinner with him.

It was walking straight into the lion's den and she knew it. It felt dangerous – stupid even. Did she think she was any more perceptive than Gina? Truth was she was putting herself into exactly the same position.

Her instinct was to tell someone about the 'date' but strangely enough the only person who came to mind was Simon Pendlebury and that was not a good idea. Nothing to do with him was ever a good idea. She'd gone far enough there. If only Alex had been around she could – no would – have asked him to keep an eye out. But of course he was not here. Not in a useful sense anyway.

He would have watched her back because this guy felt and seemed dangerous. And his bank of friends were nasty little buggers. A poisoned network of them. But could he have charmed Gina Marconi, who would have had an instinct for villains like him? No. Surely not. Someone else – and Victor Stanley fitted the bill to perfection. Donaldson could lead her to him.

He stood up once they'd arranged to continue their talk that evening at The Granary.

But even as she left his office she had a feeling of dread. No one would know where she had gone – or why.

Just before she left home she gave in and dialled Simon's number. 'Don't ask any questions,' she warned. 'You won't like the answers.'

He said nothing but she could almost hear the fizz in his mind as he raised his eyebrows. And yes, he would be smiling. And curious.

'I'm going somewhere tonight.'

'Ri-ight?'

'With someone I don't trust.'

And at that, Simon being Simon, he burst out laughing. 'And what, you want me to be your chaperone? Or your bodyguard?' He chuckled. 'Either way, I'm up for it. I could do with a bit of excitement in my life.'

'No,' she said. 'Simon. Please, take this seriously. Have I ever asked you to watch my back before?'

'No,' he said, and she could hear the smile still in his voice, which prepared her for his follow up. 'But then you always had your tame policeman hanging around somewhere in the background.'

'I did not,' she said, cross with him for putting his finger on a very tender pulse. 'And DI Randall was never tame.'

'Oh, get you,' he said, still laughing. Then, 'OK, what do you want me to do?'

'Ring my mobile at ten?'

'OK. And, umm, if you don't answer?'

'It could mean one of two things.' Martha thought for a moment then answered. 'Come and find me. We're going to The Granary.'

'Oh,' he said, then. 'OK, Martha. I take it you're doing some sort of enquiry yourself?'

'I believe he's got something to do with Gina Marconi's suicide.'

Simon sounded puzzled. 'A financial advisor?' He sounded sceptical. 'What exactly?'

'I don't know. All I do know is that she couldn't face something.'

'Something?'

Knowing she wouldn't stop at half an answer Simon waited for her to explain.

'Disgrace,' she filled in. 'She couldn't face disgrace. It's a common reason for a suicide.'

'I thought depression would have been the main reason for suicide.'

'You'd be surprised at how often a person can't face criminal accusation, financial hardship, exposure.'

'Oh. OK. So disgrace – what for? Do you mean professionally – that she'd done something shameful?'

'Maybe.' She plunged on. 'But I think our Gina was too canny for that and she'd understand the pitfalls only too well. I don't think it was a professional thing at all. I suspect it was something much more personal. I think somewhere there will be compromising pictures of her just like there were of Patrick Elson. I don't know who set her up, how or why. The thing is, Simon, it's easy to understand a child's mind. The two bullies simply hated Patrick because he was something they weren't. He was clever. And they had help. But Gina – how was she set up? By whom, why and how? What did they have to gain by it? Revenge? She did her best, defended the criminal fraternity.' Thoughts were buzzing through her mind now even as she was speaking. What if the punishment had been set up because she had failed them? The name Silver still sprang to mind. And then she recalled Lewinski's visits to Gina's office and the threats he had made.

Simon was still plodding behind her in his thoughts. 'OK. Well, whatever, have a good time.' He couldn't resist a further dig. 'Enjoy your dinner with Al Capone.'

Putting the phone down, she could still hear him chuckling, but at least Martha felt happier.

But that feeling began to wear off by the time she was dressing for the evening in dark trousers, ankle boots and a cream wool jacket. Now her mind was not on Gina Marconi but had returned, like a homing pigeon, to Alex. She felt intense frustration. What was happening? What had the test shown? Had her hunch been correct? And even if she was right, had Mark Sullivan found anything else at post-mortem? Obviously, as the funeral was in a few days' time and Alex was expected back at work, it could be nothing that was either open to question or could potentially incriminate him. But was it still something that would leave a cloud over his head? Had Erica left something behind that could incriminate her husband? What would be the fallout from that? Was it possible their friendship could *ever* resume exactly where it had left off?

In frustration Martha was tempted to give in to her red hair instinct and hurl her hair brush across the room. But down the hall she could hear Sukey's voice. And it sounded like for once she was sticking up for herself. Martha knew that voice. It was Little Miss Stubborn, the voice Sukey adopted when she'd been pushed too far and was digging her heels in.

Look out, Pom, she thought, smiling at herself in the mirror. She was tempted to listen, to open her door just a crack, pick up on the words. She could hear Pom's voice, possibly less strident than usual. Or was she imagining it? She listened harder. Sukey's was definitely the louder. And firmer.

Then one sentence wafted along the landing and Martha was tempted to whoop for joy. Sukey's immoveable voice, cold, hostile, challenging. 'I don't agree.' Uncompromising too. Yay! Was Sukey actually waking up to what a prick the boy was?

She waited for a response from him. When it came it was quiet, laced with a threat. 'Well, if you fail and that's the end you'll only have yourself to blame.'

She could listen no more. She so wanted to burst in, put her arm round her daughter and defend her, support her, but Sukey would have been furious.

And so she left her alone but, once dressed, hair brushed into submission, she knocked on her door. 'I'm just off out.' Immediately the door was tugged open and her daughter stood there with her unmistakably tear-streaked face. 'Where?'

'I'm going for dinner with a financial advisor.'

'What?' If she'd said she was having dinner with the Pope her daughter couldn't have been more astonished.

Martha gave a half-smile meant to be reassuring. 'You heard.'

'And what do you need a financial advisor for?'

'Investments,' Martha said airily and watched Sukey's face turn suspicious.

'And who is this financial advisor?'

That was when she realized, she need not have involved Simon at all. Her *daughter* intended to guard her. She chose her words very carefully. 'He's connected with a case I'm involved in. A suicide. I'm trying to find out why.'

Sukey's face twisted scornfully. 'And you think he's going to tell you, this . . .' She twiddled her fingers into speech marks. 'Financial advisor?'

'I don't know,' Martha confessed, 'but you know me. I'm fond of the truth. Clarity.'

Behind her daughter Pom was watching her very carefully. She'd thought his eyes were about to roll, his mouth twist into a snarl. But instead what she saw was a look of vulnerability. If she had been forced to interpret that look she would have guessed that if he could not control her daughter he was afraid he would lose her.

Oh, aren't lives complicated, she thought as she watched Sukey turn around and appraise her boyfriend in a cold stare. People are immeasurably unpredictable, complex and singular. There is no one category for a personality, instead lots and lots of permutations and anomalies, all of which are endlessly fascinating. A few weeks ago she had feared for her daughter's relationship. Now her fear was for Pom.

Martha transferred all her attention back to her daughter whose face was warm now she was focused on her mother. 'I know you, Mum,' she said and brushed her arm with her fingers, delicate as a butterfly landing. Then she laughed. 'Don't be late,' she said, wagging her finger as Martha never had done, having gone in for lax parenting.

And Martha echoed back a response by a raising of her eyebrows and a joke. 'I will.'

On her way out she passed Sam heading towards the front door. Sam, smelling unmistakably of aftershave and wearing a very clean sweater and well-fitting jeans. 'Off out?' she asked lightly and her son, footballing Sam, who had never shown any interest in the opposite sex, went bright red. At least the tips of his ears did, clashing nastily with his ginger hair.

She was already thinking ahead. Without Martin she was going to have to be the one to warn him about the wiles of women, about birth control, about the morning-after pill, paternity suits and the rest of the messy business that follows in the wake of the joy of sex.

For now she just patted him on the shoulder. 'Have a great time,' she said.

Her last thought as she closed the front door behind her was: *My twins are growing up.*

FORTY

Tuesday, 18 April, 8 p.m.

Unsurprisingly, as Martha had already marked Ivor Donaldson down as a man with no manners, she arrived at The Granary first. He was ten minutes late. And the ten minutes passed surprisingly slowly. She felt like a sad woman who'd been stood up. Maybe she had. Maybe the 'date' had been a tease. Maybe £50,000 hadn't been enough of a temptation. She sat at a table for two, tonic water in a tall glass with ice and a slice.

But eventually he breezed in, in a dark suit, rings flashing, ostentatiously glancing at the Rolex on his wrist.

OK, she wanted to say, *I've noticed it. Now tuck it away.*

'Sorry, love,' he said as he sat down. And it was that epithet that increased her dislike of him tenfold.

'That's OK,' she answered sweetly and put a bite in the tail. 'The wallpaper's interesting.'

He did a double blink, apparently unsure whether she was being ironic. Then he gave a loud laugh full of capped teeth. 'Wasn't sure,' he began, and Martha saw he still wasn't. Good. She wanted him on the hop, unable to put a finger on what she was up to. And she didn't want him to find out either.

'So,' he said when he'd ordered a whisky, 'you want to make some investments.' He could not disguise the little gleam in his eye at the thought of money – more money. And yet more money.

'I've got fifty grand – well, actually I want to invest more – but I want a high return. The interest rate is hopeless these days.'

She was watching him, trying to gauge his interest.

'Pooh.' Donaldson blew out his cheeks. 'Interest rates. Tell me about it.' He wafted a plump little hand, Rolex still exposed. 'I can get you a lot more than that, Mrs Gunn.' He'd taken a quick glance at her ring finger. 'And tax-free.'

She put her elbows on the table in spite of hearing her mother's staccato *'tut tut'* quite distinctly in her ear. 'What are your charges, Mr Donaldson?'

He wasn't in the least bit fazed by her bluntness. 'Ten, twelve per cent,' he said quickly, eyeing her to gauge her reaction. 'Depends.'

She nodded. 'Over?'

'Three years minimum.'

'And if I need access to funds?'

All the time she was trying to imagine Gina Marconi dealing with this guy. How had he fixed a hold over her? How had he put her in a position where she would choose death knowing what legacy her decision would leave behind? Wounds that would never heal.

And then she caught a whiff of it, in the way Donaldson was eyeing her up. Speculatively, greedily. Not because he wanted sex with her but because he wanted her money. She had hinted at fifty K but let him think there was plenty more where that had come from. He was a man who would always want something out of a woman.

When he had looked at Gina, what had he wanted? Oh, Mr Donaldson, she thought. You are giving yourself away.

But the question was stubborn. How had he done it, gained control over a woman with such experience of criminals? Or had it been that very experience that had let her down, tripped her up? Had she thought she could handle it without realizing how deep the waters were? Had she paddled right out of her depth?

She met Donaldson's dark gaze and felt he was being just as speculative as she was. 'Why are you really here, Martha Gunn?' His voice was oily smooth, menacing.

That was when two things happened simultaneously. The door to the restaurant swung open and Simon Pendlebury walked in, but just before that she had felt a chilling, paralysing fear. Donaldson was on to her and she had no defence. Except . . .

Simon was leaning against the bar, pretending not to know her or see her. Instead he was ordering a drink and flirting with the waitress.

His very presence gave Martha confidence. She decided to play it straight. 'You knew Gina Marconi.'

The look he tossed back at her was mocking. 'I didn't realize a coroner's remit was so broad or so detailed.'

So, the gloves were off.

'My remit,' she said, deliberately averting her eyes from Simon, 'is to find out why a beautiful, clever young woman with everything to live for gets up in the middle of the night, puts her clothes on, leaves her mobile phone by the side of the bed and drives into a wall at speed, destroying her life and the lives of those who loved her.'

His response was unfazed, mocking and chilling. 'Who knows?'

She didn't answer.

He regarded her steadily and then gave a little smirk. 'An interesting evening,' he said and stood up. 'I'll pay the bill on the way out,' he said. 'Thank you so much.'

Martha simply smiled. It was stupid but she felt she had one over on him because *he* might know who *she* was but he hadn't realized Simon was keeping an eye on her. Or had he? He'd left pretty abruptly and soon after Simon had arrived.

Simon wandered across, mischief in his eyes. 'Abandoned, Martha?'

'Oh, shut up,' she said. 'He was right on to me and I've learnt nothing.'

'Haven't you?'

'He's learnt more about me,' she said. 'He knew exactly who I was and what I was after.'

'But you've rattled him?'

'I'd like to think so but I very much doubt it.'

Outside the restaurant they heard a car rev up and speed away.

FORTY-ONE

After Ivor Donaldson left The Granary, Simon glanced at Martha awkwardly. 'Don't suppose you need babysitting now?'

She shook her head. They had a quick drink together and parted, Simon still, apparently, in happy-happy mood. Outside he kissed her lightly on the cheek; she climbed into her car and he into his, waving through the open window as he navigated the narrow archway back out on to the road.

Back at the White House, Sam's car wasn't in the drive; Sukey's red Mini was parked in exactly the same place as it had been three hours before when Martha had left.

There was no sound from their rooms.

Martha returned downstairs and sat with a goodnight glass of wine, thinking to herself. It was at moments like this, the house quiet, Sam and Sukey safe, that she allowed herself to dream. The log-burning stove was still alight and she put another log on it, watched the sparks drift upwards, kicked her shoes off and tucked her feet underneath her on the generously sized sofa.

There was plenty to occupy her mind but sometimes in the day events jumbled themselves together – the two suicides, Erica Randall's death. She still didn't know what the post-mortem and subsequent results would prove. Probably inconclusive, she thought glumly. Then there was Sukey's awkward relationship, Sam and his emerging rather belatedly into adulthood. In the quiet of her home and an empty room she could put things into perspective, fit the puzzles together, analyse each event separately. See a way through.

These were her treasured times, the times when she felt truly at peace.

She heard the front door open and close very gently. Sam walked into the room. 'Hi,' he said. He had a mark of very pink lipstick on his left cheek and a suspicion of more around his mouth. Martha smiled up at him and he came and sat in the chair beside her as she'd hoped he would. She felt a wave of affection for this lovely young man – her son who always reminded her of Martin. He was so like his father.

'Did you have a good night?'

'Yeah.' He scratched his head, rubbed his cheek, smeared the lipstick. 'Yeah. I enjoyed it.'

'Go anywhere nice?'

'Yeah,' he said again. 'A film and then on to Nando's. You know – nowhere special. And you?'

'Even less special,' she admitted. 'Dinner, which didn't quite materialize, with a financial advisor.'

Sam looked appalled. 'God, that sounds awful. Really boring.'

She laughed. 'It was rather, except Simon Pendlebury turned up thinking he was my knight in shining armour.'

Sam made a face.

'You don't like him?' she asked.

He shook his head. 'Do you?'

She gave a smothered yawn. 'Put it like this,' she said, setting the now-empty wine glass down on the table. 'He's beginning to grow on me.'

Sam gave a wise nod as though he was some ancient guru who understood these things.

'And now,' she said, rising, 'it's time for me to go to bed. I'm interviewing a young lad in the morning who's lost his mother. And I have an inquest on another boy.'

'Ouch,' Sam responded. 'I'd hate to do your job. Always dealing with death.'

'I don't see it like that. And you?'

'Training,' he said, 'and more training. The new manager's keen on us upping our fitness levels so we're expected to turn up for every single training session. He's very ambitious.'

She laughed. 'It's paying off, though.'

Sam nodded, serious now. 'Yeah,' he said. 'Stoke City are back where they belong, in the Premier League. But you know what they say – the higher you climb . . .'

'Mm. And don't forget the other cheery mantra. *Those whom the Gods wish to destroy . . .*'

Sam nodded then looked away. 'People think it must be wonderful – life in the fast lane – but . . .' He suddenly looked affronted. 'Do you know?'

She put her head to one side.

'Someone on Twitter said how they hated my freckles.'

She gave a sigh and smothered a giggle.

'I can't help having freckles.'

'No.'

'You know what pisses me off, Mum?'

She nodded. She already knew.

Why was one twin so perfect while the other shouldered the flaws for both of them? To which there was no answer. She merely gave him a hug. 'Goodnight, darling.'

'Night, Mum.'

FORTY-TWO

Wednesday, 19 April, 9.30 a.m.

Rather unexpectedly, considering she'd been rumbled, Ivor Donaldson rang Martha in the morning asking if she'd come to any decision about the investments. 'Not yet,' she said, stalling him for now. 'I need to think about it.' She couldn't work him out. Surely as he knew who she was he must have realized the investments story was simply a ruse to speak to him?

She could, she knew, have asked Simon for advice. If anyone understood the complexities of financial management and investment he surely did, but she'd pestered him enough for now. Leave him alone.

*　　*　　*

Eleven o'clock brought Terence Marconi in with his grandmother. Bridget appeared to have recovered some of her equilibrium. She was smartly dressed in a pair of well-fitting black trousers and a black and white striped sweater. She wore little jewellery but her air of dignity suited her. Terence was in his school uniform, dark blue and black. He looked less self-conscious this time but clung to his grandmother's hand as though she was a lifeline and he was about to drown. He gave Martha a tentative smile, met her eyes for a while longer than he needed to. Was she imagining a surreptitious message from an eight-year-old?

Martha decided she should take her cue from Bridget, who spent some time sitting down in the chair, fiddling with her handbag straps, removing her jacket, generally fussing and stalling. Finally she was still and looking across at Martha. Then she gave her a bittersweet smile.

'Terence and I have had a talk,' she began. The boy was taking his cue from his grandmother. He gripped her hand even tighter.

Bridget bent down and opened the fastening on her handbag, pulled out an A4 brown envelope. Martha already knew what it would contain. She met Bridget's eyes. Bridget nodded and Terence looked at the floor. They were both waiting for her to look at the pictures. She pulled them out – three photographs – and the contents made her gasp. If that was Gina she was practically unrecognizable. She looked like a . . .

Martha met Bridget's eyes but Gina's mother simply nodded.

'It rather explains things, doesn't it?'

Gina was wearing scraps of garments, bits of cheap red satin, nipples exposed, tiny bit of lace, split at the crotch, her dark pubic hair visible, making the picture even more obscene.

In the second photograph, her legs splayed, Gina looked drunk, with wet, whorish lips. The man with her was at the point of penetration, Gina's legs wrapped around him, urging him on. The detail was remarkable and intrusive. Full colour. What had they given her to make her like this? Cocaine? Rohypnol? Ecstasy? Alcohol? Worst of all she was wearing her barrister's wig, lopsided in a parody of her court appearances. She could never have worked as a barrister again. The pictures could not have been more damning. They were awful. Lipstick smeared on like jam on a toddler's face, legs apart like a desperate whore. What had turned her into that?

Who had been behind the shutter? Or had the camera been set up remotely?

And Martha could see every pornographic detail in glorious Technicolor.

She moved to the next one. Gina, wearing different scraps of clothing this time. *So there had been more than one occasion.* She was on her knees, her mouth closed around . . . She could only see the man's torso, slim, muscular, skin tone a light coffee.

Martha looked away.

But she was being asked to look at them and understand. Not turn away but face it.

So . . . what now?

She looked at each of the photographs again and then slipped them back in the envelope, looked across at Bridget. And the three of them – even if Terence was only eight and they had kept the worst of the pictures from him – all knew the contents of the envelope would have destroyed everything Gina Marconi had held dear: lover, mother, son, profession. If the tabloids had got hold of these, even with modesty strips over the most explicit bits, Julius's career too would have gone down the plughole unless he had distanced himself from her post-haste.

Someone had planned this. They had set her up and recorded the occasion.

Martha thought back to the man in the picture. He had a body that would create waves on the internet. Muscular. Olive skinned. Black or very dark brown curly hair. Possibly Moroccan? Algerian? Even Italian? You couldn't see his face but his body was enough. Physique powerful. But who was he?

Bridget answered her silent question. 'We don't know him,' she said while Terence shook his head, mute.

'I've never seen him before in my life.' The boy's expression was disgust.

'Someone set this up,' Martha said. 'They wanted to destroy your daughter.'

Terence was now fighting to hold back the tears. 'Mum,' he said. It was all he could manage and that one appeal made Martha realize she owed something to him and to his grandmother.

Question: Is a coroner a sort of avenging angel?
Answer: Sometimes.
'May I keep these?'
Bridget nodded.
'Would you mind if I let the police see them?'
Bridget shook her head.
Martha reached out with two hands, one on each of their shoulders. 'We can suppress this,' she said. 'It need not come out in the inquest. There's no point and it would defeat your daughter's last hope. For privacy and dignity.'
Bridget let out a long sigh of relief. 'Thank God,' she said.
'You've been very brave and . . . very trusting bringing these to me. Thank you.'
Bridget hadn't finished. 'The little boy? Patrick – the one who jumped off the A5 bridge?'
Martha nodded.
'And the policeman's wife?'
Startled now, Martha could hardly make any response. She was frozen – paralysed. 'I read in the paper,' Bridget continued, 'that they thought she was mentally unbalanced and threw herself downstairs deliberately.' Her eyes were watchful. 'I wondered if there was a connection.'
'I don't think so.'

FORTY-THREE

To have any chance of suppressing this vile pornography, Martha needed to know who the man in the pictures was. At one time she could have clicked her fingers and Alex would have identified him within minutes. But . . .

She needed to be resourceful.

So she picked up the phone, spoke to Curtis Thatcher and described the man in the pictures, without giving away any detail. 'Do you know of anyone fitting that description?'

'No.' He sounded puzzled. 'It certainly doesn't sound like Lewinski.'

'I didn't think it fitted his description.'

'Do you think it's important? Does it have any bearing on Gina's . . .' His voice tailed off.

'It might. I think so. I have some photographs of them together.' No need to enlarge.

He was hesitant for a moment, as though thinking. Then he added, 'She did have a couple of funny phone calls in those last few days. She'd shut the door so I couldn't overhear. But that's not unusual. Clients have a right to privacy. I didn't intrude.' And Martha could hear his regret, that maybe he should have done, that maybe that intervention could have saved her life.

How?

The word stumped in angrily and clumped away down the corridor of regret.

When she had seen the pictures Gina had known, as Martha understood now. Her life was over. It wasn't just the pictures – it was that lascivious look of relish, captured so graphically, that had made her face look so dissolute, so debauched. Yet recognizable. The horrible, tacky scraps of material, a bra with holes for the nipples, a G-string. Cheap, nasty. The barrister's wig. Those pictures, she knew, would have flashed around social media quicker than the speed of light, circumventing the world in the time it took to blink an eye, making her a pariah to everyone. The *Have you seen . . .?* which lasts for a minute and the 100,000 shares which ensures it lasts a lifetime.

Her mood was sober as she put the phone down. It immediately rang again. And the voice was so familiar it made her heart skip.

'Martha.'

'Alex?'

They spoke simultaneously.

'How are you?'

'I'm sorry about your wife.'

It was Alex who put the conversation back to one-to-one rules. 'I'm all right, thank you.' But there was a distance in his voice that had never been there before – even in their early days of working together. It was as though moss had grown over a wall, concealing the stones and the cracks between, smoothing over rough surfaces with polite exchanges.

'I understand that you made a suggestion to Mark Sullivan.'

'I did.'

Silence.

'It appears you were right.'

One of the times when she could feel no joy in being *right*.

'I . . .' He couldn't say it, instead switching subject. 'The funeral's next Thursday.' A pause. 'I don't suppose many people will attend. Erica didn't have many friends.'

And because Martha had so much she wanted to say to him she continued on the same vein. 'No family?'

'Her mother, of course. Her father left years ago. I don't have contact details for him. A sister who couldn't stand her and two elderly grandparents who are so demented they probably wouldn't know whose funeral they were attending.' It was an attempt at a joke. 'Erica was tricky, you know.'

'Yes – you've said.'

'It wasn't her fault.'

'No.'

Alex briefly cleared his throat. It sounded an apology for what he was about to say next. 'This is so difficult. I wish we could speak face-to-face. I'm no good on the phone.'

Martha paused before responding. She had so much to say to him and similarly felt she could not speak. When she did find the words they were the wrong ones. 'I don't think it's a good idea for us to meet up, Alex. Not right now, anyway. I mean, our . . .' She stumbled over the word but blundered on regardless: 'Friendship. That was the reason I asked David Steadman to look into Erica's death and handle the inquest. It wouldn't have been fair.' It burst out of her then. Unrehearsed, spontaneous, heartfelt. 'I couldn't have been impartial, Alex. You must know that.'

The silence on the other end was thick as velvet.

And now she didn't know what to say. Oh, fuck, she thought. When did life and relationships get so bloody complicated?

Finally he spoke. Or at least cleared his throat. 'Umm. This is difficult for me, Martha. I wish . . .' His voice was gruff.

What do you wish, Alex? Could she have coaxed it out of him?

She sensed whatever it had been, he was not going to say it. Maybe never would now.

'I'm sorry,' he said, 'sorry about everything.' And he put the phone down, leaving her reflective. She couldn't pretend there was nothing between them, nor did she want to. It had been a long time since Martin had died and she had largely been content on her own, focusing on bringing up the twins. But now she felt a fierce longing to be with Randall, and it hurt because the murky waters that lay between them were never going to clear.

And if, as he seemed to have hinted, her hunch was indeed right and Mark Sullivan had proved it, those waters, murky as they were, could get a whole lot murkier.

FORTY-FOUR

I t took Martha a while to move. She had been sitting still for more than ten minutes, ten minutes of paralysis both in thought and deed. Then she shook herself. This was no good. She had a job to do and she would do it. She needed to pass on the details of these photographs. The police needed to know. Would they be able to prosecute the man in the pictures or the person who had photographed the session or even the person who had sent the images to her?

She doubted it.

What she didn't expect was that someone would approach her.

She couldn't know that at that very moment in a murky corner of a beautiful town there was a coffee bar. Not one of the chains, not a Starbucks or a Costa, but somewhere privately owned, up a tiny, narrow cobbled side street to the side of Waterstones known, tellingly, as Grope Lane where plots had been hatched for centuries. Sitting in the corner, even with his clothes on the man in the photograph would have been easily recognizable. Tall, muscular, handsome in a ballsy, dissolute sort of way. And the man speaking to him? Recognizable too. 'Put these pictures in the right place and we've got enough to compromise her.'

Martha would have recognized the pictures, known exactly when and where they had been taken. But what she would not have known was that they had been Photoshopped. Only a touch, only a tinge, a matter of an inch or so, but it looked as though she and Alex Randall were practically welded to each other. His lips were a hair's breadth from her cheek. But what they needn't have Photoshopped or done anything else with was the look they were exchanging. They had been in a public place – the quarry. It had been a hot day and they had shared a picnic. This was no bedroom and they were not panting to rip each other's clothes off, but looks can speak more eloquently than a thousand words and the look was unmistakable. But while she was a widow DI Randall had, at the time, been a married man. And this picture had been taken before his wife had died in suspicious circumstances.

This photograph would not help his career or the investigation into Erica's death. It would compromise her too. That was the way *they* were thinking.

But for now, in the steamy little coffee bar, both men were simply enjoying the power these pictures gave them. Victor Stanley was a minor thief. He'd also been accused of rape – quite unfounded from his point of view; the girl had been gagging for it. And, with a bit of persuasion, had withdrawn her allegation anyway. She'd nearly got into trouble for wasting police time. Stanley's speciality was hanging around rich women, compromising and blackmailing them with the help of alcohol and sometimes a bit of chemical help. There's plenty of stuff out there. With his good looks and deceitful manner it was an easy and lucrative business. He tanned easily, was athletic and strong, a good swimmer and fit. Women always noticed him as he noticed them. He wasn't too fussy, which helped his cause, and he was perfectly capable of seducing them with practically a hundred per cent success. He was what you might call an actor – both a romantic lead and a minor villain. Don't women just love a bad guy? He played all parts to perfection. Trouble was no one, least of all the women who were his target, realized it was all an act.

Underneath Stanley was mean-spirited, emotionally frigid, narcissistic, vain and self-absorbed. But boy, could he put on an act. And he could produce an erection practically to order.

That helped.

Equally at home in a tux or a diving suit, casual chinos or smart, navy business suit, his age also worked for him. He was forty-six, but he could look thirty-six or fifty-six. He was a chameleon – that was what Ivor Donaldson called him, The Chameleon. With Donaldson's access to the wealthy, the lonely, the frustrated and the bored, he would form the introductions and The Chameleon would play his part. It was a lucrative business. Between them they would extract money as easily as squeezing juice from a lemon – with the right equipment – and Victor Stanley had that all right. In fact, he had all the gifts nature could bestow and looked after them with some hefty workouts at the gym.

To help matters along Victor Stanley had a little issue with the coroner. Years ago she had directed the police towards a finding of vehicular homicide. And the person who had been subsequently convicted had been a friend named Harris. OK, she had not actually convicted him and sentenced him to a nasty long stretch in a prison built for villains in the Victorian era, but his mate, Harris, had just been a car mechanic and the bloody thing that he'd worked on had crashed. On the A49. OK, the brakes had failed. OK, a few other people had died and a couple had been hurt. But Martha had come down on him like a ton of bricks at the inquests. She had well and truly pointed the finger at the person who had knowingly or carelessly fitted substandard brakes forgetting, as his mate had said, that they were half the price. But his mate had ended up going to prison – poor defence, useless lawyer. He'd got her already. In prison his mate, Harris, had died of drug-related hepatitis which was, in his mind, very unlucky. But his mate had been clean before he'd gone to prison. The coroner, he believed, had executed him. So he owed her one. Little red-haired cow.

Look out, Coroner Gunn. I'm coming for you.

He was a guy who liked to settle his scores.

And he always had a grudge against the police. And lawyers.

Two birds with one stone was the way he looked at it when he'd seen the pictures snapped of the pair of them, sitting together. Always worth having someone with a camera keeping an eye on people, particularly detectives off their guard – and in this case the coroner. They should have been more careful. You never knew who was watching. Nice warm sunny day, she in a sleeveless dress, he in a short-sleeved shirt. Sometimes these schemes worked better than others. But one needed apprentices to train up and since Jack was in prison he'd sort of taken the two lads under his wing. It helped that Jodi Silver was a looker. Bloody gorgeous and canny too. And lonely without her husband. So he'd taken it on himself to coach Warren and Sean in 'life sciences' – teach them how to make someone hurl themselves off a bridge rather than face continuing torment. The only thing that had gone ever so slightly wrong had been that silly trip out to the coroner's office and scratching the message on the car. But Sean had insisted. And maybe learning a bit about the business or perhaps because they were, underneath, a chip off the old block, when they'd heard he intended to give the coroner a warning both boys had wheedled Stanley. 'Go on, let us have a go.' And when he hadn't obliged they'd tried a threat. 'Take us out with you. Otherwise we could be telling our dad on our next visit that you're bonking his wife.'

He'd given in. What harm could it do? Though what they could have had against the coroner was beyond him. Maybe nothing. Maybe it was just a trip for the fun of it.

FORTY-FIVE

Wednesday, 19 April, 2 p.m.

Patrick's inquest was always going to be a difficult occasion, but just before it started Martha had spent some time with Amanda and her sister and helped them compose themselves.

'The police have an idea how, where and when he was victimized. None of this,' she assured them, 'needs to come out in the inquest.' They clutched each other's hands and Amanda gave a watery smile.

'There will almost certainly be a conviction by the police but Patrick's name need not be mentioned.'

'Thank you.'

'So now shall we go through?'

Jericho did his duty, thoughtfully providing them with a glass of water each before standing back, chin in the air, standing to attention as though on military parade.

Both Patrick's mother and his aunt were dressed in dark skirt suits. Amanda, in particular, now wore a determined, dogged air, chin up, teeth gritted, lips set firm, hands gripping the arms of the chair. She was going to get through this. Martha had already performed the preliminaries to the court and now she invited them to speak on the boy's behalf.

As they spoke she listened. It gave her a chance to get a handle on the boy she would never meet. She would never see the bright-eyed lad with big teeth who had grinned at her from a school photograph. She would never be impressed by his skill with mathematics and physics, never hear him recite *The Lion and Albert* (with actions) from beginning to end. This was their chance to bring him back to life. Suicide wreaks vengeance on the family, trailing miserable guilt in its wake, only conscious of their failings. They should have picked up . . . But as Martha listened to Amanda Elson's description of her son, her thoughts tracked away, searching for some other explanation so she could avoid adding to the burden of bereavement with a verdict of suicide. But facts were incontrovertible facts.

He had been alone on the bridge. No one had pushed him. Eileen Tinsley had seen him reach the second rung, balance on the top rail and dive down on to the road. No hand had pushed him. And there were plenty of other witnesses who all testified to the same sequence of events. What else could it have been?

Freddie Trimble, still in sports jacket but wearing a black tie, gave his testimony in a clear, slow description, using notes he had made. Both Amanda and Melanie smiled as he evoked the solemn boy.

Mark Sullivan's evidence was more difficult to handle. Martha had asked him not to list his injuries or mention the signs of abuse. That, she felt, would have been much too harrowing. She'd asked him simply to state what Patrick's cause of death had been.

'He died of shock and haemorrhage due to multiple injuries caused by contact with several motor vehicles which were travelling at speed.' He eyed Martha, who nodded.

And she had no option but to give the cause of death as suicide while the balance of his mind was disturbed. The court was silent in response.

On occasions Martha made some social comment but in Patrick's case the only comment she could have made would have been to expose the exploitation of a boy by two children the same age, encouraged into violent acts and the manipulation of a minor by a felon.

On the way out she had a word with Mark Sullivan. 'Thanks,' she said. 'You handled that really sensitively.'

'I'd like to say it's a pleasure,' he said, 'but that sort of case is just tragic.'

She nodded in agreement.

'On a more cheerful note,' he said, 'there's nothing to implicate Alex in his wife's fall. And,' he said, his hand on her shoulder, 'your hunch paid off. Well done you.'

'Well, I thought it very unlikely that you would link Christopher's congenital abnormality with Erica's mental state.'

'You're darned right,' he said admiringly. 'I would never have thought of that.'

'Maybe I know more about DI Randall's home circumstances?'

His eyes twinkled. 'Maybe you do, Martha.'

'Can I have a quick word with you on another matter?'

He nodded, wondering what on earth was coming next.

Thursday, 20 April, 3 p.m.

She hadn't meant to go. She had no business going. It was not a good idea. In fact, it was a really bad idea. There was no place for her here in any role. Not as coroner or friend or even nosey bystander. She knew few people would be there which meant her presence would be noticed. She didn't even know why she was going. What did she hope to achieve? What was she playing at?

She went anyway.

The funeral service was to be held at the crematorium. Possibly it only made things worse that it was a glorious April day, daffodils well out, wafting in the breeze, lambs playing in the field. England, and particularly Shropshire, is at its best on such a beautiful spring day. It was a day when no one would want to leave the world. Erica Randall had been forty-six years old, she learned by reading through the order of service. The photograph on the front, she guessed, had been taken a few years ago.

Before . . .

Erica Randall wore a determined look, dark eyes gazing outwards. Martha studied it and saw a woman who could have been beautiful had she not worn that look, determined to take on the world. She guessed even before her mental problems that

Erica Randall would not have been a comfortable person to live with.

Out of respect for Alex's wife, Martha had worn a dark grey suit. Not black. Not deep mourning. She'd held back there. That would have been too hypocritical.

She sat down at the back and bowed her head.

The organ music was muted, soft and recorded and, like supermarket tunes, seemed to have no beginning, no middle and no end. It just dribbled out like a musical stream, flowing and unthreatening. Martha did not recognize it.

The coffin with just two wreaths of lilies and roses on top was wheeled in. Coffins usually seem too small to contain a person one has known and loved but this one looked too big for her image of Erica Randall. Alex trailed behind with an older woman Martha guessed to be Erica's mother. She took a surreptitious glance at him. His face was set as though in granite in an expression she knew well. Gritted teeth. Like Patrick's mother and aunt yesterday, this was something he just had to get through. He didn't look either to his right or to his left but straight ahead so he didn't see her. He was wearing a black suit, black tie, white shirt and looked taller and thinner and older than when she had last seen him. Surprisingly behind Alex and, presumably, his mother-in-law, trailed both Paul Talith and Gethin Roberts in uniforms so well pressed they looked like members of the armed forces.

And now she noticed, three rows from the front, David Steadman, head bowed, and by his side Mark Sullivan. Whether both were there out of a sense of duty, loyalty or friendship she could only guess. Probably a mixture of all three.

The service began.

Alex gave the eulogy, his head also bowed, his words muffled, in a voice so quiet she had to strain to decipher what he was saying.

'My wife had her problems,' he said, suddenly looking up as though to have admitted this was a relief. 'She had been unhappy ever since the birth of our son, Christopher, who was born with a birth defect. He lived for less than an hour. Erica was never well after that. And now we know the truth.'

His eyes flickered across the front row and Martha saw him exchange a glance with Mark Sullivan, who almost smiled. Encouragement? Maybe.

Alex continued. 'It is only since Erica's death that we have any explanation for all that happened.' He looked up then and she read intense pain in his face. 'For everything that she went through. That carries with it a burden, a sense of failure, a sense of guilt that will stay with me.' His face was pale as he continued. 'I regret much of my poor wife's unhappy existence and . . .' Now he looked farther into the room and his head jerked back as he caught sight of Martha. His face was pinched and he was temporarily lost for words before continuing bravely. 'I shall remember Erica as she was in the early days, the days before she was sick, before Christopher. The happy days.' Perhaps lost in this past crevice, he smiled then and Martha was reminded of the moment in *Pilgrim's Progress* when Christian's burden rolls off his back. She caught a glimpse of an Alex who smiled, who looked younger, someone without cares as he finished his speech. 'Please,' he said, 'let's remember an Erica before our little boy, before illness, a happy, intelligent, beautiful . . .'

Martha slipped out of the crematorium. She didn't want to hear any more of this eulogy. Her last glance before exiting was Alex, still reading from his sheets of paper. He did not look up as she opened the door and passed through.

FORTY-SIX

The next few days were noteworthy by the lack of phone calls from anyone connected with either the two suicides or Erica Randall. Martha had released Patrick's body for burial and expected the funeral to take place in the next few days. She wondered when Erica's inquest would be closed and waited for either Alex, Mark Sullivan or David Steadman to let her know. There was a certain courtesy to be observed.

Her interest in the three cases was diluted by a sudden flurry of deaths due to what the newspapers were calling 'spring flu' which was, in fact, a cluster of viral infections that felled anyone with respiratory disease, other chronic illness or simple old age. The young, the sick and old were culled and it kept her busy.

On 21 April, the nation had celebrated the Queen's birthday (one of those not felled by the nasty little viruses) and Sukey came home alone, pale, tired and looking slightly depressed. Martha avoided the subject of Pom, though it was hard. A mother naturally frets about her children, however old they are. But, she told herself, her daughter would confide in her when she was ready. All she did was give her an extra-warm hug when she greeted her and murmured in her ear that she was always ready to listen, but the nearest Sukey got to confiding in her mother was the brief announcement that she had decided to accept the part in the soap and Dominic was currently drawing up the contracts.

Yay! Good, she cheered silently, giving her daughter a kiss but otherwise outwardly merely nodding her approval. She didn't want to put her off by being too enthusiastic. But she liked and trusted Dominic Pryce. He had come to stay once or twice, a sharp shooter in his forties who could read contracts like a horoscope, seemingly seeing right into the future where the wording would lead them and sniff out a dodgy clause. He was not above squeezing out a few extra pounds a week but also knew when to accept a lower offer that might lead to greater things. He had a number of production companies tucked in his belt and, Martha thought, was perceptive, appreciating both Sukey's talents but also her limitations. He also knew when to back off. He would have fumed at Pomeroy's interference but in the end would have assessed that the decision would be Sukey's. Knowing Dominic, he would have simply planted the one phrase: *Offers don't last forever.*

It was the theatrical equivalent of *plenty more fish in the sea.*

Sam, in the meantime, was saying nothing about the various signs she was picking up that he had finally discovered the opposite sex. Only a newcomer to that particular club could possibly imagine that the clues were invisible – the scent of perfume which clung to him on his late returns home, the smears of lipstick and when he had given her a lift, in his Fiesta, to collect her car, she had noticed a mascara rolled almost underneath the seat. It wasn't hers; neither was it his twin sister's. One of his friends had a younger sister called Rosalie whom, he had said gruffly, '*isn't too bad*'. And from that she was building up a picture. Her children were growing up fast, Martha thought. It wouldn't be too long before she would be living in the White House all alone.

And that thought chilled her.

The one bit of tangible news was about the damage done to her car. The police had shown her the images from her CCTV camera. They were too grainy to be sure but she thought the boy could well have been Sean Silver. It was her first sighting of these shadowy figures bent on destruction. The question was what on earth was all this to do with her? Why had they vandalized *her* car? Had they realized the depth of her interest in the two suicides?

She wondered when she would have an answer.

FORTY-SEVEN

Monday, 24 April, 10 a.m.

Martha didn't have to wait for long.

David Steadman was, by nature, like many coroners, a curious beast. He and Martha had known each other for years, sometimes working side by side in deaths that crisscrossed their borders. They pooled knowledge, shared information, met on various courses and had bumped into one another at various social events, and yet he retained this formality that was so stiff and starchy it made her want to giggle. Sometimes she even had to cough to try and disguise this unfortunate tendency. She wondered why he'd rung and wondered whether he had noticed her brief appearance at Erica's funeral.

'Martha.' He sounded almost disapproving. 'It was good of you to pass this case on to me.'

Not exactly good, she thought, *more expedient*. But still . . .

'It's proved most interesting.'

'I'm grateful to you,' she said. 'I've worked closely with DI Randall. I would have found it . . . difficult. And in the light of Doctor Sullivan's findings almost impossible to conduct the inquest. But it didn't stop me speculating.'

'Quite. I understand you made the suggestion to Mark Sullivan that he perform genetic tests.'

'That's right,' she said. 'I put together the fact that Mrs Randall had had a child with anencephaly and thought it was worth him testing Mrs Randall's blood for a genetic defect.'

'Which he found,' he said. 'And which explains everything: her son's death, her poor mental state and probably loss of consciousness which in turn caused her to fall.'

'Tragic. Had she ever had a brain scan?'

'No. I thought that might be something I could pick up on. Her strange behaviour was put down to prolonged puerperal psychosis rather than being properly investigated.'

'But with all the investigations in the world there would have been nothing anyone could have done.'

'Maybe one day, Martha, we'll have genetic engineering for such conditions.'

Her outlook was more glum. 'More likely we'll have more tests done to pregnant women and eugenics.'

'Oh, really.' He snorted and continued in the same vein. 'I did discuss with DI Randall that there was possibly a case for medical negligence against one or more of the psychiatrists whose help he sought, but he isn't interested.'

'So how is he?'

Steadman paused. 'It's hard to say really. He's quite a . . . contained man, isn't he?'

'Yes.' *Most of the time. The times when nothing is bursting out.*

'Will you be homing in on the failure to diagnose at the inquest?'

'No,' he said. 'It'll do neither Mrs or Mr Randall any good now. And it isn't what he wants. But . . .'

She might have known there would be a '*but*'.

'I might have a few words to say about making an assumption of psychiatric illness before excluding physical disease. That would be appropriate,' he finished airily, 'don't you think?

'It's your case, David.' She was smiling. 'So your verdict will be . . .?'

'Natural causes. A bit unsatisfactory under the circumstances but there is no question of either homicide or suicide and even I baulk at the idea of dragging in medical negligence. There was a failure to diagnose but no one is to blame for Mrs Randall's death. However, it would be interesting to interview the psychiatrists Mrs Randall had been under, don't you think?'

'There would have been quite a few,' she mused. 'The DI has had a few moves in the last six years.'

'Quite,' he said. 'But the change in care came with a diagnosis firmly in place. Mrs Randall had, apparently, not had a fit or headaches or any other physical symptoms which might have led to a brain scan and the discovery of her condition.' He couldn't resist giving himself a swift pat on the back. 'I was most particular about asking DI Randall about this.' She could imagine his tight little lips curving in a self-congratulatory smile as he carried on with his summing up of Erica's death.

'She was not properly investigated for an organic cause for her odd behaviour. And we can understand why. The malformation of her son would be enough to account for prolonged grief.'

'But also it was a pointer,' she said, thinking, *poor Erica.* Aloud, saying, 'Poor woman.'

'Indeed,' Steadman said, pompously. 'A sad state of affairs and bound to have a negative knock-on effect on her husband. He will be feeling guilty that he didn't insist she seek medical opinion for a very long time, I'm sure.'

Thanks for that, Steadman.

He continued seamlessly. 'The funeral has, of course, as you know, already taken place.' So he had seen her there.

He finished with: 'And I've set a date for the final inquest. I don't know whether you'll feel you want to attend?'

'I don't think so.' She thanked him again and the conversation finished.

FORTY-EIGHT

Martha had been half expecting this. The envelope was exactly the same. And she had an idea what might be inside so she didn't open it but rang the police station and asked to speak to DS Talith. She couldn't face Alex. Not now, not yet. Not with this in her hands. But this little missive they'd sent her meant that she was getting close.

She had found the link between the criminal world, a

high-profile lawyer about to be exposed, a schoolboy being bullied
and worse, both resulting in what she called determined suicides.
And now it was up to her to move in, prove that connection without
publicly sullying the reputations both had died to preserve. Once
she had learned the full ugly truth about the reasons behind these
two apparently unrelated deaths, she could hold Gina's inquest
and Amanda and her sister could arrange Patrick's funeral. Leave
their dear ones privacy and space to grieve. In camera. There was
no need for the public to know. The person who had orchestrated
all this was both clever and evil. For Gina he had wanted both
death and public humiliation. Not only her body but her soul, her
reputation and memory. And Patrick? He had got in the way of
two boys, apprentices. And he had . . . Martha could hardly bear
to think.

The weak link had been the two boys who had taken Patrick
Elson to their house. Thanks to the information from their teacher,
it had led her to connect the two suicides. But this envelope was
a warning. If Gina could be so manipulated, then she, Martha
Gunn, coroner of North Shropshire, was not proof against that
person. They were on to her. She was their next selected victim.

Right on cue there was a knock on the door. 'Martha.'

She could hardly believe it. Here he was, in person. 'I thought
Talith would come.'

He simply shook his head.

'How are you?'

He simply looked at her.

'I was sorry to hear about . . .'

'Yeah. You heard about the . . .?'

She pre-empted him. She knew. 'Yes, I did.' She tried to reassure him. 'When I put the two histories together, Christopher's
and Erica's, I just wondered whether there could be a connection.'
She cleared her throat. 'I don't think anyone could have known.'

He gave the vaguest hint of a smile. 'Are you defending the
medical profession or me, as her husband?' His tone was curious
rather than challenging. 'You think *I* should have picked up on it?'

'I'm not trying to defend anyone,' she said steadily, 'or let
anyone off the hook. I'm simply pointing out that with Erica's
psychiatric diagnosis after such a tragedy I don't think a doctor
or you would have looked for another cause for her behaviour.'

There was a pause before he spoke again, as though he had been digesting her words. 'But you did. Mark told me you had suggested we test for a genetic link.'

She was silent.

'I still think,' he said, 'I should have trusted her character better. I think,' he said again, 'that I shall always feel guilty that I didn't. I failed her, Martha. I let her down.' He crossed to the window and stared out. 'I should have picked up on it, had more faith in her. Truth is, Martha, after Christopher's sad, brief little life ended, we were both destroyed. When her grieving became prolonged I lost patience with her. After all, we'd both been through the same thing.'

'Not quite,' she said. 'A woman holds a child inside her for the months of pregnancy and then has a labour.'

He turned. 'And a man has hopes for a son.'

'Yes.'

'I should have taken her to a doctor and insisted she be investigated. As it was I simply accepted the psychiatrist's opinion that she had changed because of our loss. It's an unfortunate coincidence, a horrible trick of nature that had a dreadful effect on both our lives. And now Erica is dead too. It's cruel.'

And she could do little but agree with him, her thoughts swirling round and round. *Poor woman, labelled mad, labelled bad, disliked by her husband.* 'So,' he said. 'Why the summons?'

She dropped her eyes to the envelope on the desk.

He nodded. 'Talith's filled me in very well.' He slipped on a pair of latex gloves and slid out the photographs. He looked at them carefully, one at a time. 'I see,' he said. 'I understand.'

She looked too at the obvious connection between two people. But when she met his eyes now that connection had vanished. Melted away like ice cream in a heat wave.

'Leave this to us,' he said. 'Leave it, Martha. Don't get involved.'

She met his gaze now without flinching. She could ride this one out.

'The link,' she said, 'I'm sure, is a man called Ivor Donaldson who is a financial advisor.'

'He's on our radar.'

He turned to leave. 'So that's that?' she demanded. 'You expect me to just leave it all to you?'

He turned back then, his eyes warm, his mouth twitching, hinting at a smile which never quite completed. 'We-ell,' he said. 'It would be a good idea but I can't say I expect it.'

And with that he left.

She hadn't even had the chance to speak her prepared neutral line. *It'd be great if we could meet up sometime.*

Agitated, she went into the kitchen, passing an affronted Jericho who considered the room his domain and the task of coffee-making his duty. But she needed to walk. To move. She had too much work on to stroll into town or even take a spin up Haughmond Hill but she did need to stretch her legs, get away from the four walls of her office. Breathe. She felt Jericho's eyes on her, reproachful, but couldn't find the right response. Then thought, *Why not the truth?*

'I needed to stretch my legs, Jericho,' she explained. But it didn't quite extinguish the reproachful look so she didn't offer to make him a coffee.

She strode around the garden for an hour breathing the fresh air deeply, only returning when the exercise had calmed her. Back in her office she closed her door firmly behind her. She needed to focus. And for that now she needed peace, quiet and privacy. She had an idea.

FORTY-NINE

Once safely inside, with no witnesses and no one likely to burst in, Martha drew a spider's web on a sheet of paper. In the centre she put Gina and Patrick. The victims. And the spider? The olive-skinned man who had reduced Gina Marconi to a whore. How had he done it? More importantly, who had introduced her to him? How? And why? Was he a criminal she had defended or failed to defend? And, Martha thought, why me? What do I have to do with this man? Those photos of her and Alex looking like lovers had been taken last summer. Long before these two suicides. So who else was in his sights, apart from her?

She recalled the man who had been with Gina on that night when their planets had brushed together. And that was it. He had been her escort. A handsome, suave man whose olive skin showed well against the white of his shirt. So Gina had paid for a male escort to the ball because Julius Zedanski was probably halfway across the world. Was it possible that Gina had mentioned her name, joked with her escort? *The lady with the red hair. That's the coroner.*

And that had been it? Enough to make her a person of interest? Or was it something else? Maybe he or one of his associates had had indirect dealings with her?

And now she knew a little more she wanted to understand the rest. Victor Stanley had been Gina's escort that night. And without realizing who she was tangling with, she had walked right in to what was so obviously a trap.

Martha frowned as she recalled the pictures.

What had they given her to make her like this? Cocaine? Rohypnol? The pictures could not have been more damning. She could never have worked as a barrister again.

Work was a welcome diversion and calmed her down, finding the rhythmic groove of more routine cases. Not all coroners' work is so dramatic.

She'd almost forgotten about the conflict when, at six o'clock, her mobile pinged with a message. *Enjoyed the other night. A friend of mine would love to meet up with you. Ivor D.*

She stared at her phone screen. *Will you walk into my parlour*, said the spider to the fly. It was an invitation to sup with the Devil.

She felt the sour taste of fear even as she tapped out her response. It was dangerous. It made no sense. It was stupid. She knew exactly who the friend was, knew she was putting herself at risk. Did she think she was cleverer than Ms Marconi? Did she think she had less to lose? Position, family et cetera, et cetera. As Gina had had a position, so did she. As Gina's had been destroyed, so could hers. She was no better, no wiser, no more in control than Gina Marconi had been and yet she knew her own nature. Blame half-Irish, half-Welsh. She was a risk taker, a rule breaker. She liked adventure and she liked the truth. And so she would do it. Find out how all this had happened. More than ever she wished she had Alex Randall to watch her back. But she didn't because paradoxically, now he was free, now they could be open about a friendship, he was further away from her than ever. And the photos could always be aired to indicate a relationship between them *while his poor, damaged wife was still alive. And then she'd died. Of natural causes, they'd said.*

Oh, Alex.

She responded to the text message with just the one word. *Saturday?*

So the trap was set. She knew exactly what she was doing. Or did she? She sure as hell knew *why* she was going. This persistent search for the truth behind the obfuscation. And to find that out she was walking not just into the lions' den but right into the lion's mouth close enough to pick between his teeth. And she had no one to look out for her – just as Patrick's mother had been at work blissfully unaware of her son's intent, Terence and Bridget had been asleep and Gina's fiancé halfway round the world reporting on others' desperate situations. She was similarly alone. If she got it wrong she knew what the consequences could be.

The image of the boy's face as described by the witnesses loomed in front of her, determined as he had stood on the rail of the A5 bridge looking at the traffic. Gina's face would have been similarly determined. And now, in the gilded mirror hanging on the wall near the door, she caught sight of her own face with that same look, gritty determination. That was where she was heading. To hell? Surely not. Not if she was on her guard. Forewarned. Forearmed.

Friends and relatives had painted the pictures but there was something she did not understand. While Gina had made enemies through her work, what interest could Victor Stanley possibly have had in one twelve-year-old boy? She was still missing some connection. Was it because he preyed sexually on young lads as well as available women? Or was there something else?

Before she could speculate further her mobile phone buzzed again. *Great. The Armoury? 8 p.m.*

She tapped out *Fine*.

The Armoury was an unusual choice for an intimate meeting. Almost a student pub, it wasn't particularly private but open plan and noisy. The food was great but the atmosphere was not exactly conducive to winkling out secrets. But . . . and when Martha realized this her feet went cold. It was somewhere where people could easily watch you, take photographs without being noticed because, being open plan, lots of people were taking pictures and selfies with their mobile phones ready to display to all their Facebook friends what a great life they were having. It was, in other words, public. Not intimate but jolly, reminding her of the student pubs she and Martin had frequented all those years ago, places in Birmingham, which fairly buzzed with the excitement of the young and which they had invented new names for: The White Swan became The Mucky Duck. The Gun Barrels became The Beer Barrels and so on. Silly student jokes.

But there was a difference. Geographically The Armoury was on the banks of the River Severn, its level currently high following heavy rain but held back by flood defences. As coroner she presided over about three drownings a year in that wicked old river. A friend on summer days when the folk of Shrewsbury strolled along its banks or sculled over its surface, but like a dog that bites its owner a river is wild, untamed. However picturesque, tempting artists and trippers, a river is still a river. Water can drown you. You can sink or swim. She had another thought that chilled her even further: if she had ever planned her own suicide it was possible this would have been the route she would have chosen. Not an overdose or a slash of the wrists, not a hanging or the suffocation of carbon monoxide poisoning from a car exhaust. It would be a dive into the river. Welcome water dragging her down, closing over her head.

And then rationale took over.

That, she thought, is not how he works. He needs time for his punishments to mature. To prolong and extract the suffering. She was supping with the Devil. She could do with back-up.

But she couldn't call on Simon Pendlebury again. Friendship was as far as they would go. She'd seen him out with his new secretary a year or so ago and knew his predilection for beautiful young women would always prove to be his weak spot. Seeing his attractiveness only too clearly through their eyes, rich, polished, handsome, they would succumb. But unlike poor little flawed Christabel who had been his previous squeeze, naive and blinded by love for him, in contrast Cerys Watkins, his secretary, could probably look after herself. She was a Welsh beauty with the loveliest hair Martha had ever seen, long, straight and black falling to her waist. Combined with the scarlet lipstick Cerys wore she had reminded her of a witch queen. But Cerys had an extra quality that made all the difference. She was clever and when Simon introduced her into the conversation he brought her name up with respect.

The real question was whether Cerys was strong enough to withstand the onslaught of Simon's two daughters.

So Simon was out and so was Alex.

'Martha,' she spoke aloud, 'this time you really are on your own.'

FIFTY

Saturday, 29 April, 7.25 p.m.

The day rolled round soon enough. Sam was distracted with a major match and Sukey had returned to university so Martha was alone as she showered and chose an outfit. What did one wear for such an ordeal? A chastity belt? She was aware she hadn't addressed the question of whether Gina had been drugged. She felt a strange mixture of excitement, exhilaration and apprehension. Which was winning, she couldn't even begin to guess.

The Armoury was not a dressy place but neither was it somewhere you would wear jeans. In the end she opted for some black trousers (safer in them than a skirt, surely?), high-heeled boots and a rather flashy pink jacket. She tried to erase the expression of anxiety from her face and replace it at least with something neutral but wasn't sure she'd quite succeeded. She left the house wishing she was already returning. She felt hugely apprehensive and scolded herself as she turned the car around in front of the White House. She paused for a moment. The name often made her smile and she could not see the name on the gate without remembering her and Martin's giggles at the name. Yet what else could you call a large, square house with a balcony central on the first floor and a snowflake facade? It might have a pretentious name but it was a beautiful place. High Georgian, perfect symmetry. When she and Martin had turned into the drive on that first occasion they had fallen in love with its square symmetry, the sash windows, the solid front door, portico over to protect visitors from rain. Standing outside it, they had decided then and there it was the place for them to bring up their twins. Once inside, the rooms had not disappointed. Square and neat, easy to furnish, light and bright. They had quickly imagined the function and colour scheme for each room. But she had not thought she would be inhabiting it alone.

She turned away. Time to go.

She headed down the drive and out on to the Shrewsbury bypass, turning in on the road that passed the crematorium towards the town. She could park in the nearby car park and walk down to Frankwell and the river.

It was darkening, the sky streaked with silver, the town already bustling ready for its Saturday evening jollities. The Armoury looked welcoming as she peered in through the tall windows. As usual, when she entered it took a while to adjust to the noisy, friendly place and the sound of chatter and laughter. No background music was necessary. No one would have heard it anyway and the place had enough atmosphere without it. Lined with bookshelves and old prints of the town, it was almost collegiate.

She spotted him straight away, to the right of the front door, sitting at the back, not at one of the long refectory tables but in the far corner, his eyes watchful. He'd already picked up on her entrance. There was a touch of triumphant humour around his mouth.

She gulped in a deep breath. The friendly atmosphere receded. She was in enemy territory. She squared her shoulders. What could he do to her here? It was a public place.

She would be safe. Surely?

Gina Marconi must have believed that too. He stood up politely, smiling but making no attempt to make the greeting physical – neither kissing one or both cheeks or even a formal shake of the hand. He simply smiled at her. The camera had not lied; neither had her memory. Victor Stanley was as handsome as a film star, tall, dark haired, olive skinned, with white teeth and brown eyes which smiled at her from underneath heavy lids. His dress, she noticed, was casual, grey chinos, a dark blue sweater over an open-necked pale blue shirt. No tie. 'Good of you to come,' he said, eyes roving over her but not making a personal comment. There was nothing lascivious about it. He was too clever for that.

She smiled her response and sat down but already she felt uncomfortable. He was too smart for her. She realized then what a stupid move this had been. She should have thought this one through. Martha looked around her and ordered herself not to let her guard drop. Even here, in this crowd of Saturday-night revellers, couples, work colleagues, bands of friends, families, she might not be safe. It was even possible that the very public venue in the town where she both lived and worked was the most dangerous place to be seen with him. He could slip something into her drink, as he might have done to Gina. She felt panicked, looked around for someone – anyone she knew. Did not recognize a single person. And no one appeared to recognize her. No one even looked her way.

'Hungry?'

She looked down at the menu. 'Not terribly.'

He gave a bland smile which could mean anything. And then the conversation seemed to stutter and stop. He asked a little about her work and she trotted out the same old points – that she was a voice for the dead. A mouthpiece for those who had lost the power of speech. They talked around this issue but it was desultory conversation, neither leading anywhere nor, she suspected, was it what either of them had come here tonight to discuss. It didn't answer the question: *Why me?*

So she needed to skirt around it.

'And you?' she finally asked, quite pleasantly, half interested. 'What do you do?'

'I run my own business,' he said, a challenge in its wake. 'A timber yard.'

'A timber yard?' Why, she wondered, had he chosen this?

'That's right. I import most of my wood from the Far East,' he added, an engaging twinkle now in the heavy-lidded brown eyes. 'They grow lovely hard, dark woods over there. And there's an inexhaustible supply.'

She stared at him. What was he really talking about? Not wood, that was for sure.

She had to remind herself why she was here tonight. She met his eyes and read determination, steely, unforgiving and with a hint of mischief. She didn't feel afraid of him. Peering into this face with its neat features and reassuringly clear brown eyes hoisted no red flag. Her warning voices were all silenced.

It was that that made him dangerous.

She didn't realize she had been staring at him, searching for some alert until he interrupted her thoughts. 'So, would you like to eat?'

'Yeah.' She looked around. The menus were on the table, the specials on the board. She chose beef wellington and he a steak, and he wandered over to the counter to put the order in, returning with a welcome glass of blood-warm Rioja. He asked her a little more about her work, her background, her training, her family, and she gave away as little as possible – nothing he couldn't have found out through Google. The food arrived and they ate, still making that desultory conversation.

Finally he put his knife and fork down. 'We-ell?'

It was a challenge. 'Time to stop playing games, I think.'

Was this the moment when he morphed into the villain of the piece? Was Dr Jekyll about to turn into Mr Hyde?

He took a sip of his beer, wiped the foam from his lips. 'Let's get down to business, shall we? You must be wondering why I invited *you* here.' He didn't wait for a response. 'Does the name Harris Palliser mean anything to you?'

She shook her head and saw a glint of anger in his eyes.

'Years ago you were conducting an inquest into the deaths of three people killed in a multiple vehicle car crash.'

'Unfortunately, Mr Stanley,' she said, 'I deal with many fatalities following car crashes.'

'Hmm,' he said. 'You . . .' stabbing her with an index finger, '. . . directed the police towards a finding of vehicular homicide. And the person who was subsequently convicted was a friend. OK,' he conceded, 'you didn't actually convict him but you pointed the finger. He was subsequently sentenced to a long stretch in prison.'

She blinked.

'My mate was just a car mechanic and the bloody thing that he'd worked on crashed. The brakes failed because my mate,

Harris, fitted faulty brakes because they were half the price and you drew attention to this. Made a little speech damning cheats who put in substandard parts in the cars they serviced. My mate died in prison of hepatitis. He was clean before he went in. You executed him by your little comment. So, Mrs Gunn, I owe you one.'

'I stand by what I said.'

His face showed no sign he had even heard her. 'You don't know what to say, do you? So why are you here?'

'Because I believe,' she said, 'that you set up two suicides.'

'Really? And how do you think I did that?'

'Photographs,' she said, 'taken of people in compromising situations. One just a boy.'

He smiled, reached across the table and stroked her hand. 'What an imagination you have, Coroner Gunn.'

'Why? What's in it for you? How does it benefit you?'

He watched her steadily for a few minutes then smiled. 'What makes you so sure I'm involved, let alone responsible?'

'I've seen the photographs. You're in them.'

'Sure about that?'

She nodded, then leaned forward to make her words score a direct hit. 'Why? What did they ever do to you?'

He drew in a deep breath and his answer, in a pleasant, polite voice, was chilling. 'Are you talking about Gina?'

'We can start with her.'

'She was going to . . .'

'Struggle to convince the jury that Pete Lewinski was innocent? That the knife somehow magically appeared in his hand?'

She sensed a grudging respect as he nodded.

'Besides, Gina was a beauty.' He folded his arms and grinned. 'Sometimes, Mrs Gunn, I really enjoy my job. You want to know why? Money. Mrs Gunn, some people have brains, others looks. Whatever you have you trade.'

'Wasn't it a bit risky when she had protection?'

He smiled again. 'All jobs carry risks.'

'Who took the photos?'

'My friend.' He blinked then smiled. 'You have no option but to find her death suicide.'

Martha smiled back. 'That might be what you think. I couldn't possibly comment.'

He looked angry at that. Victor was a man who did not like to lose.

She pressed on. 'But Patrick?'

'Let's just say I owed a friend a favour.'

'Jack Silver?'

He wagged a finger in front of her face. 'You don't know everything then, Mrs Gunn.'

Now she was sensing his overt hostility.

'Not Jack Silver,' he said impatiently.

She shook her head, unsure now.

'Jodi,' he supplied, 'the lovely wife of the currently imprisoned Jack.' He paused. 'And mother to two boys.' He paused.

'Warren is . . .' He thought for a minute. 'Well, to put it frankly, Warren is a devious little rat. But Sean, Jodi's younger son, he's labelled dyslexic or . . .' He frowned. 'What do they call it these days?' He scrabbled around in his brain. 'Oh, yes – learning difficulties. He was always bottom of the class. A plodder, the butt of all jokes.' He smiled abstractedly.

She tried to flush him out. 'You're fond of the boy.'

His eyes grew hard. 'I tell you what I choose to tell you.'

He was silent and she wondered if he was going to keep his story to himself after all, but then he kicked off again. 'Patrick Elson was in the same class as Warren and Sean. Patrick wasn't just bright, he was a show-off. Laughed when poor old Sean got all his questions wrong – mocked him. And one day it just got to Sean. He chucked the boy's new and probably hard-earned shoes over the telegraph wire. But that wasn't enough. He asked me to teach the boy a real lesson. So I did.'

And the result of that lesson had been . . . Arms outstretched, the boy flew across her mind's eyes. 'He didn't deserve to . . .'

Victor Stanley interrupted her right then with a voice as sharp as a stiletto, displaying the anger he had kept so well hidden until now. 'You still don't get it, do you? Strength and sheer bloody mindedness – it's all Sean's got. That was his gift and he used it. We used to meet at their house and he probably heard me and Pete jawing off about Gina, how we'd paid her back. Humiliated her. I remember saying that. Humiliation works a treat. Very destructive force is humiliation, Martha Gunn. Make a fool of them. They never get to you again because everyone sees only the fool. I think the boys must have been listening and they asked me to intervene with their troublesome classmate. As it happened it suited me. I can bat for both teams.' He stood up. 'And now, Mrs Gunn, I think it's time we settled our bill. Paid our dues.'

He crossed the room. Her eyes followed him. He had a plan, she sensed, but she didn't have a clue what that plan was.

There was a queue at the counter, people arriving and setting up tabs, people leaving and paying their bill, others ordering their meals, starters, desserts, more drinks. He was a full ten minutes gone and she didn't know what his intentions were. She watched him surreptitiously. Unlike many of the impatient customers, with their fidgeting or hopping from one leg to the other, the wait did not seem to faze him. He stood still, not glancing back in her direction. This was a man who was perfectly comfortable in his own skin, happy with his rotten ways, and he would continue. There was nothing she could do to stop him.

When he came back he was still in arrogant mood. 'No crime was committed,' he said, pocketing his wallet. 'No money demanded, nothing. They both chose to die. The police have absolutely no chance of conviction. They have nothing against me.'

'They have pictures of you committing an indecent and humiliating act with a twelve-year-old boy.'

'Prove it.'

'I believe the police will be able to.'

He shrugged, a casual, contemptuous gesture. 'Believe what you like,' he said. 'I really don't care what you believe. It doesn't matter to me.'

Martha looked around her. The place seemed busier than ever, full of decent people having a good time.

Oh, how she wanted to win this round. And then . . .

The entrance to The Armoury is three steps down, in a well. Two men were walking in. She saw their heads first. DS Paul Talith, Alex behind him. Talith looked around for an empty table – or perhaps a reserved one, and spotted her . . . and him.

Martha's heart sank. Because she'd felt nervous about the outcome of the evening she'd wanted someone to be there for her, but not him and not like this. Not without a chance to explain.

She felt hot with embarrassment. She could see this from their perspective. Having what would look like a friendly dinner with a good-looking man ten years younger than herself.

They would assume the worst. She was trying not to look across the crowd but her eyes seemed magnetized. And even from this distance she could read Alex's expression. He was staring at her with a look of utter bleakness.

Victor Stanley followed the direction of her gaze and for a moment he looked furious, until his demeanour slowly changed as he thought of a way he could capitalize on this late arrival. His smile broadened; his face looked malicious. Martha almost shrank away from the expression, it held so much spite. She hadn't seen this level of hatred since a girl had pulled her ponytail and said how she hated people with red hair. Martha had been six years old at the time and it had been the first time she'd encountered ginger prejudice.

'Well, look who's here,' he said. 'The recently widowed Detective Inspector Alex Randall.'

FIFTY-ONE

S he would have given anything not to see the hurt, the shock in Alex's face as he looked from one to the other. She felt frozen. Hopeless. Victor Stanley leaned in to her, eyes steady. He smiled into her eyes as though romanticizing her. All a deliberate act. As though they were already lovers and she knew that in this way he was laying a little trail of breadcrumbs that would mislead. She knew that in this restaurant, if she turned around, she would see someone with a tablet or a camera phone. All this would be recorded. She had walked into the trap fully aware and still been caught. What a fool. She looked at Stanley and knew it. He'd set the whole bloody thing up. He'd probably suggested that DS Talith and his recently bereaved senior officer have a nice cosy drink right here.

He almost brushed her lips as he spat out his next few sentences. 'Poor little Erica,' he said. 'Funny old thing, wasn't she?'

'I never met her.'

'Oh, no. Of course you wouldn't have, would you? Too busy making up to him. We have the photos of you two having your jolly at the quarry.'

'I handed them straight to the police.' It was up to her to turn this around. She stood up, faced Stanley, who looked surprised at this turn of events.

Alex Randall and Talith had crossed the floor in a couple of steps.

'Victor Stanley.' She had never heard Alex's voice so stern. 'We are arresting you on suspicion of people trafficking and also the rape of Patrick Elson. You do not have to say anything . . .'

She watched as though in a nightmare. She wanted to explain what she was doing here.

Alex gave her a swift look. 'DNA,' he said. 'And there are the photographs.'

Stanley's response was predictable. 'Prove it.'

'Certainly. We are not short of evidence which will convict you.'

Then Alex Randall smiled at her and the warmth and shared friendship held in that smile was as comforting as cocoa on a cold day, ice cream on a hot one, an umbrella in the rain and a glass of wine after a hard day's work.

Alex spoke very softly, for her ears only. 'So what,' he asked gently, 'are you up to now, Martha?'

She met those hazel eyes, part grey, part a warm treacly colour. 'That,' she said, her mouth close to his, speaking in a soft and quiet voice, 'was purely business.'

'Purely business? Didn't look like that to me.'

'I can assure you that is what it was,' she said quietly.

His eyebrows rose.

Later she would learn that in Patrick Elson's schoolbag left on the bridge over the A5 they had found a tissue. And on that tissue was semen which would be enough to convict Victor Stanley.

Not quite so clever then. Sometimes condoms leak.

FIFTY-TWO

Victor Stanley was charged, put on remand and the case against him assembled.

But when Martha had the chance, she asked Alex, 'And the boys? The Silver brothers?'

'Some day,' he said, 'they'll overstep the mark.'

So it proved. Martha was called three months later. A boy's body was dragged from the River Severn. Witnesses testified that they had seen two tow-headed boys with buzz haircuts push him in. There was photographic evidence. And CCTV.

And so the wheel of life and death, evil and good turns continued.

There was one last service she could perform.

Wednesday, 10 May, 11 a.m.

They were all there at the Coroner's Court in Shrewsbury, waiting to hear the verdict on Gina Marconi's death. Bridget and Julius were sitting so close together they appeared welded as one. Terence would be at school.

They'd listened to the pathologist's evidence, the evidence of Graham Skander, of the police and the emergency services. Julius had spoken about their planned wedding and Bridget had described her daughter's intelligence, beauty and anticipation for September's wedding.

Martha was summing up. And she still had a card up her sleeve. She would win this one.

'I think it probable that Gina was excited that night about the wedding and couldn't sleep. Tell me,' she addressed Bridget Shannon, 'was your daughter fond of animals?'

Bridget nodded without a clue where this was leading.

All faces were turned towards Martha.

'So she got out of bed and drove.' Martha smiled and to give her version authenticity she added, 'I've done the same myself – on occasions. I think it possible that approaching Mr Skander's wall she saw an animal in the road – a squirrel maybe or a fox. There is road kill on the verges. She swerved to avoid the animal, and the rest we know.'

Mouths were open as she announced her verdict. 'Accidental death.'

Nobody asked the questions they could have about the seat belt. No one asked any questions at all.

Images could have been out there, never erased, but public interest soon wanes and moves on to the next scandal. The press look for new headlines. There is always something to replace a dead lawyer, a schoolboy.

Except for their family.